THE BRITISH KNIGHT

LOUISE BAY

Published by Louise Bay 2017

ISBN – 978-1-910747-51-3

BOOKS BY LOUISE BAY

The British Knight

Hollywood Scandal

Duke of Manhattan

Park Avenue Prince

King of Wall Street

Love Unexpected

Indigo Nights

Promised Nights

Parisian Nights

The Empire State Series

Hopeful

Faithful

Sign up to the Louise Bay mailing list

www.louisebay.com/newsletter

Read more at www.louisebay.com

ONE

Violet

Men and cocktails were two of my favorite things to waste time on, and I made sure my day always had plenty of either one or the other. "Cheers." I raised my drink and clinked it against the glasses of two of my most treasured people in the world—my sister, Scarlett, and her sister-in-law Darcy. We were at some fancy bar in SoHo where the drinks were twice the price of a car. It was Darcy's first night in New York City, and I wasn't going to worry about how I was going to pay for anything tonight when I had no job to go to tomorrow. I adored her and didn't get to see her as often as I'd like as she lived in England, so I was all about the positive. Maybe I could get her laid as a welcome gift? Sex always put me in a good mood. I was certainly going to find someone to go home with. I needed to forget what a terrible week I'd had, and I wasn't sure just *one* of my favorite things was going to be enough. It was going to take alcohol *and* a man.

"Is there anyone special in England at the moment?"

Scarlett asked Darcy. "Someone to sweep you off your feet?"

I groaned. "She's not Cinderella. She's a capable, confident woman who needs no sweeping. The question you should be asking is whether or not she's had any good sex lately."

"I'm not saying she's not capable and confident, but a knight in shining armor is always a good thing," Scarlett replied.

"I wish I had sisters," Darcy said, grinning at the two of us.

Scarlett and I bickered because we were opposites. She was married for a second time. I had no desire to tie myself down to one man. Scarlett had a successful career whereas I couldn't even keep a waitressing job. She had two kids and I wasn't allowed a cat.

She was going to kill me when she found out I'd been fired.

But she was my sister and I loved her.

"It's the best," Scarlett said, "though I wish she'd listen to me a little more often."

"You just need to accept that not everyone wants the house in Connecticut with the perfect husband and two perfect but very loud children." I glanced around the room. What I wanted was *ferocious* sex with someone who could make me forget about what was or wasn't going to happen tomorrow. But no one had caught my eye so far.

"I just want you to be happy," Scarlett said, tilting her head to the side.

"Well that makes two of us." The last thing I needed was my sister's pity. Especially today. "Anyway, what are you going to do while you're in New York?" I asked Darcy. "I can come on the tourist trail with you if you'd like."

"Don't you have work?" Scarlett asked.

The problem with being close with my sister was that as much as we might be dissimilar, we couldn't hide things from each other.

"Sure, but I can fit my shifts around Darcy. I want you to have a good time." I took another sip of my cocktail, avoiding my sister's burning gaze.

"Oh, Violet. You didn't quit your job again, did you?"

From the corner of my eye, I caught the sag of Scarlett's shoulders and the bow of her head.

"Not exactly," I said.

I didn't want to see that look of disappointment in her eyes. Couldn't she just accept that I wasn't interested in a highflying career? Life had taught me more than once that the moment was to be enjoyed and that tomorrow could be figured out when it arrived.

"Not exactly?" she asked. "I thought you liked the girls at that place?"

"I did." The other waitresses had been a lot of fun and the tips had been amazing. "But I don't think I should put up with it when my ass gets grabbed at work."

"Who grabbed your arse?" Darcy asked.

"This regular we have. He does it to all of us, but I don't see why it's okay."

"It's totally not okay. So you quit?" Scarlett asked.

"No, I called him a sleazy prick and I got fired," I explained, ready to move on. I'd dealt with enough assholes in my time—I didn't want to waste any time thinking about them. "Hopefully it will mean he'll lay off the other waitresses. At least for a while."

I'd discovered that the way not to be disappointed in life was to have few expectations and the easiest way to keep expectations to a minimum was not to get too involved. It didn't matter if it was a job or a man—I didn't keep either long enough to emotionally invest, and that meant I could walk away from either without it hurting. Losing a job wasn't a problem—I was over it the moment I left. Not having any money was more of an issue.

Scarlett sighed. "It's not like you to lose your temper like that. I totally know he shouldn't be grabbing anyone's ass but . . ."

"You expected me to suck it up?"

"Absolutely not. I'm just saying it's not like you to lose it. I'm worried about you. Is this about the news yesterday?"

"News?" I asked, feigning ignorance. I was a terrible liar. The worst. But the last thing I wanted to do was discuss my ex-boyfriend and the fact that yesterday's business pages had announced he was taking the company we'd founded together public.

This was exactly the conversation I'd been avoiding.

"Are you upset?" Scarlett asked, clearly knowing I was full of shit.

"Not at all. You know I'm totally over it—it was years ago." It had been almost four years since I'd been betrayed by my college boyfriend and had the company I'd worked so hard to build taken from me. "I've told you before, life is good."

I'd genuinely thought I was over it. But yesterday's news had been a shock and brought back a lot of emotions. I enjoyed my life—most of the time. I had an amazing family, good friends, and I didn't have to worry, make difficult decisions, or do any of the stressful stuff that came with running your own business. I just didn't have the life I'd thought I'd end up with. I'd expected to be in the photograph alongside David. We'd be married—maybe with a kid or two—a tech power couple. Instead he was standing with his new wife, months away from winning the IPO lottery, and I was a waitress.

Scarlett reached across the table and squeezed my hand. "I think it's great you're happy. But honestly, sometimes it's good to have a plan, mix things up a bit. Isn't that right, Darcy?"

It was a low blow bringing Darcy into this conversation. She didn't know how loaded the question was.

"I love to plan," Darcy said. "I'm slowly increasing profits of the estate. We're looking at a fifteen percent jump over the next three years. If that happens, I want to open a farm shop, selling local produce. Also, I want to adopt a kid before I hit thirty-five. Oh, and if a knight in shining armor shows up, I don't need to be swept off my feet, but if he wants to take me to dinner and give me a foot rub then I'm not going to say no. Business, kid, foot rub. In that order."

I laughed at her to-do list. Darcy always seemed so happy-go-lucky, but now I thought about it, running her country estate must take a lot of planning and skills. And she was obviously good at it.

"Have you thought about going back to school?" Scarlett asked me.

"Are you serious? School?" I had so many bad memories intertwined with my college experience that repeating it was the last thing I would consider. David and I had met as sophomores and stayed together four years. We'd been lovers, business partners, and now strangers.

"I mean, if you're not sure what you want to do. And now that you don't have a job or a plan it might be the perfect place to figure stuff out," Scarlett said.

"Why give up today to make tomorrow better when you don't know if you'll live to see it?" Having my business taken from me when I'd spent so much time and effort building it into something I'd been so proud of had been devastating. I was determined not to repeat that mistake. I'd sacrificed so much of my early twenties for . . . nothing. The past few years I'd been trying to get that time back—partying, living life in the moment, dating lots of guys.

"That's a little depressing," Darcy said.

"It's just the opposite," I replied. "I don't waste all that time planning for things that might never happen. I don't have a rainy-day fund, so I don't have to spend time *planning* for a rainy day—that's what's depressing. Better to enjoy the sunshine."

"And when the rain falls?"

I was pretty sure getting fired qualified as a rainy day and I was still having fun—now I was with Darcy and Scarlett. "I find a hot guy and have some wild sex until the clouds pass."

Scarlett shook her head. "What are you going to do about a job?"

"I have no idea. Get another, I guess." I had about three hundred dollars to my name, which wasn't even half what I needed if I wanted to renew my lease next month. The problem was, waitressing was getting old. I was growing tired of the drinks after work and the making up for lost time. I just didn't know what else I could do. I might have a computer science degree and a couple of years' experience at running a start-up, but the last few years had qualified me for nothing other than being able to memorize the specials and carry three dishes at a time.

"Why don't you come back to England with me?" Darcy said. "You don't have to be out with me in the country. You could stay at the London house and wait for the clouds to pass for a couple of months. You never know, the city might inspire you to find your passion."

I'd never been to Darcy and Scarlett's husband's London house, but Scarlett had told me it was like something out of a Jane Austen novel.

London could be fun, but there was no way I could afford to go.

"That's so nice of you but . . ."

"The place is totally empty and it's right in the center of things," Darcy said.

I glanced at Scarlett, waiting for her to interject and tell Darcy it was a crazy idea and that I needed to buckle down and find another job, but she just stared straight back at me, waiting for my answer.

"I can't. I have my apartment and I need to start job hunting. But thank you."

"Didn't you say that your lease was coming up for renewal anyway?" Scarlett asked. Was she on board with me just abandoning New York?

"You were all for me going to college five seconds ago."

"I just think a change would be good for you. Maybe London is what you need—a few weeks to reassess what you want from your life. Since the start-up you've . . . With this IPO coming up in a few months, a break from New York might be good."

"I'm happy, Scarlett." I really didn't want to talk about my ex. "Surely, that's the most important thing?"

Scarlett smiled reluctantly. "I hope so. Because that's what I want for you above anything else."

My heart tugged in my chest. I hated that my sister worried about me. Most of the time she was completely overreacting, but today she'd caught me at a weak moment. The news about David had been a shock. It was a reminder of what my life could have been and had brought into focus everything my life wasn't. I was feeling less than happy. I just didn't know how to make it any better.

"I think you're more cut up about David and this IPO than you're admitting," Scarlett said. "And I'm not surprised. I would be too. What happened was awful. He betrayed you and worse he got away with it. You had every right to take a time-out. It was perfectly natural. But it's been four years and I miss my bold, go-getting sister who was ready to take on the world. I feel like he stole her, and I want her back."

A tide of emotions passed over me at my sister's words— I didn't know whether to throw up or cry. I'd worked hard not to repeat the same mistakes I'd made with David and my business by not getting emotionally invested in anything, but something was missing. As much as I hated to admit it, Scarlett was right: part of who I used to be, a good part, had disappeared. I closed my eyes and exhaled, trying to stop myself from breaking down in tears in public. Once I had been the girl who was ready to take on the world. I wanted that person back too.

My sister's hand covered mine and I looked at her. "I love you," I said.

"I love you too, but don't get soppy on me. You have to get over this guy and what he did to you, but you seem stuck," Scarlett said.

I was over him, wasn't I? We lived in the same city, but I'd deliberately made sure we occupied different worlds. It wasn't as if I was pining for him, but Scarlett was right—I did feel stuck.

"Please consider going to London," Scarlett said. "That way you're not in New York when this whole IPO thing happens, and you can just get some inspiration, get unstuck, and figure out what you want to do when you grow up." She grinned, always happy when she was reminding me she was older than me.

"If you've got nothing keeping you in New York, why not come over for a few weeks, even a few months? It could be a way of pressing the reset button," Darcy said.

"You are always saying how you want to live moment to moment," Scarlett said. "Except every moment seems a lot like the last. Why not live a few of your moments in London? You can come back reinvented. Violet King 2 point O."

I hated it, but Scarlett had a point. The last twelve months, bouncing from waitressing job to waitressing job, hadn't been fun, however much I tried to insist otherwise. I'd had to change the plan on my cell to the basic, and I'd eaten a lot of toast. I needed a change but going abroad hadn't even occurred to me. Would going to London really press the reset button? Provide inspiration? Create a Violet ready to take on the world?

"Ryder's coming back with me, so obviously he's insisting we take a private plane. You wouldn't even have to worry about booking a ticket."

I chuckled. There was a whole world out there I really didn't understand. Private planes were at the top of the list. But if I didn't have to spend my last few hundred dollars, and some borrowed ones, on a plane ticket, the list of reasons why I shouldn't go to London was running short.

"London, huh?"

Darcy squealed. "Yes! And you can come up to the country on weekends to see me."

"I'd need to get a job out there," I said, thinking out loud. My three hundred bucks wasn't going to get me far even if I wasn't paying rent.

"Restaurants are two a penny in London. You'd walk into a job," Darcy said.

I wrinkled my nose. "Honestly, I might look for something different. Like Scarlett says, switch things up a little." I avoided looking at my sister. No doubt she was wearing her I-told-you-so grin.

"Well, let me speak to a few family friends and see what I can do," Darcy said. "There might be someone looking for something."

"Are you sure? You letting me stay at the house is so generous and—"

Darcy lifted her palm to face me. "Don't mention it. I can't promise anything, but I'll see what I can do."

"Thank you." I grinned and nodded slowly; maybe a change of scenery was exactly what I needed. If nothing else, the men there had an accent. And judging by the guys in this bar, I had to find a new hunting ground. I might even be able to start thinking about my future for the first time in a long time.

TWO

Violet

London was exactly how I imagined it would be. The black taxis, red phone booths, the rain and old buildings—I loved it all. After locking Darcy's townhouse, I turned and took the three steps down to the sidewalk. Or *pavement*, as the British would say. I was going to go back to America as British as I could. As well as the differences in language, I had to master an ability to talk incessantly about the weather. British people talked about the weather as if it were a dysfunctional member of the family they were constantly disappointed in. Even if the sky was blue and the sun was out, they'd complain that they'd not been expecting it and had too many layers on. If it was raining they certainly weren't happy but, interestingly, if it hadn't rained for a few days they were all shaking their heads concerned with the lack of precipitation. It was totally bizarre, but I loved it. I'd learned if I wanted to strike up a conversation with a stranger, the weather was my Trojan horse. The topic was the equivalent to the Super Bowl in America, except it was a 365-days-a-year event.

I had a good feeling about today. The sky was blue, I didn't have too many layers on, my travel pass had twenty pounds on it, and I was about to ace an interview that Darcy had arranged for me. I could feel it in my bones. Today was my day. It had to be. I was down to my last fifty dollars, and if I didn't get this job I was going to have to call my sister and have her buy me a plane ticket back to the US and the nothing that awaited me.

I'd moved three boxes of things from my apartment the day before I flew to London, plus the suitcase I'd brought with me. Three boxes that included all my clothes, books, mementos, and jewelry. I had no furniture. I didn't own so much as a fork. For years I'd reveled in my lack of things, and for a long time I'd thought it was super cool I wasn't tied down to material possessions, but seeing the three boxes in the back of my sister's car had made me feel pathetic.

Today I was going to resist feeling pathetic. I was all about the interview and the three-month contract it offered. Darcy had heard that one of her grandfather's friends had a temporary job opening at some barristers' offices doing administrative work and had arranged an interview. It wasn't a sure thing—I could still mess the interview up, but I would do my best. I didn't want to let Darcy down, and I liked the idea of working in a law office. It was something new. The job description hadn't been specific, but Darcy had told me they needed someone *robust* and that an American might just work out.

A quick scan of Wikipedia had given me the basics on barristers. I'd figured out that unlike the US, the Brits had two types of lawyers—solicitors and barristers. Barristers wore the weird wigs and gowns and went to court. Solicitors were stuck in the office, in suits, dealing with clients. I had no idea why there had to be a split, but barristers seemed more British with their old-fashioned costumes, and I was obsessing about the British so that worked for me.

I peeked into my tote. The folded square of paper with the address copied out was still there, alongside my cell phone, so I headed to the tube station. I'd planned out my route and left plenty of time. I needed to get off at Holborn tube station and from there I could figure out where I was going with the aid of Google Maps. I had such a great feeling about today.

I reached the entrance to the tube and pressed my travel pass against the payment pad. If I got this job, this would be the route I'd take every day for the next three months. It would be as if I was really *living* in London. I couldn't remember the last time I'd been this excited about anything, let alone a job or a commute. It really did feel like the start of something—a new beginning.

A seasoned New Yorker, I was used to *subway face*. There were certain rules you had to abide by when taking public transit—a zipped bag, no eye contact, and an impassive expression. I was pretty sure the tube used the same rulebook, but today, I couldn't hide my grin. I wanted to share my good mood with everyone.

The train arrived as soon as I stepped on the platform. That had to be a sign—everything was going my way. I stepped on, being careful to *Mind the Gap* as I was told to do by an electronic voice, and spotted a seat in the corner, but a man who'd got on the train with me was nearer. I watched as he spotted the seat and then turned to me. He had bright blue eyes and a jawline so sharp I wanted to reach out and stroke my fingers along it. He wasn't my usual type—suits weren't my thing—but I'd make an exception for someone so tall and handsome. Someone who wore his suit that well.

"Please," he said, gesturing to the empty seat.

A hotter-than-hot guy offering me a seat? This really *was* my day. "Thank you." I went full throttle on my grin.

He paused, our eyes locked for a second, and he nodded and turned away, pulling out a newspaper. My heart was beating a little faster from his stare, and I watched as he shook out the paper, then folded it in sharp, deliberate movements. Was he as concise and deliberate in bed? Would he study my body the way he studied that paper, be as focused? I sighed and took a deep breath. I'd never know.

I turned back to take my seat and saw someone who hadn't been as distracted by a hot guy sit down in the space that had been meant for me. Apparently, the politeness of the British only lasted so long. I sighed and glanced around, trying to find somewhere to stand where I wouldn't topple over. I tucked myself in by the door, holding on to the bright yellow handrail that five other hands were also grasping. I also just happened to be wedged right next to my handsome stranger, who was managing to read his newspaper despite the train being so tightly packed. I looked up at him. His fingers were half an inch from my shoulder. I glanced down. His foot was almost touching mine. It was so weird to be so near to a complete stranger. He was close enough to lick.

This dry spell I was experiencing was having me fantasizing about strangers on the tube. Although, I suspected the man I was transfixed with would probably have me thinking wicked thoughts even if I'd had an orgasm five minutes before I'd spotted him. He was *delicious*.

I hadn't even kissed a man since coming to London two weeks ago. In New York it was easy to pick up a guy, or respond to a man picking me up. Too easy. And just like waitressing had lost some of its appeal, so had the dating scene. I was bored with it in New York. There was no point in doing the same thing in London; after all, I was here to try something new, to start again. Instead, I'd watched a lot of British TV, practiced my English accent, and walked around exploring the city. Anything to pass the time until my temporary visa came through.

Scarlett was right: There was no point in living for the moment if every moment was the same. I needed to mix things up.

The tube stopped, and I leaned forward, trying to read the name of the station. I was sure I had two more stops to go before Holborn, but I didn't want to miss it. The stop was Piccadilly Circus, which I'd been to last week and had been disappointed when I'd found neither animals nor acrobats. Just a statue of Eros surrounded by electronic billboards. It was like Times Square's eccentric but less wealthy cousin. As I straightened out, my hair skimmed the newspaper of the blue-eyed stranger and he glanced down at me. "Whoops," I said and smiled. He just stared at me, unblinking, and I couldn't look away so I just stared back. It was almost as if he was trying to communicate with me without words, but what was he trying to say?

Can I kiss you?

Let me take you to dinner?

I'm fantastic in bed, can you tell?

Yes, yes, and a double yes *please* with whipped cream.

He blinked three times in a row as if he'd been shaken out of a trance, frowned slightly, and then went back to whatever he was reading. I continued to check him out. Even without that jaw and those piercing eyes, he would be attractive. His thick dark-brown hair, the broad shoulders, and the expensive suit—it all just fit together perfectly. His skin was bronzed and smooth and it took a ton of self-control not to reach out to see if it slid against mine the way I imagined it would. His hands were large with long, strong fingers and neat nails that had been trimmed but not manicured. Manicures had become a thing for men in New York, particularly Wall Street types, and it was another reason why I rarely dated suits. Manicures should be a woman-only activity.

Finally, the doors opened on the Piccadilly Circus stop, and I was proven wrong that the train was full because about three thousand more people squeezed into the carriage. I shifted so I was closer to my fantasy man—my foot was in between his and I stared at his chest. We'd been close before but now the sleeve of his arm was brushing my hand and if I took in a deep breath I smelled leather and woods—not strong enough for cologne but too expensive to be just deodorant or soap. Carefully chosen body wash, maybe. The doors beeped and shut, and the train started again, aggressively lurching its way forward. If he hadn't moved at the same time, I'd be flat against his chest. We adjusted ourselves and the train picked up speed, continuing to see-saw along in an almost hypnotic rhythm. If my stranger noticed me staring, he didn't say anything and even if he had I wasn't sure I'd have been able to stop. Then, out of nowhere the train screeched to a halt and my hands flew up to stop myself from falling. Lucky for me they connected with my blue-eyed stranger's broad, hard chest. For a second I was frozen, unable or unwilling to move, then he gripped my upper arms and put me back on my feet.

"Are you okay?" he asked, his British accent wrapping around me like silk as I removed my hands from his chest.

I wanted to collapse again, just to feel his strength. That was it. His scent, his stare, his voice, and his touch had a thread binding them all together. They all exuded *strength* —of mind, of body, of character.

"Yes, sorry, not used to the tube, I guess."

"Keep your legs a little further apart. You'll balance better," he replied.

Had he just asked me to open my legs? I grinned and nodded.

He inhaled, expanding his already broad chest, and went back to his paper. I sighed a little more loudly than I meant to, and the woman next to me turned away, trying futilely to get some distance. She probably thought I was medicated. Or crazy. Or both. In an effort to look normal, I pulled out my phone and connected to the Wi-Fi. I'd bring up Google Maps and figure out where I was going when I got off the tube.

We passed through the stations quickly, stopping more frequently than I was used to. With my legs braced further apart, disappointingly, I didn't fall against my handsome stranger again and in just a few moments, signs for Holborn appeared through the window. I needed to focus and stop fantasizing about impossibly handsome men on the tube. I pushed myself through the crowds of people and made my way to the doors. As they opened, I took three steps forward and just as I reached the platform someone's elbow turned and knocked my arm so forcefully that my cell phone slipped out of my hand.

My heart began to thunder as I watched in slow motion as my phone, and the map, slipped toward the infamous *Gap* we were instructed to *Mind* between the train and the platform. "No," I shouted as people filed out after me, kicking my phone onto the track.

Fuck. I covered my face with my hands as people rushed past me. I couldn't believe it. How was I going to get to my interview? All my hopes of a new life, a fresh start, had been pinned on this job. And the last thing I wanted to do was embarrass Darcy by not turning up.

"That was my fault. I'm sorry."

I turned to find the man who'd made my tube journey a little more interesting. I caught my breath. "Your fault?"

The train started to beep, and its doors closed. Maybe my phone wouldn't be crushed under the wheels, and I could jump down and get it before the next train arrived?

"I knocked into you," the stranger replied.

He must have been the one who caught me with his elbow. I hadn't realized I'd followed him out.

I shook my head. "I should have been more careful." I glanced down at the tracks now the train had left the station. "There it is." It didn't look like my phone had been damaged at all. "Do you think I have time to just jump down and grab it?" I asked him.

A look of horror crossed his face and he pulled me away from the edge of the platform. I glanced down at where his hand was touching my arm. He'd moved me with such force, as if I were just a doll, and I might have been imagining it but I'm sure I could feel the heat of his skin through my coat. He reached into his jacket pocket and pulled out a business card. "The station staff may be able to retrieve it after service closes this evening. If not, call me and I'll replace it for you."

I was so busy staring at him I almost didn't hear what he said and then it registered.

"This evening? No, I need it now." I started to panic. I had to get to my interview, and with less than five pounds in my wallet, I couldn't even buy myself a map. "I need the map for directions; I have somewhere to be." I grabbed his arm, which was still touching mine.

The stranger glanced down at our linked arms and back up into my eyes, with the same expression he'd had on the tube, as if he wanted to say more than he did.

I needed to focus. I had to get to this interview. "Maybe you can give me directions." I dived into my tote and pulled out the piece of paper that had the address of the barristers' chambers. Thank God, I'd written the address down. "I need you to tell me how I get here. I can't be late."

I showed him the address, which he glanced at, then looked back at me—those blue eyes studying what he saw. "I'm going there myself. I'll walk you."

"You will?" Even if he hadn't looked like he'd just stepped out of a Tom Ford ad campaign and had seemed to make my knees a little weak just from looking at me, I'd have broken all my rules about never getting married and accepted any proposal he had for me in that moment. There was no way I could not turn up to this interview.

He nodded. "And it's the least I can do." His voice was like crème brûlée—silky smooth with a hint of gravel. *Yum.* I'd lick the bowl if I had a dishful of him.

For a second, I forgot I was teetering on the brink of disaster.

"Come on," he said, striding toward the exit.

We didn't speak on the escalators up to the surface. He stood in front of me, his brow furrowed, as if he was thinking through a complex problem. I didn't like to interrupt him, but it seemed odd not to talk to him.

"So, are you on your way to work?" I asked as we exited the turnstiles.

"I am," he said.

His words were clipped and formal. He was hardly full of conversation. I was pretty sure he'd be happy if there was only silence between us. That only made me want to know more about him.

"I have an interview. For a job," I said, hoping it might encourage him to tell me more about himself. What did he do for a living? Was he a diamond trader? A professional polo player? Maybe he was royalty? He had a regal air about him. "I want to make a good impression. My sister would say I am unreliable, but I'm never late. I *hate* lateness. It's the worst—so arrogant." I was babbling. He was making me nervous. Men never made me nervous.

"Arrogant?" he asked, his brow still furrowed as I struggled to keep up with his pace as we headed left down the street.

Before I had a chance to answer, his phone began to ring. "Knightley," he answered.

His name was Knightley? Fuck me. A British guy with a sexy, romantic name, who might possibly be the best-looking man I'd ever laid eyes on, was rescuing me from near disaster. It wasn't just Darcy's country house that was like something out of a Jane Austen novel.

He glanced over his shoulder at me and held the phone against his shoulder. "I have to take this, but we should be there in just a few minutes."

"No problem," I said. I didn't give a crap if he was on the phone. I was still going to make my interview, and if he wasn't looking at me, it meant I could stare at him. I glanced across and took in his high, tight ass. Jesus, would he mind if I lifted his jacket a little to make *sure* it was as good as it looked? I liked a man with a nice ass almost as much as I liked a man with big hands and a strong mouth. They were all important accoutrements to being good in bed. And those eyes, the way he looked at me? I shivered.

We crossed over the sidewalk, went through a gap in the

buildings, and suddenly we'd disappeared into the back of a closet—*wardrobe*—and come out the other side. Five seconds ago we'd been surrounded by traffic, noise, and a thousand people, but here, birds sang and Dickensian buildings sat around a large square with trees everywhere.

"Where are we?" I asked, looking around.

My handsome stranger glanced back at me and then pointed toward the entrance of a park as he continued his conversation.

This didn't even seem like London. It was more like a Disney version I might discover in Florida. We crossed a cobbled street that had no cars on it, despite it being the middle of rush hour, and headed into a park surrounded by black railings. The grass was neatly mown, and a few people sat on benches enjoying their coffee or reading the newspaper. Where were we? I knew from my walks over the last two weeks that London had its share of beautiful parks. I'd visited Hyde Park and St James' Park and some of the squares had buildings on all four sides, facing a small garden. But this? It was like a square on steroids. Eventually, we came to the exit and I saw a sign for Lincoln's Inn Fields. I'd have to Google that when I got home. *If* I got home—had those kids ever left Narnia? Somehow, I'd have to find my way back.

A shrill chime of a bell caught my attention but before I could figure out where it was coming from Knightley's arm was around my shoulder, pulling me out of the way of an oncoming cyclist and toward him. For the second time this morning, my hands pressed up to his chest out of instinct as I tried not to fall over. His touch felt protective and strong like before on the tube and I just wanted to sink against his body and breathe him in. He was saving me from disaster at every turn—on the tube, walking me to my interview, and then with this bike. The bike passed, and I looked up to find Knightley's eyes boring into mine.

"Thank you," I whispered.

He didn't reply but he didn't move or look away either. For a moment I thought he might kiss me. I sensed that he wanted to, and I would have kissed him right back. But he didn't, and we just stayed there for a couple of moments. Still. Staring at each other as if this look we were sharing was even more intimate than a kiss.

Eventually, his attention caught by whoever was speaking to him on the end of the phone that was still clamped to his ear, he glanced away, and I slid my hands down and away from his chest.

We continued our journey, passing through another gap in the buildings, and I expected to rejoin the hustle and bustle of London. Instead I was surrounded by extreme cuteness. Green patches of lawn and more old buildings in different-colored brick with tin-paned windows. It was like a toy town. We made a sharp right and without even saying goodbye, Knightley pressed cancel on his phone and shoved it in his pocket. "We're here. Let me know how things work out with your mobile."

I wanted him to say something else. Ask me to dinner. Kiss me. Something. I wasn't ready for him to walk away just yet. In New York, men were everywhere, but no stranger had ever captivated me like this one. It was as if when I'd stepped onto the tube I'd swallowed some kind of potion that made me completely attracted to this Knightley guy. And he wasn't even my type.

I didn't ask guys on dates. I'd never had to. About to watch him walk away, I wished I'd had more practice. "I will. Thank you."

He opened his mouth as if he was going to say something but then frowned, clearly changing his mind. And with that he swept up some steps and through an open door. I checked the address on my printout. *Number One New Square.* The exact same address was painted in shiny black paint on the side of the building. I'd made it. My handsome stranger had disappeared into the very building where I was headed. Another sign. Maybe I'd get to see him again. Today was my day.

I took a deep breath and took the stairs, retracing the footsteps Knightley had just made.

Time to be fabulous.

THREE

Alexander

My workout this morning had been punishing. The harder I worked, the harder I worked out. I was a big believer in that if I wasn't physically fit, I couldn't perform as well in my job. And I was willing to do whatever I had to do to be the best barrister I could be. As a result, I'd been up since five, worked out until six thirty, and then had a conference call with Dubai at seven. I hated days when I was late into the office, but this morning couldn't be helped. My commute had been . . . unusual. The woman I'd knocked into while getting off the tube had been beautiful, and I couldn't keep the image of her gazing up at me in the middle of Lincoln's Inn Fields out of my brain. I needed to focus. And perhaps get laid when I got the time. But it wouldn't be tonight. I'd be working. I had hundreds of witness statements to go through and my opening statement to draft.

In three days, I'd be in court, and that was my sole focus. There was no time to be wasted on fantasizing about women.

As I trawled through my emails, trying to pick out the important ones from the hundreds littering my inbox, someone knocked at my door. I resisted the temptation to growl. I hated being interrupted—I needed a sign for the door.

"Come in," I barked.

The door swung open, and I could tell by the footsteps that the head clerk had swooped in. "Mr. Knightley."

"Craig." I didn't take my focus off my laptop screen. Craig was an avuncular and charming man in his mid-fifties. He'd been in the business since he was fifteen and had clerked my father. If anyone could interrupt me, he could. And he knew it. Over the years, I'd tried to get him to call me Alex, but he insisted all the clerks and admin staff call the barristers by their surnames. The bar could be a very old-fashioned place.

"I want to introduce you to your new assistant, Violet King."

I paused, my fingers hovering over my keyboard. I knew nothing of this and would never have agreed to it—I worked alone. Slowly, I turned to find Craig in front of my desk, his eyebrows raised in expectation.

"My what?" I asked. A figure moved in beside him and I slid my gaze to the right. I found myself staring straight at the beautiful woman who'd invaded my thoughts since I'd arrived in chambers. What was going on? I looked away from her, sure that Craig would see my attraction to her if my eyes lingered over her for more than a split second.

My breath had caught in my throat when I'd seen her this morning on the platform. I'd watched, mesmerized, as she hurried toward me, arriving on the platform just before the train arrived. She had pale blue eyes, flushed cheeks, and long, black hair that I could imagine twisting my fingers through as I fucked her over my desk. Women rarely caught my attention, but she was not only beautiful. There was something exotic about her, something that made me want to know more. I'd been warmed by her heat throughout our journey this morning and was almost pleased when I got to walk her to chambers, although I'd felt like a teenager, unable to think of anything to say. I'd been grateful when a phone call had saved me from completely betraying my fascination with her. The way she'd looked up at me with those blue eyes, as she steadied herself against my chest on the tube and again in Lincoln's Inn Fields. My pulse began to race—at the memory or at having her so close now. I couldn't decide.

Here in my office, she was just as beautiful. Just as intriguing. It set me on edge. I didn't like the unexpected. The last thing I needed was her assistance.

"She's going to start straightaway, which is tremendous news."

"And what, may I ask, will Miss King be *assisting* me with?" I'd never heard of a barrister having an assistant before. The admin staff and the clerks were all pooled between us, and most barristers were pretty self-sufficient. After all, we were all self-employed and in a set of chambers simply to share resources. We all paid a percentage of our income toward maintaining chambers, but we were fiercely independent. The independence and the lack of interaction with others were some of the things I liked about my job. Every now and then, Craig would invent some new effort to organize my billing or my office, but it never lasted long. He gave up when I didn't give an inch.

"She's going to help you with your billing. You know you should be bringing in triple what you are."

Good head clerks guided barristers through their careers, and I knew Craig was looking out for me. The problem was I didn't give a shit about the money. I made plenty, and my father's death had made me a very wealthy man. What I cared about was the work. I didn't like to waste time billing clients and then chasing them for payment once I had. When the clerks had tried to bring my billing up-to-date before, they'd required me to go through each file with them and tell them which needed billing. They weren't really doing anything. It didn't take long for my lack of cooperation and blunt responses to exhaust them; they had plenty of other things to do that were easier. But an assistant whose only job was to annoy me might present more of a challenge. Especially someone as beautiful as Violet King. Just a few minutes as strangers with her this morning had provided too much of a distraction already. I wasn't sure how I'd keep my mind on the job if she was nearby all the time. My time was very limited. I needed to stay focused.

"You work harder than any barrister I've ever worked with, and you should be rewarded for that," Craig said.

That couldn't be true. As Craig had clerked my father, he knew the hardest-working barrister there had ever been at the bar. I was always stunned to see the corridors empty when I was in chambers late at night. I'd assumed that all barristers worked as hard as my dad, and he was never home in the evenings. Often he didn't make it home at all. A couple of times, my mother had brought us up to Lincoln's Inn to drop off a clean shirt or take him to lunch. It had always felt like such an adventure—I knew my father was impressive and the work he was doing important because they were always the reasons I was given why he wasn't at home, but seeing him in this environment proved it to me.

The men in suits, the people scurrying around with armfuls of papers doing what he told them, the way everyone I met told me how talented my father was and how lucky I was to be his son—it created a craving in me and I'd known from eight years old that I wanted to be here in Lincoln's Inn, just like him. I'd imagined we'd work side by side—maybe even share an office. He'd died before I'd been called to the bar. Our careers had never overlapped.

"You know I'm not concerned about the money," I replied.

"Frankly, chambers will get a bad reputation for its clerking if things carry on, which hurts us all. We need to be seen as modern and dynamic to attract clients and up-and-coming barristers. All we're asking is for you to let someone help you out." He glanced around the room. There was paper everywhere. I liked to think it looked like a scale model of an Asian capital—tower blocks of paper heading toward the ceiling, blocking out the light. "And your filing and your archiving is completely out of control. It needs to get cleared up."

"I'll get to it," I said, knowing full well that I never would.

Craig sighed. "Throw me a bone and give Violet a chance. She's here for three months and is going to make your life easier. She's a clever, robust American, so she should be able to put up with you."

I didn't respond. No one else in chambers would dare be so blunt with me. I knew the more junior clerks and admin staff feared me, which I rather enjoyed. I liked to be left alone to get on with my work, so it suited me that I wasn't drawn into polite conversations or pestered with inane questions.

"I'm too busy to be explaining anything to anyone," I

said, turning back to my laptop, careful to avoid looking at Violet. I'd been close to kissing her this morning. She'd felt good in my arms when I'd pulled her out of the way of that rogue cyclist—as if she fit—and I hadn't wanted to let her go. I could almost still feel her against my chest while sitting here just a meter away from her. Her smile had been so warm and open and for a second I forgot how late I was. Perhaps I'd imagined it. Unable to help myself, I glanced across at her again, and she was wearing that warm smile that seemed to direct heat throughout my body. Would her full lips be as soft to kiss as they looked? Would she fit against my body as I imagined she would?

I inhaled sharply and looked back at Craig.

"I warned you he would be difficult," Craig said, presumably to my new *assistant*.

This must have been the job she was so keen to get to. How ironic that if I hadn't shown her the way to chambers, she wouldn't be here.

"Do what you can." Craig sighed.

"No problem," she replied.

I swallowed and turned back to my screen.

"I'll introduce you to the rest of the team and then you can make a start," Craig said. "Have a good day, Mr. Knightley."

The door shut and I sat back in my chair. I'd always successfully resisted any attempts to organize me or to take over my billing.

Anyone else I would have just flatly refused, but I liked Craig—respected him—and I didn't want his reputation to suffer because of me. It was true that my additional billings would reflect well on chambers and Craig personally. I also knew in the back of my mind that I wasn't going to be able to take on bigger cases and advance my career working the way I was. There were only so many hours in the day, and I wasn't doing much but working, sleeping, and going to the gym. So I needed to get more efficient if I was going to be the best at the bar. If only Craig hadn't picked this woman. Something told me that she was trouble.

FOUR

Violet

So much for Knightley being some kind of hero from a Jane Austen novel. The picture Craig had painted in the interview was of a very difficult man, but then when he'd mentioned the name Knightley, I was delighted. I knew the person who'd rescued me at the tube station couldn't be the ogre he described. We had some kind of history together—there was some kind of connection between us. But no. When Craig had introduced us, Knightley barely even acknowledged me. It was as if we'd never met, as if I'd been invisible. Even if he was ridiculously handsome, and turned my insides to jelly, he was a jerk.

But I had to make this job work. The last thing I wanted to do was embarrass Darcy, and I needed the money. It was also my first non-waitressing job in a long time, and I needed to prove to myself that I could do something else, something more, even if it was administration.

"I warned you he was gruff," Craig said as we trundled

along the narrow, dimly lit corridor back to the clerks' section of the building.

The place must have been a house at some point because the furniture and fixtures looked more at place in a Victorian costume drama than in twenty-first century London.

"It will take tenacity and a thick skin to make any progress with him, but you have no other duties or responsibilities. It's all about Mr. Knightley. We need to get his billing up-to-date, shred, file, and archive his papers as I said to him. But really your job is to do anything that makes his life easier."

I had a feeling my job here was going to be pointless. I'd spend the next three months trying to polish a turd, and probably get fired in the process. But for today, I was going to stay positive. At least at the end of the week, I'd have a paycheck. And I'd be in London.

Craig stopped before we reached his office and headed into a room with one small window at the back. "This is the clerking team."

People at the eight or so desks raised their heads to look at me.

"This is Violet. She's Mr. Knightley's exclusive assistant." There was a collection of shocked faces and groans, but I wasn't sure if it was just a general lack of enthusiasm at the thought of a new person or sympathy that I was going to have to tackle Knightley. "I need you to give her all the help she needs," he said, and then he turned to me. "The clerks are responsible for taking instructions from law firms and then giving them to the barrister they think would be best suited to do the work. Sometimes the law firms request a specific barrister, then the clerks tell the law firms how much it will cost and liaise with the law firm to make sure they have what they need. Clerks also arrange the bill for the law firms, but the barristers need to tell them what they've been working on and for how long. Then the clerk can negotiate a fee lift if necessary. The issue we have with Mr. Knightley is that he never tells us when he's completed work or what time he's spent on what. Sometimes we know, but oftentimes we don't. That's why we need your help."

I nodded, trying to take things in. "So you guys organize the work for the barristers and negotiate the fees. But the invoice is raised by finance?"

Craig nodded. "But finance won't bill anything until they've heard from us that the work is completed and how much to bill."

Okay, that seemed straightforward.

"The admin staff sit through there"—Craig pointed through an archway to a connecting room—"along with the small finance team we have. You'll get to know everyone soon enough. I'm going to leave you in Jimmy's capable hands. He'll introduce you around and show you where you're sitting."

A lanky guy about my age wearing a pink shirt and a blue-and-pink tie came toward us. We shook hands. "I'll be happy to show you around. Anyone brave enough to take on Mr. Knightley will need all the help they can get."

Brave? Maybe if it was just him and me alone, he'd be different. Perhaps that crackle of tension between us would return.

"Well, don't make her more apprehensive than she already must be," Craig said. "I've got a good feeling about her. Anyway, things can't get any worse."

Craig shook my hand and left me alone with Jimmy and the other clerks. Life in an office involved a lot more hand-shaking than a restaurant ever had; hopefully there'd be less ass grabbing at the same time.

"So, I'll show you through here," Jimmy said, leading the way through the archway to where Craig had said the admin staff sat.

Jimmy showed me to the only free desk, which was pushed up against two walls. I'd be facing the corner like I was being punished.

"And can I see what Knight—Mr. Knightley is working on from my computer?" It felt weird calling a man who didn't seem much older than me *mister*. It was so formal.

Jimmy shook his head. "No, because the barristers are all self-employed they aren't networked. Only the clerks, finance, and admin."

Well, that was going to make life difficult. How would I see what he was working on? "So, I either ask him or hack into his computer?"

Jimmy laughed, but I wasn't joking. I used to enjoy hacking into MIT's systems for sport when I was at college. I was sure Knightley's computer wouldn't be so difficult.

"He won't answer questions about his billing, not even when they come from Craig. So, yes, I guess hacking is your only option." He grinned as if we were sharing a joke, so I smiled along with him, but my stomach churned. He clearly thought that I had an impossible task, that I'd been set up for failure. At least when I was waitressing, no one actively tried to stop me delivering plates to the tables.

"You think I have no chance?"

He shrugged. "I think people before you have tried and failed."

I folded my arms. "If sorting this out is impossible, then I don't know why I'm here."

"Mr. Knightley is a very important name in chambers.

His father was *the* barrister of his generation and our Mr. Knightley attracts a lot of attention because of that. And he's brilliant—he really is. Clients love him." Jimmy seemed to have real respect for Knightley, which gave me a little hope that despite being described as a monster, perhaps there was a softer side of him that would be open to me helping him, like the one he'd shown me this morning. "He's going to follow right along in his father's footsteps, but he can't take on the bigger cases while his office is a shithole—sorry, I mean it's in disarray and he's not working efficiently. He's doing everything himself and he's going to burn out. He needs to get into the habit of letting people help him."

Disarray was right. I'd never seen so much paper in my life. There were floor-to-ceiling piles of the stuff. I wasn't sure what I was supposed to do with it all. Craig had said in the interview that I'd get some help in figuring it out, but it seemed a little overwhelming at the moment. It was weird because he was perfectly dressed and had not a hair out of place—how was his office such a mess?

"And his billing has to get sorted. Chambers can't afford to get a reputation for not billing properly or mismanaging finances. That looks bad on the clerks, particularly Craig. And if Mr. Knightley isn't earning what he should, that's bad for all of us, him included. At the bar, money equals success. Unfortunately, Mr. Knightley doesn't see it that way."

I didn't know where to even start. "So how would you go about it?"

Jimmy pulled in a long breath and shook his head. "Honestly, it's going to be tricky. I think you need to try to keep out of his way as much as possible. If it were any other barrister, I'd say go into his office when they were out and start on the filing. Once he sees how useful you can be, you might be able to help him more. The problem is Knightley works around the clock."

Jesus, who was this guy? Didn't he have friends or family? He couldn't work every hour of the day, surely.

"The only time I can guarantee he's not in his office is when he's in court."

"Perfect. So does he go to court every day?"

Jimmy chuckled. "No, but he starts a big case in three days. There's a master calendar in the clerks' office of when all of the barristers are in court."

That seemed like a good place to start, but what was I going to do for the next three days? I'd never worked in an office before, but I'd graduated summa cum laude from MIT. This job couldn't be beyond me. I just needed to come up with a plan. A way to organize Knightley and turn him into an example for this chambers rather than someone who was going to stunt his career and the reputation of this chambers and the clerks in it.

And if he asked me for a drink at some point along the way, I might just say yes. Or suggest we skip the drink bit and get right to the good part.

I'D SPENT yesterday getting to know the clerks and all the members of the admin team. I figured out that while the guys liked to tease and joke with each other, people took their jobs seriously and were hard workers. I'd asked each of them a billion questions about Knightley—his habits, his moods, his calendar, his computer. I'd extracted every last drop of information about him from the people in chambers, only to realize he asked nothing of them. I'd discovered that other barristers used the clerks and admin staff to arrange things like meeting rooms, hire couriers, and even copy and file paperwork with the court. But Knightley did everything himself. Most of the people I talked to mentioned Knightley's father and how he was the greatest barrister of his generation. Other than that, no one mentioned his personal life. I wasn't sure if that was because he didn't have one or because he was fiercely private.

From what I could figure out, the man was a driven, ambitious control freak.

Because Knightley had no boss, he could really do what he wanted, and clearly he was doing just that. I had no idea why he didn't want any help, and I couldn't imagine how I was supposed to change his mind. I needed a way in.

Now that I'd gathered all this information on him, I wanted to get into his office to see what else I could find that might give me a start. And then I could also begin his filing. He was the only barrister in chambers who didn't share an office, so I only had to wait for him to leave to have the place to myself. I wanted to take a look at some of those piles of paper that I'd seen. What the hell was all that crap? I also wanted to see if he had any photographs on his desk or mementos on his wall; maybe if I got to understand him a little, I could figure out who he was aside from a man who looked like he'd just stepped out of a cologne ad in the pages of Vanity Fair. From what people had said, he had a brain the size of Jupiter, but none of that told me what made him tick. People described him as surly and gruff, but there was clearly more to him. The way he'd offered to replace my phone and walked me to chambers, saved me from an oncoming cyclist—he wasn't a complete monster. Was he one person in chambers and another at home? Was he a loving husband and devoted father? And if so, why the fuck didn't he care about getting paid? Nothing added up.

I left my desk and made my way along the narrow corridor to the door of Knightley's office. It was closed. Opposite was a staircase with an ornate wooden banister leading up to more offices. I climbed the stairs and just as I reached the point where the steps curved and Knightley's office door was partly obscured, I took a seat. I was staking this guy out. He must leave his office for lunch or something.

After about an hour, the brass handle of Knightley's office rattled and his door opened. In confident, long strides, he strode along the corridor toward the back of the building. Even from a bird's eye view, he looked handsome. He'd removed his jacket and his shirt fit tightly over his muscular shoulders. In a flash he was gone. I wasn't even going to try to slip into his office now in case he was just going to the restroom, but my heart was still beating out of my chest. It wasn't as if I was doing anything wrong—I was just waiting for him to leave his office—but watching someone who didn't know they were being tracked felt odd. Especially when I was kinda ogling him.

This must be the strangest office job anyone had ever had.

I timed him, and exactly four minutes later he was back, shutting the door behind him. I didn't know his first name, but I knew how long it took him to pee. It felt like a small victory.

As the hours passed, I alternated between standing up, sitting down, stretching my legs in front of me, sitting on one numb cheek and then the other. Then, as Knightley's door handle rattled again, I froze. This was it, another bathroom break or something longer. I checked my watch. Or lunch. It was almost two. He appeared in the doorway, a frown fixed on his face, and this time turned right. My heartbeat pulsed in my ears. Was he leaving the building? As he disappeared out of sight, I crept down the stairs. I got to the bottom just in time to see him heading outside. This was my chance. I grabbed the brass handle and slid into his room and closed the door behind me.

I didn't know why I was so nervous. Being in here was my job and it was the approach Jimmy had suggested. I just didn't want to piss Knightley off so badly I got fired on my third day in the office. I moved between the piles of paper toward his desk. Careful not to touch anything, I tried to figure out what each stack was, but nothing made sense— just mentions of cases and respondents, court and proceedings. Thin, pink ribbons dangled from the towers of paper like ivy growing over stone. I sighed. How was I ever going to be able to go through this stuff? It was as if it were in Chinese.

I moved farther into the room. I needed to understand him better, find a way of building trust with him. I dragged my hand over the warm, dark mahogany desk, inlaid with green leather. More paper. Everywhere. And his laptop. I pressed down the spacebar. A password box popped up. Well, it couldn't be that easy, could it?

There were no photographs on his desk. No inspirational quotes on a notepad by his phone. I glanced at his walls. Only a few certificates in the name A. Knightley. I suppose at least now I had an initial. Knightley, or whatever his name was, was all work. Looking closer, I saw he'd graduated eleven years ago from Cambridge University. That made him roughly thirty-two, three years older than me. We couldn't have more different lives. Like him, I'd gone to a good college, but he'd spent the last decade building a career and a reputation that was unfathomable to me. All that time and commitment to one thing—what drove him to the levels of dedication he had? Did he ever have fun? Was he married? Have a girlfriend, boyfriend, pet hamster? In just a few days, I'd thought up more questions for him than there was time left on my three-month contract for him to answer.

I sat down and pulled out the top drawer in his desk. It was just pens and the ubiquitous pink ribbons. I pulled out the next drawer and found a collection of folded shirts, wrapped in tissue paper. All white. Why hadn't he taken these home? The next drawer was the same.

I spun the chair around and spotted a large plastic carrier bag. Had he been shopping? I crouched down to see what he'd bought. Rumpled shirts clearly waiting to be taken to the dry cleaners. Well, that was something I could do. Craig had said I should do anything to help Knightley out, and he did seem to have a shirt obsession. Maybe he'd let me on his computer if I took care of his dry cleaning? It was unlikely, but it might be the first step. I resisted the urge to bury my nose in his shirts just to smell that scent of leather and wood that I'd taken in on the train. I picked up the bag and, careful not to knock any of the stacks of paper over, made my way out of his office, shutting the door behind me.

I waited for Knightley to come back into chambers so I could be sure I wouldn't run into him with his bag of dry cleaning, then pulled on my jacket and headed out. Jimmy had told me that all the barristers, including Knightley, had accounts with a particular dry cleaners, which was perfect, since I couldn't afford to pay for this on top of a new phone, which reminded me. I had Knightley's business card in my coat pocket. That would tell me his first name. I stopped on the path and pulled out the card. What would his name be? Something poetic and British.

I scanned the card. *A*? His name was just printed as *A*.

Knightley. Who in the hell didn't put their fucking name on their own business card? I stuffed the card back in my pocket and picked up my pace. It was as if A-fucking-Knightley was *trying* to be difficult. Well, it wouldn't work. The handsome genius with a potential personality disorder had intrigued me. Now, I wanted to beat him. I would succeed where no one else had ever come close. I needed this job. I wanted to be good at something other than taking orders and dodging grabby hands. And the dry cleaning might be my way in.

FIVE

Alexander

"Come in," I barked, unused to being interrupted so often in a single week.

The door opened and I continued with my work, but when no one said anything, I glanced up to find Miss King taking my coat from the back of my office door. "What are you doing?" I couldn't help but run my glance down her legs, up to her perfect arse. When was the last time I noticed a woman in the office? When was the last time I noticed a woman?

She didn't turn around. Instead she just heaved as she hooked a bunch of cellophane-wrapped dry cleaning on the back of the door. "I had your shirts laundered."

What? "How did you get them in the first place?"

"I came into your office while you were out and found them." She turned to look at me and I avoided meeting her eyes, refocusing on my laptop. I needed to minimize this pull I felt toward her.

I should be angry. She'd been snooping, removed personal items from my office without my permission. But she'd also done me a favor. I couldn't remember how long that bag of shirts had been there. Two, maybe three weeks? Each day when I arrived, I resolved to take them to the cleaners at lunchtime, but then I'd submerge myself in work and I'd forget all about them. She had guts to come in here and just take them, I'd give her that.

"Did you put them on my account?" I asked, keeping my gaze on the computer screen.

"I did," she replied. "Also, I wanted to ask you, the instructions you got last month from Spencer & Associates regarding their client—"

"Dr. and Mrs. Foster." I knew every single client I'd had since my career started. She didn't need to remind me. "I don't have time for this. I'm in court tomorrow."

"I just want to know if you completed the opinion they asked you for." I glanced up, and she was hovering by the door, her hand on the doorknob as if she were ready to duck out of the room if I threw something at her. It wasn't like I hadn't lobbed a book at a bothersome clerk before. She must have heard the stories, so I admired her for having the nerve to ask me questions she knew I didn't want to answer. She risked me exploding at her, yet she still asked me. Was it guts or did she not care what I thought?

If I'd really wanted to discourage her from bothering me again I wouldn't have said anything, but despite myself, I found I wanted her attention. "It was completed. You can bill the agreed amount."

She tilted her head and raised her eyebrows but didn't say a word. She was silent in her victory, and I liked her more for it.

"Did you retrieve your phone from the tube station?" She'd worn her hair back today. I preferred it loose, but this way I was able to see her fine features a little more clearly. Her generous lips were free of any enhancement and naturally red, as if five minutes ago she'd been kissing someone with fervor. The curve of her neck begged to be stroked; the angle of her breasts had my mouth watering. I cleared my throat. I couldn't say if half the staff in this place were men or women. I was always too focused on the job, which made Miss King a distraction.

She pulled in a breath and I wasn't sure if it was because she'd seen me staring or it was a natural gesture from her. I wanted to know.

"Nope," she replied. "It was totaled. Do you need any assistance with preparing for court?"

There was no doubt that she could help, just not in the way she thought. My heartbeat pulsed in my neck as I imagined her pulling up her skirt and leaning over my desk. Her pale skin would look magnificent against the dark mahogany of the wood. Perhaps I'd leave her like that while I worked—bent over and ready for me. Or have her sit across from me, her legs open, and underwear free. Yes, that would be of great assistance.

"Mr. Knightley?" she asked, and I had to swallow down a groan.

"No, nothing," I said as I turned back to my computer. She slipped silently out of my office, leaving me with a hardening cock under my desk.

Fuck. Nothing ever broke my concentration, but Miss King had found a way. I was in court tomorrow and I needed to be the most focused I'd ever been. Every case this year was going to be important for me, but this had come from an American law firm that had never instructed chambers before. They'd specifically wanted me, and I wasn't going to be anything other than my best for them. The last thing I needed was to be distracted by some pretty American who doubtless would have handed in her notice by the end of the week.

SIX

Violet

It was official. I had a crush.

I'd practically skipped to work today. Just the thought of seeing Knightley had my stomach swooping and my nipples hard. He was gruff, antisocial, and sexy as hell. He hadn't thanked me for sorting out his dry cleaning and he'd in no way made me feel welcome, but I was sure there was a different side to him. The side that had walked me to my interview just a few days ago, the side that yesterday had looked at me like he wanted to fuck me for days. I recognized that look. I just wasn't used to guys not acting on it. Maybe he was married or had a girl-friend? Or maybe he just didn't fuck people who worked for him. I liked all the contradictions and complications about him. Most of the men I'd dated in the last few years were simple—easy to read, easy to understand. And boring.

I couldn't hide my grin as I walked into the clerks' room. It was before eight and only Jimmy and a girl—Becky, I thought—were behind their desks. I'd come in early, just in case Knightley needed anything from me before court.

"You're very chirpy today," Jimmy replied.

"Of course, it's a beautiful day." I wasn't sure if the British weren't morning people or whether my enthusiasm for the day would be categorized as *American*.

I headed left toward the admin area, and as I approached my desk I could see a small white box, right in the middle of my workspace. I knew I hadn't left it there last night. I glanced around for signs that someone had been in the office before me. But there were no coffee cups, coats, or other signs of life. As I stepped forward, I took off my jacket and peered at the box, recognizing the familiar picture of an iPhone. Turning it over, I saw it still had the security label intact on the back.

Knightley. He'd got me a phone.

I lifted the top of the box to discover the latest, top-of-the-line, rose-gold iPhone. It might be the most beautiful thing I owned. I collapsed in my chair and turned over the smooth metal object in my hand. There was no note. No explanation. As if it was nothing . . . but it wasn't. He hadn't needed to replace my cell, and he definitely didn't need to replace it with something so expensive.

There was that softer side again.

I pressed my lips together, trying to disguise my smile.

I put down the phone and logged on to my computer. As much as I might be crushing on Knightley, I still wanted to do good work for him, and I still needed this job.

Jimmy put his head around the door, and surreptitiously I slid the phone into the top drawer of my desk. For whatever reason, Knightley had clearly left it when no one else was in the office. Maybe he'd just been in early. Perhaps he'd wanted no one to see. But I was nothing if not discreet.

"Well done for getting that Foster case billed yesterday. That was twenty-five grand I never thought we'd see."

"Small steps," I replied.

"That counts as a giant step from my perspective."

I nodded. "I don't want to push too hard, too soon. Especially with this case he's on now."

"Agreed, but you're on the right track. Good job." He disappeared and I brought up my email, scanning the messages to see if anything had come in from the day before, but there was nothing so I headed to the kitchen. I had no idea if Knightley drank coffee, but it was the least I could do given his desk delivery this morning.

With two mugs clutched in one hand, I knocked on Knightley's door. I heard him sigh before he replied, utterly exasperated, "Come in."

I turned the brass door handle and walked in. "Thought you might want coffee before court."

He looked up at me with a frown. "I don't drink coffee before court," he snapped. Apparently, his softer side was hiding today. That didn't stop his gaze drifting down my body, focusing on my chest and my ass.

I pulled the cup back from where I'd been about to set it down. Oh well, all the more for me. "Thank you for the new cell phone," I said as I turned and headed back out.

"I owed you a replacement, Miss King."

"Please, call me Violet. And thank you anyway." *Tell me what the A stands for.* I didn't want to ask, didn't want to risk being told to mind my own business.

He stood and began gathering papers from his desk.

"Do you need assistance with anything?"

"Yes," he barked.

My heart leapt. Had I won him over? Was he going to let me help him?

"Please close the door behind you on the way out and ensure I do not have any further interruptions this morning."

What in the hell had crawled up his ass this morning? Was he like this every time he went to court? "Yes, sir," I said as formally as my sarcastic tongue could muster, pulling the handle until the old-fashioned door mechanism clinked shut.

Two cups of coffee later, as I was headed to the restroom, I bumped into Knightley coming out of his office.

"Miss King, please watch where you're going," he snapped. His bad mood was lingering apparently.

He'd been just as much at fault as me. "We all bump into things by accident from time to time, Mr. Knightley. I trust your mobile phone is safe?"

I swear I saw the corners of his lips twitch, but if a smile was threatening, he managed to suppress it. He stared at me as if trying to figure out how to respond, but he simply took a deep breath, shook his head, and strode out of the door.

I turned and leaned on the ornate wallpaper as I watched him leave. He had a mighty fine ass. It was a shame his attitude needed a workout even if he had his body covered. He should change his mind about coffee before court. It might help.

I stood there for fifteen minutes, watching the door, waiting to see if Knightley came back. But he didn't. That meant the coast was clear, and for the first time since I started, I had free rein in Knightley's office. I was going to start filing and archiving today, although I had no clue where I'd begin.

I took a deep breath as I turned the doorknob. It squeaked, as if warning me I was in for trouble. I shut the door and leaned back. Now I knew Knightley would be out of the office all morning, I was better able to take in the room and the size of the task ahead of me. I'd never seen anything like it. Where did I even start? There was barely a path of free space between the door and Knightley's desk, just stacks of manila files, loose papers, and rivulets of pink.

Several chairs were scattered about the room. All had a stack of paper seated on them, and in the far corner, there was actually another desk, buried under piles of paper and barely visible. I could start there, that way Knightley wouldn't notice and I wouldn't feel overwhelmed. I took the first slice of papers from the top of the pile. I might be forty by the time I'd finished.

As I headed back to the door, I glanced around the room, imagining Knightley at his desk. Despite him being moody and mercurial, there was a pull I felt toward him that was something more than his nice ass. I wanted to please him, have him understand that although I had no career, money, or prospects, I could if I'd made different choices. I also wanted him to kiss me, hold me like he had in Lincoln's Inn Fields.

SEVEN

Alexander

Court had been a shambles. I'd been completely prepared and then totally let down when six days into the trial, five more witness statements landed in front of me just minutes before we were due to start closing arguments. The judge hadn't been impressed, and he'd adjourned the trial for three weeks. My client was unhappy, the solicitors were furious, and although I had to act as if I was taking it all in my stride, if opposing counsel had come near me, I was likely to have punched him.

I pushed open the door of chambers with my foot, my arms full with my wig, robe, and stack of files. The door smashed into the wall, the whole building vibrating with the force. But at least it released *some* of my frustration at the other side's incompetence. I'd need to drink, run, or fuck to get rid of the rest.

Clerks backed into doorways as I stormed up the corridor to my office. I slung my wig and gown across the floor, narrowly missing several towers of paper.

"Knightley?" a woman asked from just in front of my desk.

It wasn't as if I hadn't noticed Violet King had been coming into my office each time I left for court. She tried to cover her tracks, but the whisper of her jasmine perfume lingered in the air, reminding me of the summer I spent in India before my final year at Cambridge, and gave her away. Well, that and the fact that the papers in the far corner of the room had been disappearing. She couldn't think I wouldn't notice. I knew the exact location of each and every thing in my office.

"Miss King, what are you doing in my office?" Today was the wrong day for her to push her luck. Unless she was handing me a glass of whiskey or prepared to slide to her knees to suck my cock, which twitched whenever she was close, she needed to leave me in peace.

She regarded me from over her shoulder, her red lips parted slightly. "I didn't expect you back."

"That doesn't explain why you're on your knees in front of my desk." I had to hold back a growl as it was exactly where I wanted her.

"I'm doing my job," she replied.

"Your job is to assist me. You're not assisting me if you're distracting me."

"I'm just picking up some files for archiving," she said, looking up at me, her forehead bunched. "How am I being distracting?"

I shouldn't have used the word, but distracting was exactly what she was. Did she have no clue how sexy she was? Just the way she moved, the curve of her mouth, the way her skirt was a little too tight and a little too short, it was all too tempting.

I realized I was fixating on her hips, her legs, her heels and when I quickly looked up and met her eyes, she looked back at me, her eyebrows raised. She knew that I'd been taking in her phenomenal body, trying to commit each part to memory so I could imagine it later. Instead of admonishing me or scurrying away, she simply let her gaze trail down my body, her tongue darting out to wet her lips just before her eyes met mine.

"Yeah, well, you're pretty distracting too," she said. "But I'm not complaining. I'm trying to work. I don't know who the hell stuck a pole up your ass today, but it sure as hell wasn't me, so be nice."

"Be *nice*?" I bellowed, moving toward her. No one had spoken to me like that since boarding school.

"Yes. Stop being an asshole for a second of your day. I'm trying to help you and you're not going to frighten me off."

Oh, she was so sacked. "I'm an arsehole? Is that what you called me?" I stood over her, looking down as she kneeled in front of me. Christ, I swore her mouth was twenty centimeters from my dick.

"It's good to know you're not deaf," she said, her blue eyes gazing up at me so innocently I could almost forget how insolent she was being.

"Is this normally how you speak to your employer?" I asked, fisting my hands. I had the distinct urge to pull this woman to her feet and kiss the impertinence right out of her.

Her eyes narrowed a little as if she was really trying to remember whether this was normal behavior for her. I didn't want it to be. I wanted the side of her that I saw, however challenging and inappropriate, to be reserved especially for me.

"Maybe," she replied. "Is this normally how you speak to women who are on their knees trying to assist you?" She gasped as she realized how provocative her question was. She'd gone too far and she knew it.

My heart slammed against my chest and our eyes locked. I didn't respond. Didn't trust myself not to reach for her. All I could hear was my heavy breath as she got to her feet and stood in front of me. We were just a finger's width away from each other. She tipped her head back as she continued to hold my gaze.

Neither of us looked away as if we knew whatever happened next would be crucial. If she touched me I wouldn't be able to hold back.

"Miss King," I said, my tone warning. She needed to understand the next thing she said would have consequences. I couldn't remember the last time I wanted to fuck a woman so badly. I'd always enjoyed sex. It was the ultimate way to blow off steam, but it was rarely much if anything to do with the particular woman in front of me and rather just an internal desire. In that moment I wanted to fuck, but more importantly, I wanted to fuck *Violet King*. I was pretty sure she was encouraging me, so she needed to be careful. She was playing with fire.

"Mr. Knightley," she replied, her breathing uneven.

I clenched my jaw, trying to regain control of my instincts. I was a second away from cupping her face and kissing her into next week, a minute away from yanking down her underwear and thrusting my fingers into her. I couldn't look away. Something was pulling me toward her, drawing me in.

Her teeth plunged into her bottom lip as if she were considering her options.

My heart racing, I reached out and swept my thumb along her mouth, and she released her lip. I paused, enjoying her hot, soft flesh and the buzz that hummed under my skin where I touched her. She was beautiful and I wanted her but we were in my office, in the middle of the day and she was a member of staff. This couldn't happen however much I might want it to. Even if she was encouraging me.

"I suggest you get out of my office and let me get back to work," I said. "Now."

She blinked and turned away sharply.

I exhaled, grateful that she'd freed me from her spell.

"Shit," she said, grabbing her hip. "My good skirt."

She'd caught herself on the corner of my desk and ripped the black fabric of her skirt, creating a large hole, exposing her pale skin.

"God damn it. This place is such a mess." She stomped over to the exit without looking at me and my jaw began to unclench as the distance between us increased.

With one hand on the doorknob she turned to me. "The Jenkins case—how long did you spend on it?"

"Seven hours," I said without hesitation. I needed her to leave and would tell her whatever she wanted if it made her shut that door with her the other side of it.

She nodded. The neediness in her eyes had subsided, and she was back to business after whatever it was that had passed between us. "Good." She swept out and I sat back in my chair.

That had been dangerously close.

If she'd not turned away when she had, my desire for her may have overridden my self-control. The way she looked at me, it was as if she was waiting for me to do just that—like she wanted me just as badly as I wanted her. Even though I knew that mixing business with pleasure couldn't be a good thing, if I found her in my office again, I wasn't sure if I'd be able to hold myself back. The girl was dissolving my focus, my control, my defenses.

EIGHT

Violet

It would be two days until I got paid for the first time since arriving in London. I'd eaten grilled cheese for dinner the last two nights and it had gotten old already. Friday night I was going to go wild and order pizza. I might even treat myself to a bottle of wine. I straightened my gray skirt before slipping on my jacket. I was going to have to wear this skirt—my only office-appropriate skirt since I'd ripped my black one—every day until I got my paycheck, so I had to do everything to avoid spilling anything. Or ripping it. Again.

I picked up my bag and headed out to the tube station. I wasn't quite sure what had passed between Knightley and me in his office yesterday. I just knew it was something—he knew it too. He looked at me as if he were half enraged, half desperate to kiss me. And I'd been waiting for him to touch me, press my lips to his, smooth his hands over my body.

I needed to shut thoughts of him down and keep things professional. I'd been rude to him and he could easily have had me fired, but something told me I had to match him, not submit to him, if I was going to get anywhere with this job.

As I got to the platform, I scanned the people left and right of me. Knightley had gotten onto the same train that first morning, but I hadn't seen him since.

Today I was going to avoid him, which wouldn't be difficult. I'd never seen him in the admin room, and I wasn't sure if he'd ever even been into the clerks' room. I was going to focus on billing and the paperwork I'd managed to sneak out of his office while he wasn't there.

"Good morning," I said as I passed Jimmy's desk on the way to mine.

"All right?" Jimmy asked.

I'd figured out "all right" was the standard greeting between the clerks and admin team. They weren't actually asking if you were okay, it was just meant in the same way that Americans would say hello. But they were much more formal with Craig and the clerks. It was almost as if we were the servants living downstairs in Downton Abbey—it was a different world.

"You're always so cheerful, Violet," he said, leaning back in his chair. "And good job on that bill yesterday."

I wasn't sure if he'd be so impressed if he knew how I'd spoken to Knightley, what had almost happened between us, but hopefully he'd never find out.

"Thanks, Jimmy. Baby steps," I called over my shoulder as I walked into the admin room. I was the first to arrive again this morning. I squinted as I walked closer, focusing on a shallow, glossy black box on my desk. As I got closer, I could see it was tied with a black bow. What the hell?

I peeled off my coat and dropped it on my chair before reaching for the package. My heart was thumping. Why would anyone leave me a gift? I slid the bow off and lifted the lid of the box as I sat down. I pulled open the white tissue paper and pulled out what was buried.

Oh. My. God.

A skirt. A *Dolce and Gabbana* skirt.

Knightley. Who else?

I exhaled. I didn't know what to think. I couldn't accept a freaking designer skirt. The one that had ripped had been from Forever 21. And it hadn't even been his fault. So much for avoiding him today.

I slipped past Jimmy and knocked on Knightley's door.

"What?" he barked.

I grinned and then stopped myself before I went in and closed the door firmly behind me. He didn't look up.

"Mr. Knightley," I said.

Slowly, he lifted his gaze to mine. "Miss King."

I tilted my head. "It was such a thoughtful gift, but I can't accept the skirt."

He frowned and blinked, once. "Of course you can," he snapped. "The damage to your other one was my fault. This office is indeed a mess. I've scraped my gown on that corner several times. I should have had someone mend it. It's a simple replacement."

I took a step forward. "You don't replace Forever 21 with Dolce and Gabbana."

He turned back to his computer. "It would seem you're wrong about that."

Arrogant ass. "Well, I can't accept it."

"You can, Violet, and you will."

My breath caught when he used my name.

"You will displease me if I don't see you wearing that skirt tomorrow."

I put my hand on my hip. Seriously? "I'll *displease* you?"

"Yes, now leave. I have work to do."

"Tell me about the Generide Corporation case. How many hours?"

He didn't respond, but kept tapping away at his computer.

"Just tell me how many hours and I'll go," I said.

"Patience, Miss King. I'm checking."

I pressed lips together to stop my smirk from forming.

"Ninety," he said, looking me straight in the eye.

"Nine zero?"

He nodded.

Holy shitballs; Jimmy was going to love me. Without another word, I turned and left the office, grabbing a handful of papers from the pile I was working on before I left. If he was going to buy me Dolce and Gabbana skirts, then he could give up a few more files.

I closed his door, clutched the papers to my chest, and hurried back to my desk. Another day, another invoice raised, another day I kept my job, but I hadn't managed to reject the skirt. Worse, he'd commanded I wear it. Like the lawyer he was, he wanted *evidence* that I'd accepted his gift to me. Did I want to *displease* him? I landed on my chair and turned to my desk. And the wall. No. I wanted to please him. I wanted him to want me. I wanted him to fantasize about his hand up my skirt, fucking me over his desk. Despite him being moody and bad-tempered, it felt as if I'd pierced a part of his armor, as if I were part of some secret, seductive world—his world that only a few were even invited to.

"Violet," Jimmy called, and I spun to face him. "Could you take minutes of our chambers meeting tomorrow night at six?" he asked. "I wouldn't ask but Becky is out—"

"Yes, that's fine," I replied. It wasn't as if I had anything else to do, and I found chambers life more and more fascinating. I'd learned that Lincoln's Inn, this little tucked-away haven in the middle of one of the busiest cities in the world, was one of the four Inns of Court that gave barristers their certification. These grassy enclaves in London had housed barristers for the last six hundred years—way before the city around them had grown up into the modern metropolis it was today.

The Inns of Court had stayed constant while the rest of London metamorphosed.

It explained why everything was so old-fashioned. I'd spent lunchtimes exploring tiny streets that led to dead ends or another collection of buildings that wouldn't be out of place in a Dickens' novel. I'd wandered into law libraries, and once found myself in what was described as the Great Hall and must have been the inspiration for JK Rowling's Hogwarts dining room—floor-to-ceiling oak paneling dotted with portraits of judges and barristers and colored coats of arms alongside huge, arched, stained-glass windows. It was all so different to what I was used to in New York and different was exactly what I needed.

So I was more than happy to take minutes at what felt like a meeting of a secret society, to see how all these barristers interacted with each other and Knightley. He seemed to have so many sides to him, arrogant lawyer, kind stranger, prolific gift giver. What else would I discover about him?

Alexander

After Violet had burst into my room yesterday to tell me she wasn't accepting my gift, I kept waiting for her to reappear. But she never did. I hadn't seen her all day today, either. Normally I wouldn't notice if I'd seen Craig or Jimmy or any of the staff in chambers from one week's end to the next, but Violet King had caught my attention.

Today, I'd wanted to see if she'd complied and worn the skirt I'd bought her. She'd acted as if I'd made some huge, inappropriate gesture, but I'd just gone online and had it delivered to my desk. It wasn't like it took any effort. After all, it was my desk that had ruined the original, and I knew she didn't have many clothes. I'd quite enjoyed picking it out on the website—imagining what she'd look like in it, how the material would bunch with my hand up it. But now that I'd not seen her, I was concerned that I'd gone too far. Not that Violet seemed to be the kind of woman who was easily frightened off. But I did have to wonder if the episode in my office and my subsequent gift made me look like a kind of pervert.

Since my wife and I separated three years ago, I'd had a series of one-night stands, but I'd not *dated* anyone, and the women I'd fucked had nothing to do with chambers. Somehow, Violet, with her smart mouth and long legs, had worked me up to a point where I'd allowed myself to lose focus. I couldn't give in to my desire for her. My work had to have my sole focus—it was who I was. In fact, wondering how she'd look in the skirt I'd bought should be the last thing I was fixating on.

Further down the corridor I heard Craig knocking on office doors. The dreaded monthly chambers meeting. I normally managed to double-book myself a client dinner or something equally as immovable, so I didn't have to attend. But my mind had been elsewhere. I'd show my face and then fake an emergency call after thirty minutes or so.

I came out of my office and turned left down to our largest conference room and found myself following Miss King. So she hadn't run off after all. She'd just not been into my office today. Interesting. I glanced down and noticed she was wearing the skirt I'd bought her. It had a thick, red seam that led to the split in the back, a pathway to a promised land. I trailed my eyes back to her neck. She'd worn her hair up today. I preferred it down.

"You look like you've got something on your mind, Mr. Knightley," Jimmy said as he came up next to me. Violet turned her head slightly, as if she were going to look over her shoulder, then had thought better about it.

"Always," I replied. Except I was usually fixating over work, and not the nape of a woman's neck.

"I'm sorry to hear about the Mermerand case being adjourned."

Jimmy didn't give a shit about the Mermerand case. And I was fine with that—it wasn't his job. "It's fine," I replied. I didn't need to be his friend. I had no patience for small talk. I just needed him to do his job. Apparently, he'd not realized that yet.

The carved oak door of the conference room was propped open and barristers filled up the seats around the table. There were a few spaces still available, but there wouldn't be by the time everyone had arrived and so some barristers, normally the more junior in chambers, would take one of the seats around the outside of the room. Jimmy headed to one side of the outside circle of chairs by the arched windows while Violet headed to the other. I followed her. I'd always sat at the table, even when I was newly called to the bar. My father's reputation may have been an albatross around my neck in some ways, but it also provided certain privileges, such as automatic respect among more senior members of the bar, including judges. It might not be fair, but it was how life at the bar worked. Nepotism was an accepted way of life. There were plenty of advantages it afforded me, but there was also a downside that no one saw—the expectation, the reputation to live up to.

I took a seat next to Violet. Charles, one of the barristers I respected, pulled out the chair next to him. "There's room at the table," he said.

"I'm fine here," I replied.

He frowned, clearly a little confused, but turned back to the table.

I wanted to be able to make a discreet exit before the meeting ended, so sitting here was better. Besides, it put me next to Violet. I'd not been this close to her since the episode in my office. The scent of jasmine wafted my way, releasing the tension in my muscles. I leaned back, my thigh nudging hers. She didn't flinch, didn't react at all. Did I have any effect on her? Fuck, why did I care?

The meeting was called to order and Violet began scribbling away. I wasn't interested in the pedestrian agenda that included the proposition of renting space next door for additional conference rooms and the number of places we had for pupils—trainee barristers—for the coming year. It was just an excuse for certain members of chambers to hear more of their own voice as far as I was concerned. But Violet was recording everything as if she were reporting for Parliament's official record.

Two of the most senior members of chambers began to trade opinions about a current pupil and whether he should be offered tenancy—a permanent place in chambers. They were diametrically opposed, one thinking he should take a spot, the other believing he wasn't good enough. I didn't have a view. I hadn't worked with him. I hated working with people generally, but particularly those who hadn't already proven themselves. My reputation was too important, and I was too much of a control freak.

Except, there was nothing freaky about wanting to be in control—it was a natural survival instinct. One that had served me well. Voices became raised and Violet turned to me, her eyes widening as if she were sharing her shock with me. It was the first time she'd acknowledged me, and I was puzzled at how much I enjoyed the intimacy of her looking to me for answers. As if we had some kind of connection or history.

What the fuck was happening to me?

This girl had cast a spell on me.

The room was uncomfortably hot and my clothes unusually tight. Trying to give myself room to breathe, I ran my index finger around the inside of my collar. It seemed to do the opposite, and I found myself gasping for air as if I'd become allergic to this meeting, or worse, overwhelmed by the possibility that a woman was getting to me.

I stood abruptly and left, not bothering to excuse myself. I needed to create some distance between Violet and me. I'd never been unsettled by a woman before. Even my wife had found it difficult to get my attention, which I guess was part of the reason I'd spent the last three years living in a hotel.

It wasn't as if Violet King was so special, despite her perfume of the Indian twilight and her legs that looked like they were the perfect length to wrap around my waist. No matter the delicate curve of her neck and the press of her hands.

No. Violet wasn't special and I was done thinking about her.

NINE

Violet

Despite knowing it would make her English ass uncomfortable, I hugged Darcy as hard as I could. It was Friday. I'd been paid. I was ready to flirt with some British boys and drink some London cocktails. Luckily, Darcy had saved me from an evening in front of the TV with a pizza. I was excited to have my first real night out since I'd arrived in London.

"Put me down, Violet," she said. "Anyone would think you'd just been released from prison."

I laughed and sat down on the low velvet chair in an uber-cool bar in the center of Soho. "Some would say I have."

"How is the job?"

Darcy lived in a world where it was possible to survive without working—not that she didn't work. She did. The responsibilities of running her family's estate swallowed up her life. She just didn't *have* to work. I wasn't sure what that would feel like.

"Good. I'm a 'proper' commuting Londoner," I said, waving at a waiter to get his attention.

"I'm sorry I couldn't find you something more exciting."

"Are you kidding? It was so great of you. And actually, I'm enjoying it. It's distracting." I hadn't thought about David and the IPO since I'd started.

"Aren't they a bunch of snooty arseholes who were born with a silver spoon in their mouths?" she asked.

I raised my eyebrows at her. "Seriously? This coming from the granddaughter and sister of freaking dukes?"

She laughed. "I suppose when you put it like that . . . It's just that barristers are an odd bunch. They seem to exist in a different world. I dated one once."

She'd caught my attention. Were they impossible to date? Knightley worked so much, I wasn't sure he'd have the time for anything other than sleep. "I didn't know that. What happened?"

"He was emotionally stunted, obviously."

I nodded. That sounded about right. And a mass of contradictions. Formal and polite in some circumstances, not so much when he was looking at me as if he wanted to devour me. But smart as anything and complicated as anything. And I really liked that.

The waiter delivered our cocktails—my favorite: a French 75.

"And he was a total workaholic."

Hmmm, that sounded familiar. It was a wonder any of them managed to get laid. As much as he was a workaholic, I bet Knightley made time for sex. Although I couldn't imagine he prioritized a relationship. People didn't seem to be his focus. He was all about the paper.

"And the sex just wasn't that good. He had a premature

thing happening. Came from kissing me one time," Darcy continued.

I shuddered. "Oh wow." Knightley seemed too much in control to have that issue. "Doesn't sound particularly fulfilling."

She laughed. "No. Not in any way. But I guess you don't have to fuck them."

I kept my face passive, careful not to give anything away. Darcy didn't need to know I wanted to get naked with Knightley. Since our encounter in his office, I'd avoided him as much as I could. Then, in the meeting yesterday, he'd sat next to me despite seats available at the table. Maybe he'd wanted to reassure me that I shouldn't feel uncomfortable, but then I might be overestimating his softer side.

In any case, he'd left the meeting in a bit of a rush and I'd found myself missing the warmth of his body next to mine. He'd sat closer to me than he'd needed to, and I'd enjoyed it, reveling in the buzz between us. At least I'd thought there'd been a buzz between us. Maybe I'd imagined it.

"Violet?"

"Sorry," I said, realizing Darcy had been talking while I daydreamed. "I just remembered I forgot to finish something off at work."

"So you're enjoying it?" she asked.

I nodded. "I've never had an office job before. At the start-up we were working from our apartments or coffee shops and after that I've always waitressed or worked in hospitality. But yes, it's better than I expected." For so long I'd rejected any job that involved a computer; I'd not wanted any association with my past disappointment.

When Darcy didn't respond, I glanced up from my drink.

She grinned at me. "You never know, this could lead to something."

"It's a nice thought, but I doubt it." Clerical work would do for now. But I didn't emotionally invest in anything for the long term. It wasn't who I was. Not now. At least, I didn't think it was. Swapping New York for London had been the biggest change I'd made in my life since David and I split after college, and it had awoken something in me. I craved something more; I just wasn't sure what. "Enough about work. I want to hear about your dating life."

Darcy groaned. "What dating life? I never meet people. If I wanted to date a horse, I'd be perfectly placed."

"I like to think I'm open-minded when it comes to dating, but I don't think going out with a horse should even be a consideration." I grinned. I was pretty sure she was joking, but the more time I spent around the British, the more I realized anything was possible. "Come on, I'm sure I can find you a cute guy. You know I found your brother for Scarlett. I think I have a bit of a magic touch for these things." I scanned the room. The lighting was dim and the walls a bronze color. There were no windows and the floors were black so it felt intimate and almost sullen, but it was small and the tables were close together so I could make out most of the other patrons. "What kind of guy do you go for?"

Darcy sighed. "Someone who's not a total shit," she said, in a way that said she didn't think that should be a complete no-brainer of a requirement. As if she expected me to suggest she date a total shit if he took her to a nice restaurant, or was a good kisser or something.

"Okay. Any other criteria?" I asked.

"Well obviously someone who loves the country. I mean, I like town and everything, but my heart aches if I spend too long without seeing miles of green fields and acres of trees."

"I'm sure we can find someone who likes the smell of cow shit." I grinned and Darcy chuckled. "What about physically? What's your type?" I narrowed my eyes, trying to take in all the men in the bar who looked potentially single and in the right age bracket. This was clearly some kind of Mecca for the good-looking and rich, because there were plenty of handsome men in expensive suits. I spotted the back of one man's head that looked very familiar and my breath caught. Shit, Knightley.

I shouldn't be surprised. This seemed like his kind of place—moody, with overpriced drinks. I pulled my shoulders back and kept my gaze fixed on him, waiting for him to turn around. Would he come over? I glanced at his companion, who was facing me. She was a beautiful blonde woman around my age who wore a very low-cut blouse. My gut churned. They looked like they were on a date. My pulse sped as he grasped the arms of the chair and stood. As he headed to the other side of the bar, I realized it wasn't Knightley at all, but rather someone not half as broad, or tall, or handsome.

Fuck, I was *imagining* him.

What was the matter with me? I grabbed my glass and downed my cocktail, wincing at the burn of the alcohol in my throat.

"I like blonds," Darcy said. "That floppy-haired, laid-back thing always gets me."

I nodded. "Like that guy?" I lifted my chin to indicate a guy ordering drinks at the bar who wore a very loud pink shirt and a pinky ring.

She shrugged. "Maybe. But my life is the estate. There's no point boyfriend hunting in London."

"You're only an hour away, and like you said, you're not going to find Mr. Right on your doorstep. You don't even *have* neighbors."

The floppy-haired blond collected a couple of drinks and went to one of the tables on the other side of the bar where a taller, dark-haired guy was sitting who wasn't wearing a tie or a jacket. He must have been the least formally dressed guy in the place. "Let's just wait to see if that blond one is with a woman." If he wasn't joined by anyone, then it was Darcy's lucky night. I might not be the world's best waitress, but I could pick up a guy without any trouble at all.

"Any hot barristers caught your attention?" Darcy asked as I was staring at our two potential dates.

Knightley had definitely caught my attention. That brooding, English-hero thing he had going on worked for him. "I'm still scoping them out." I grabbed the cocktail menu and wafted it toward my burning cheeks. Jesus, what was I so embarrassed about? Men never embarrassed me. "They all hide down this rabbit hole of a hallway. I don't think I've even met them all." I'd seen most of them at the meeting last night, though, but none of them had been as handsome as Knightley. Or had the same commanding presence. I shifted in my seat, trying to shake visions of a naked Knightley from my head.

I took a sip of my cocktail. "They're definitely not waiting for anyone," I said, refocusing on the floppy-haired guy and his friend. "It's just the two of them at that table and neither of them have looked over at the door once, although they have scanned the bar, which makes me think they're up for company." I turned to Darcy. "Are you ready?"

She frowned. "For what?"

I wasn't interested in getting to know either of these guys, which made no sense because I'd not kissed anyone since arriving in London. Tonight would be all about Darcy. "Bring your drink and follow me. There's no point in going boyfriend shopping and not trying anything on."

"You're crazy."

I stood and grabbed my cocktail. "Let's have some fun. It's my first night out in London, despite the fact that I've been here weeks. I need to make up for lost time."

I strode over to the table where the two guys I'd been watching were sitting. "Hey, do you mind if my friend and I join you?" I acknowledged them both but my gaze lingered on the dark-haired guy. I didn't want either of them to be under any misunderstanding as to who we'd allocated to whom.

"We'd be delighted," the dark-haired one said, standing and offering me a seat. "Can I get you a drink?"

I shifted down the bench that he'd left warm. "Maybe in a few minutes. I still have my cocktail," I said, raising my glass to him.

Darcy hovered a few feet away from the table.

"Darcy, let me introduce you to our new friends," I said. "This is . . ."

The blond one stood and held out his hand. "Edward," he said, ignoring me. There had definitely been a twinkle in his eye when he caught sight of her. Perfect.

"I'm Violet," I said, as my allocated man sat down next to me.

"And how lovely you are, just like the flower."

I managed not to laugh.

"My name is Reginald."

I couldn't hold back anymore and I chuckled. "Your name is *not* Reginald."

"Well, no, but if it had been, it's not very nice to laugh when someone tells you their name." He grinned at me. "But I'll forgive you, given you're American. My name is James."

"Nice to meet you, James." I made up my mind about men I met very quickly. I liked men who knew how to fuck, otherwise I didn't have a type. It shouldn't have been a particularly high standard, but it wasn't easy to find a guy who knew how to fuck *me*, and even when I did find one, he always wanted to cuddle afterward, or take me to dinner. I got bored very quickly—sometimes it took an evening, others a month or two, but it was never long before I went back to being single and unwilling to commit to anything for long. Knightley was probably the same way.

It wasn't that James didn't have potential. He was cute, and funny and flirty. The jury was out on whether or not he'd know how to fuck, but there was something missing. Something that wasn't pulling me toward him, making me want to imagine him naked.

Unlike Knightley. Shit, why was my mind wandering to Knightley again? I squeezed my thighs together and turned to James.

"You live over here?" he asked.

"Just for a few months," I replied, trying to pay attention to him and not betray that I was sitting here thinking about another man.

"And then you'll head back to the States?"

"Sure. That's where my family is." Christ, was that all I had in the US? No job, no apartment, nothing. Just siblings who were all moving on to the next stage of their lives and three boxes of God knew what in my sister's garage.

"What about you? You live in London?"

"Islington."

I nodded even though I had no clue where that was.

"I'm a banker. We both are," he said, lifting his chin toward his friend.

"Is he single?" I asked.

James chuckled. "You interested?"

"Oh, no. I meant for Darcy. I'm looking out for her." I hadn't meant for it to sound like I wasn't interested in the handsome guy I was talking to, who was so far perfectly charming, but he'd picked up on something. The fact was, I wasn't that interested in him.

Knightley had gotten under my skin, and although I wasn't about to march into his office and request he take me on the desk, I also didn't want to fuck one person while thinking about another. Somehow it didn't seem right. I glanced across at Darcy and the floppy-haired blond who was making her laugh. Tonight was about her.

I was happy to play wingman and be left to my fantasies of a naked Knightley.

TEN

Alexander

After only four hours of sleep, I'd been at the gym doors when they'd opened at five thirty, but even a brutal workout hadn't exhausted me. My mind was all over the place. I just couldn't concentrate. I screwed up the paper I'd been making notes on and threw it in the bin in the corner of my office. I had too much energy. I'd worked all weekend in the hotel, gone on two long runs along the Thames, but still hadn't slept well.

After sitting next to Violet during last week's meeting, I'd done my best to rid myself of all thoughts of her. I hated the way I'd changed my behavior because of her—even if it was in the smallest way—by sitting in a different spot in the conference room. Even though I'd told myself that it was a better position from which to make a surreptitious exit, I knew the truth.

I was full of shit.

I'd wanted to be near her, to breathe in her scent and feel the heat of her body next to mine.

It pissed me off.

No woman made me lose focus on my work. Ever. My broken marriage was a testament to that.

"Fuck," I said under my breath at the knock at the door. I could tell by the confident rap it was Violet. She was probably the only one in these chambers who wasn't scared to interrupt me when she needed to. "Come in," I said, turning my attention to my computer screen. I didn't want to have to look at her, didn't want her to see how much she'd gotten under my skin, or how much I resented her for it.

"Do you have any more dry cleaning?" she asked. "I'm happy to take your shirts to be laundered."

Fuck, she sounded so innocent, but I suspected she was anything but. "I don't need you to babysit me," I said. "I can arrange my own laundry." Perhaps, if I was less than polite, she'd leave me alone.

She didn't respond, and I looked up to see if she'd left me in peace. "What are you doing?" I asked as I saw her squeezing between two towers of paper.

"Knitting a sweater. You? Trying to get into the finals for asshole of the year?" she said as she disappeared behind the piles of paper.

I didn't know whether to laugh or spank her, but my twitching cock told me I wasn't mad.

I got up from my desk and moved toward her. The last thing I wanted was for her to knock one of the piles over—they'd all go down like dominoes. "What are you looking for?" I asked, taking in her tight arse as she bent over in front of me. If I took two steps forward, I'd be able to skim my hands over her waist. She'd probably gained confidence and was trying to take some more of the Ellington case papers she'd been slowly stealing each time I left the office.

"I'm taking some of these," she said, her arms full of

witness statements by the looks of it. "You might be smart, but you haven't noticed that I've been taking bits of this pile when you're out of the office." She stood up and turned to stare at me defiantly. I wasn't about to spoil her fun and tell her that I knew exactly when she'd been in my office and what she was taking. I wouldn't give away that her jasmine perfume clung to every part of this office, including me, or that I'd imagined smelling it all weekend.

"So you're stealing from me?" I asked, folding my arms.

"I'm doing my job." She shook her head and bent to pick up a single sheet of paper that had escaped from the pile she was holding.

Fuck she was sexy. Every move, every curve—the confident way she met me head on—equal to equal.

"I have no idea what has crawled up your ass," she said, stepping toward me between two towers of paper. "But pull it out, get out of my way, and let me get on with this."

I stayed right *in* her way. I didn't want her to leave. Not yet. "What have you got there?" I placed my hand over hers to adjust the papers she was holding so I could see. Her skin was soft and smooth, and she gasped but she didn't pull away. Instead her eyes flickered to my face and I met her gaze. My resolve to keep my distance from Violet was wavering.

She inhaled as we looked at each other, neither of us speaking, my heart thudding against my chest, my dick straining in my trousers.

I wanted her.

I was sure she wanted me too.

Her tongue dipped out to wet her lips and my self-control evaporated.

I reached out and cupped her neck, sweeping my thumb over her cheek. She closed her eyes and sank against my palm. My eyes darted down to her chest and back up to her beautiful face. Sliding my hand around, I finally sank my fingers into that glossy, silky hair. It was just as soft and inviting as I'd imagined when I'd seen her on the tube

There was no going back now.

I grabbed the papers from her and tossed them over my shoulder, vaguely aware of the oversized confetti floating to the ground behind me.

Her eyes flung open wide. "What the—"

Before she could ask me what else had crawled up my backside, I pulled her toward me, one hand around her waist, the other tangled in her hair, and pressed my lips against hers. For the first time in days, my mind was focused on one thing and one thing alone—Violet King and the way she felt under my fingers, the way she tasted. It was like I'd arrived back home after a long, arduous trip.

Her knees buckled, and for a second I thought I had her immediate, unwavering submission, but then, as if she'd changed her mind, she pushed at my chest with her tiny hands.

"What?" I asked, pulling away slightly. I knew this was what she wanted.

She looked at me like she wanted to murder me. Her eyes piercing, her lips reddened and pursed—she was beautiful.

"What are you doing?" she asked.

"I'm kissing you, and in case you haven't noticed, you're kissing me back." It was the best I'd felt since she'd been this close on our walk to chambers the first time I'd laid eyes on her.

Her lips were slightly parted and her chest pressed against mine. She didn't really seem like she was wanting me to stop. I dipped my head again and delved into her mouth with my tongue. She met my energy and need, but then stopped and pushed at my chest once more.

"No. We can't. I need this job."

"*I* need *this*." I couldn't remember the last time I'd felt I *needed* a woman. I'd craved sex, release, but not hungered for a particular woman as I'd seemed to since Violet appeared at my side on the Green Park platform. I pressed my hands against her arse and cupped her buttocks. "And so do you." This feeling couldn't be one-sided, could it? "Besides, nothing we do here will affect your job. You know you want this as much as I do."

She groaned but not in the way I'd hoped. It wasn't out of lust; it sounded like frustration. "Yes you're attractive but you're an asshole to me. You can't want to kiss someone you think is stupid."

I reached for the hem of her skirt, dipping beneath the fabric, encouraged by her admission that she found me attractive. "I'm an arsehole to everyone." She rolled her eyes and I dipped and kissed her briefly before pulling back. "And I don't think you're stupid. You went to MIT, for crying out loud." The fact that she was clever was part of the attraction. Maybe that was the reason she wasn't intimidated by me. Her confidence around me was the ultimate aphrodisiac.

She narrowed her eyes. "You looked me up." She smoothed her hands over my chest, and my muscles beneath her fingers buzzed from her touch.

"You're in my office stealing papers." I slid my hand further up her leg, my fingers finding the top of her stocking and her hot, soft skin. Fuck, she was delicious. I twisted my hips against her. "I took a look at your CV."

"You knew I was taking stuff?" She bit her lip as I traced

my finger around the lace of her stocking and she sank against me a little.

I walked her back toward the wall. I wished we had more space. More time. I could lose myself in her for hours if I had the chance, I was sure of it. "I'm not an idiot either. It may look like chaos in here, but I know exactly what everything is. I have an excellent memory."

She pressed her fingertips against my cheekbone and sighed. "I don't think you're an idiot. I just thought I was covering my tracks."

I smoothed my palm up her inner thigh, and she tipped her head back and gasped. I took my time, taking in her heat and her sounds, greedy for everything about her. Her skin was smooth and tight like a drum. My hand went higher and higher wanting more and more and I tried to silence the sound of my heartbeat so I could hear when she said no. But I got only encouragement from her sounds. Had she fantasized about this like I had? Was she ready for me?

I slid my hand further up, my finger reaching the edge of her underwear. I drew my fingernail along the lace and she shivered.

"What's your name?" she asked and a shot of desire spiked through me. I had my hand up her skirt and she didn't even know what to call me. "Or do you just like to be called sir?"

As much as I had a healthy ego, and I liked to dominate in the bedroom, I didn't want her to call me anything but my name. I slipped my fingers beneath the lace. "Alex," I replied, stroking up and down her folds, pressing against her, breathing her in.

She gasped as if I were talking dirty. "Alexander."

I paused. No one other than my family had ever called me Alexander, but the way it rolled over her tongue in her lazy, sexy, do-anything-for-me drawl stopped me from correcting her. I found her clit and circled it with my finger. She arched her back.

She pushed her hands through my hair as I pulled her skirt to her waist. "Alexander," she whispered, making my cock rigid. I slid the heel of my hand down my erection. How the fuck was it possible to be this hard and not have passed out with lack of blood supply to the brain? "What if someone comes in?" she asked. But I knew she was beyond caring. Her eyes were sleepy with lust, and her hand fumbled at my fly, as she tried to get access to my dick.

I glanced over my shoulder. "No one would fucking dare. Only you." I reached between her legs and pulled at the lace—I needed to feel her pussy. The snap of the elastic as I tore her panties made her groan again, but this time, it was the timbre I'd been waiting to hear. "You've got to be quiet. I know it will be difficult because I'm going to fuck you so hard you're going to want to scream the place down. But, you've got to hold it in."

She shook her head. "So confident, Mr. Knightley."

"I'm about to prove it to you." She released my dick and I grabbed my wallet and found a condom. I couldn't handle her fist—I was too close to the edge—so I rolled on the latex, grabbed her under her thighs, and pressed her against the wall.

"You ready?" I asked.

"You better be good."

Little witch. I'd show her how a real man fucked.

I slammed into her and she grabbed onto my shoulders, her eyes wide and filled with panic. I knew she'd have a hard time staying quiet, and now she knew it, too.

I stilled, buried deep in her and we stared at each other in silent understanding. We both wanted this. Needed this.

Since the first day we'd laid eyes on each other we'd been heading to this exact moment. What had gone unspoken had finally been confessed. This wasn't a look, a touch, a kiss. Her legs were spread and my cock was inside her. There was no going back. And for the first time I understood why it was said that sex is intimate. Before I'd assumed it was due to the lack of clothes but right there, I understood it was much more than that. Having crossed this line in the sand it felt like we'd shut a door on the rest of the world leaving only Violet and me on this side. We were joined.

Slowly I began to move out, not wanting to leave the grip of her but needing to fuck. Needing to pin her against the wall with my cock. I buried my face into her neck, trying to muffle my own sounds—not trusting myself to be able to hold back.

"Alexander," she whispered in my ear as I pushed back in, deeper this time, and it was *so* deep, so very, very tight. I'd thought about this so much, imagined it, wanted it and it was even better, even *more* than I thought it would be.

I wanted her to say that she'd been waiting for this moment, had fantasized about me fucking her against my office wall. I wanted to understand this longing I'd felt these last few days wasn't one-sided. I needed her surrender. Her fingers tightened in my hair as her body relaxed in my arms. She'd given up, given her control to me—her fight had been replaced with her need for me. It was a victory.

As I began to thrust in and out of her, she clawed at my chest, undoing my buttons, almost desperate for me. Christ, I wanted her naked. I'd like to make her come with just my mouth on her nipples. She was so fucking responsive, I knew I'd have her writhing and begging for release within seconds. If I had longer, I'd spend hours enjoying her body, my tongue finding every sweet spot and I was sure there would be plenty. The grip of her perfect pussy was just the tip of the iceberg, I was sure of it.

"You walk around this wet? Ready to be fucked at all times?" I asked, grunting out each word. "Or is it just for me?"

"Don't stop," she whispered. "Please God, don't stop."

No way—I didn't think I ever could. I wanted to stay here, fucking her forever, experiencing this delicious slide as I plowed into her, this feeling that if I went deep enough, it would be all I'd ever need.

Her breathing became choppy, her fingernails dug deep into my shoulders and her whole body tensed as she bucked against me, her mouth open, her eyes screwed shut, I nearly lost my grip on her as she began to pulse around me, coming silently on my cock. Fuck, I wanted to hear her scream. Annoyed that the environment dictated how we fucked, I continued to pump into her, watching as she floated back to consciousness with a smile, then dipped her head and pressed a kiss to my jaw. It was so sweet and sexy and caring it nearly broke my rhythm.

I wasn't done with her yet. I wanted her to understand what I was capable of doing to her. This wasn't just a fuck. I wasn't just some guy she worked with. I had the urge to be indelibly etched onto her brain—to have the impact on her that she had on me. And as far as Violet King was concerned, in this moment, I was done fighting urges. I was giving into them all.

She gasped, and I could tell by the way she tightened around my cock that I was going to be able to hold out long enough to make her come again. I twisted my hips and her eyes met mine in panic.

"No, not again," she said, shaking her head.

"Yes."

"Alexander, I can't."

"You can and you will."

Her hands fisted against my shoulders but her body relaxed. She was giving herself to me—giving her next climax to me—and there was nothing sexier. I dipped my head to kiss her, wanting every inch of connection that she could give.

She knew now that I wasn't just some casual guy who didn't see how truly beautiful she was, didn't comprehend how smart she was. She knew that she wasn't going to be able to get away with faking her orgasms like she normally did. No. I'd make her come not once but twice. I'd make her see how good it could be.

I thrust harder, grinding my cock into her until she arched her back and threw her head forward, her mouth against mine, open, desperate, and intimate. I was going to come if we stayed like this and I wasn't ready. Not yet. Sharply, before it was too late, I pulled out and I released her legs, bracing myself against the wall to catch my breath.

He hands skimmed my torso. "You've not—"

I liked that she wasn't done either. "Nearly," I whispered. "You just feel so fucking great." I took a step back. "Turn around and put your hands on the wall." I could barely get my words out, I was so hard but without a question, she turned and did as I'd asked.

Perfect.

She might have a smart mouth in the office but she clearly knew how to do as she was told when it came to sex.

After surveying her for a few seconds, taking in the beautiful lines her body made, I stepped forward, and placed my hand between her thighs. "Open."

Her legs spread, she sighed and stuck out her arse, tempting me like the little witch she was.

I stepped closer to her, and dipped my head. "I know you like to get fucked, Violet but it's not normally like this, is it? Not usually this good. This is as good as it gets. And you're so desperate for me to make you come again."

Her fingernails scratched the wall as she fisted her hands. "Just as desperate as you," she replied.

I chuckled. She had some fucking nerve. I'd show her who was desperate. I nudged my thumb to her entrance, pressing and flicking my fingers across her clit.

She snapped her head around and looked at me desperately. "Please," she said, her words coated in her need.

She pulsed beneath my hand and I found myself relaxing, knowing that she was as tightly wound as I was.

Pressing her lips together, she tried to stifle her own sounds. Her body jerked and she looked at me as if she were pleading for mercy as my fingers worked her into a frenzy. I wasn't about to stop. She'd asked for this. She needed to be careful what she wished for.

Her engorged clit throbbed under my fingers as she began to whimper and her wetness seeped over my hand. God, I wanted to lick her, suck her, taste her, and for a moment I almost sank to my knees and did just that. I stopped myself as her groans became more pronounced.

I needed to be inside her. I wanted to feel her tighten around my cock as she climaxed.

I rammed in and nearly blacked out at the overwhelming pleasure coursing through my body. I couldn't stop now. I knew she was close and I was chasing her, trying to get to the finish line at the same time as I fucked and fucked. Her pussy clenched around me and I pushed in one final time, coming as if it were my first time, my body stiff, desperate to prolong our connection as long as I could.

I was sure our heavy breathing could be heard echoing through chambers, but I was too sated to care. She was the fuck of the year. Of the fucking decade.

"See? I told you you'd be coming so hard you'd see stars," I said as I released her legs and slid off the condom.

"Get over yourself. There were no stars," she said, still panting as she straightened out her skirt.

I chuckled. Her flushed cheeks and ripped underwear told a different story. "Is that right?" I raised my eyebrows.

She shrugged, but for once didn't argue.

I'd seen fucking stars for Christ's sake. It was great. It had been *more* than great. And I could tell by the softness in her eyes and the way she was still unsteady on her feet that she felt it too. But I liked the fact that she wasn't swooning and telling me how great I was—it wasn't what I was used to but I respected her for it. Liked her better because of it.

Maybe now she'd stop invading my thoughts and distracting me from what was important but as I stood captivated by her neck as she smoothed out her glossy black hair, focused on her legs as she slipped her high heels back on, something told me it wasn't going to be that easy.

ELEVEN

Violet

No more fantasizing about Alexander Knightley. No more *anything* to do with Alexander. And definitely no more office sex. I had to put myself on a time-out from being reckless. I wanted to keep this job—I was enjoying it. And I wasn't sure which member of chambers was Darcy's grandfather's friend, but the last thing I wanted to do was embarrass Darcy by getting caught fucking one of the barristers.

"Violet," Jimmy called from behind me.

I jumped and spun around in my chair. "Hi."

"Any luck in getting more invoices raised for Mr. Knightley's clients?"

Thank God. For a second, I'd thought he was going to tell me I was fired. Or that everyone knew what Alexander and I had been up to yesterday in his office—I was being completely paranoid. Ordinarily I flitted between waitressing gigs, quitting when I got bored or tired or just wanted to try something new. I found myself enjoying this job—it was so different. The fear of crossing paths with

David had always driven me away from trying anything again in the IT sector. But here in chambers I was a world away. I'd started to use my brain again and it felt good. The tasks were relatively straightforward, but it felt good to be counted on, to be doing a good job because I wanted to and not just for a tip. And I liked that I'd been given this almost-impossible task and been trusted to make it happen. No one had relied on me, counted on me, for a long time.

"Not yet. I've been working on this instead," I said, indicating the spreadsheet I'd opened earlier. "It's all the instructions that have come through, but haven't been billed. I've added in the estimate given by the clerks. That way, Knight—Mr. Knightley can just confirm the ones that are correct. The ones that are left over we can deal with separately."

"Great idea," Jimmy said, perching on the end of my desk. "And you're finding it okay? I mean, he's not too much of an . . ."

"An asshole?" I finished for him. "Sure he is." I shrugged as Jimmy winced. "But I can handle him." I squeezed my thighs together at the thought of his hand up my skirt and his tongue in my mouth.

Jimmy nodded. "That's great. Probably shouldn't call him an asshole anywhere he might hear, though."

"Good tip," I said, tapping my pen against the spreadsheet.

"And you're settling into London?" he asked, clearly not ready to give up his seat on my desk quite yet.

"Sure," I said. "It's a great town. And so many of the museums are free, which is a bonus."

"Well, if you ever need a tour guide, this guy doesn't charge," he said, pointing his thumb at his chest.

I smiled. "Good to know."

He opened his mouth, no doubt to suggest he give me a tour this weekend, but thankfully the Head of Chambers, Lance Eddington, one of the most senior barristers, interrupted us. What the hell was he doing in the admin room?

"Ahh, Jimmy, I was looking for you." Jimmy jumped off my desk as though someone had stuck an electrical charge up his ass.

"What can I do for you, sir?"

"We have the Lawyer of the Year awards next week and people are dropping like flies as usual. I've had three cancellations this morning."

I'd heard about this. Apparently, these awards were a big fucking deal—it had all the clerks excited, anyway.

"All that's left is a bunch of crusty old men who shouldn't be out that late and you. We need some fresh blood. I've just told Alex he has to attend—no excuses."

At the mention of Alexander, my stomach thrummed and I gazed at the floor, hoping no one saw the heat that crept across my cheeks. How the hell did this man have me blushing? I was sure I'd never blushed at anything ever in my life.

"But we need more young ones. And more women," Lance continued.

"Of course. I'll ask Miss Atlee and Miss Jenkins."

Lance shook his head. "No, neither of them can make it. One is on holiday, the other in court that week. And I've already asked Pollyanna and Bea—they can't come either." Lance sighed.

It was no wonder they were having difficulty trying to find more women to join them. Chambers was completely male-dominated. Not just among the barristers but also the clerks.

"We need more diversity in chambers," he said. "I've been saying it for years."

"We're much better than we used to be," Jimmy said, and Lance mumbled under his breath.

"What about you, my dear?" Lance asked, squinting at me.

"Oh, I'm just temporary."

"Violet, is it?"

How the hell did he know my name?

I nodded. "Yes, sir."

"Call me Lance. I hear you've been doing an excellent job. And you're American," he said, as if my nationality was a disability I'd miraculously overcome. But I wasn't insulted. My heart swelled with pride that he knew who I was and that he'd heard I'd been doing a good job.

"Yes, sir."

"Are you free next Tuesday evening to come to the Grosvenor, Park Lane? Black tie. You'd get to watch a bunch of lawyers get drunk."

"I'm not sure," I said, surprised that he would have thought of me. "I think I may have plans. I can check." Of course, I knew I was free, but I also knew that I had nothing to wear.

"Oh, I'm delighted. You'll be the breath of fresh air we need. Put Violet down for a ticket, Jimmy."

"Yes, sir," Jimmy replied and Lance swept out.

"How did that happen?" I asked when he left. "I didn't say anything except I would check and apparently now I've RSVP'd yes?"

"That's why he's one of the top lawyers of his generation. He gets what he wants. Knows exactly how hard to push." He sat back down at my desk.

It was a free meal, right? And maybe I could borrow a

dress from Darcy.

"I guess I'm going to the Grosvenor, Park Lane, next Tuesday." At least I wouldn't have to drop money on a cab—the hotel was within walking distance from Darcy and Ryder's place. "Is it fun?"

"Of course it will be fun," he said with a wink. "*I'll* be there, which means?"

He cocked his ear waiting for me to finish his sentence.

"Banter?" I responded.

He clicked his fingers and pointed at me. "Exactly."

I smiled thinly. I was pretty sure Jimmy was testing the waters with me, seeing if I responded to his not-so-subtle flirting. Hopefully he'd get bored quickly and move on. I had enough to handle in the office already. Jimmy didn't look like he was moving, but I wanted this conversation to be over, so I stood, and Jimmy followed me down the hall, chatting about what to expect at the awards ceremony until finally, I ducked into the restroom.

On my way back, I turned a corner to find Alexander and another barrister coming toward me. Fuck. I'd been trying to avoid Alexander. I couldn't turn around and head back without looking like an idiot. It was unnerving. I lost control when he was around. Just knowing he was in the same building was bad enough. Somehow, he seemed to strip away my defenses and see right into the core of me.

I smiled but kept my head down, avoiding eye contact with both of them, but once we had passed each other, I couldn't resist taking a glance over my shoulder at that tight ass. As I turned my head, my eyes caught his. Apparently, he was checking out my ass, too. It was hard enough to stay away from him without knowing he wanted me, maybe as much as I wanted him.

I was so totally fucked.

TWELVE

Alexander

I came back from lunch to find a spreadsheet on my desk. Of course, I knew before I'd sat down that she'd been in my office. Violet's scent had now almost permanently invaded my space. It was just stronger when she'd just been in. I found I rather enjoyed it. Since my wife and I split up, I'd worked harder than ever. My encounters with women had been fleeting and purely physical. And there was good reason. I understood there were things I was good at and things that I wasn't. Women weren't my strong suit. I never understood what they needed from me and I was sure I had nothing to offer. Keeping things physical meant I didn't upset anyone; I didn't send any mixed messages. My wife told me I always put my work first and it was true. I was good at the law. I understood it and it didn't want more from me than I could give. The more I worked, the better I got at my job. The longer I was married, the worse things had become between my wife and me.

My concentration had been off since Violet had started.

I'd hoped to fuck her out of my system, but that hadn't happened. Just a glimpse of her in the corridor yesterday had my dick straining for more.

But enough. No more. I was here to work, to concentrate on what I was good at. This was an important year for me. My career could be made or broken with the next few cases I had lined up. I needed to be at the top of my game. And I'd hurt enough women in my time to know I could only ever bring Violet pain and disappointment.

I scanned down the spreadsheet, seeing the familiar names of cases and advice. Shit. There was a lot of stuff I'd not billed. I hadn't realized that I'd let this get so out of hand. I picked up a pencil and began to work my way down the list. Violet had been clever in how she'd arranged everything, grouping all the similar work together and then estimating what the bill should be. It made it easier for me. I went line by line either ticking the amount Violet had suggested or putting a cross through it and writing in the figure it should be. If I finished this, hopefully Violet would have no need to bother me.

Despite being overwhelmed with work, I spent longer than I should have on the spreadsheet. I wanted her to have everything she needed. Partly so she'd have no reason to ask me for anything but also because I wanted her to be well thought of in chambers. She was intelligent, and although most clerks and admin staff were frightened of me, Violet certainly wasn't. I enjoyed the way she gave back as much as I dished out. I liked her. Too much. Which was exactly why I needed her to keep her distance.

I ticked the last one off the list and went to find Violet. I needed to rip the plaster off, tell her straight that nothing more should happen between us and that we should keep our relationship purely professional. Better sooner rather than later.

I swung the door open and headed right toward the clerks' room, nearly walking right into Violet.

"Vi—Miss King."

She dipped her head and moved to the side, trying to pass me.

"Actually, I was coming to find you." I held up the spreadsheet by way of explanation.

"Oh," she said, scanning it. "You looked at it?" Was she not meeting my eye on purpose or was she really just enthralled by paperwork?

"I did. Can I have a word in my office?"

She narrowed her eyes and pursed her lips. "Okay," she said.

I turned and opened the door.

"Close the door behind you, will you?"

The door clicked behind me as I headed to my desk. When I turned, Violet was still by the door.

"I think it's best if I stay here."

I rolled my eyes and sat on the corner of my desk. I might want her to keep her distance, but she didn't need to act as if I were toxic waste. Jesus, this woman did nothing to flatter a man's ego.

"I just wanted to give you your spreadsheet and suggest—"

She put her hand up to silence me. "I just want to keep things professional," she said. "You over there. Me over here. The less we see each other the better. You can just email me if you need anything. Professionally, that is." Her eyes trailed over the room, fixating on anything that wasn't me. "As your assistant."

This wasn't how I'd seen this conversation going. I'd

expected to have to explain myself, convince her that we needed distance.

"I agree," I said, standing and thrusting my hands into my pockets. "We're colleagues. I don't think we should be blurring any lines."

She looked at me for the first time since she'd come into my office. "Oh." She nodded. "Good. Just what I was thinking."

"I'm glad we're agreed," I said, not being able to stop a grin from tugging at the corners of my mouth. She'd clearly been expecting me to protest. I imagined most men did when she turned them down. Thank God she'd made this easy for me, for us both. We could be adults and now go about our jobs like nothing had ever happened between us.

"I'll come and collect files when you're in court or at lunch."

I nodded. "Sounds sensible."

"Any questions I might have, I'll email you or leave a note in your office."

"That's fine." She really did want to keep away from me and, despite me wanting the same just a few minutes ago, her need to keep away intrigued me. Did she find me so irresistible that she couldn't trust herself to be around me? That was exactly how I felt about her.

"Good," she said.

"Excellent," I replied.

As she looked at me with those blue eyes and blinked slowly and deliberately, I wanted to unbutton her blouse and feast on her breasts. To shove my hand up her skirt and feel her silky pussy just one last time. She inspired a primal urge in me that I'd never felt before.

What was I thinking? She must be wielding witchcraft. There was no other explanation. Women didn't get under my skin like this, didn't ever hold my attention like Violet did. I cleared my throat and held out her spreadsheet. "So, if you'd close the door on your way out."

She stepped forward tentatively and reached for the spreadsheet. "Thank you," she said, our fingers touching. Her touch magnified my need for her, the desire to pull her toward me. I resisted, stepped back and watched as she turned away, a crease between her eyes as if she were thoroughly confused.

I looked up as the brass handle of the door squeaked. She glanced over her shoulder. "Goodbye, Alexander."

"Goodbye, Violet."

I turned back to my laptop. Back to my work—something I could easily navigate, the part of my life I knew I was good at.

THIRTEEN

Violet

"You're welcome to any of these, really," Darcy said as I sat cross-legged on the floor at the foot of her huge four-poster bed, facing into her closet.

I winced at the scrape of the hangers against the rail. Darcy was going through her closet looking for dresses I could borrow to wear to the awards ceremony.

"But which one do you like the least?" I asked.

"They're dresses, not ex-boyfriends," she said. "Take whatever you like." She snatched a hanger off the rail and spun, holding the plastic-covered dress in front of her. "This color would look beautiful on you."

"Purple?"

"It has a diamante belt. It's so pretty." She unzipped the bag and pulled out a fountain of purple-blue chiffon. "It's cornflower blue."

I leaned forward to grab some of the vast amounts of material. "It feels expensive—it's way too nice for me to borrow."

"Don't be so ridiculous. Try it on."

I stood, deliciously tempted by the fairytale dress but unable to escape the feeling I'd never pull it off.

"Come on. Strip and take off your bra. It's one-shouldered."

Darcy looked at me expectantly and I began to undress. "So, how's the man situation?" she asked, her eyes dancing as she spoke.

I still hadn't told her about Alexander. "No situation," I said simply, peeling off my jeans.

"Surely another whole week hasn't gone by without you having a man under your spell?" Darcy handed me the dress and I stepped into it. The chiffon floated against my skin like a thousand kisses. I shivered.

"Wow. That looks amazing on you." She fiddled with the material at my shoulder. "The shoulder kind of acts like a train or a scarf," she said as the material of the sleeve floated behind me. On the hanger the bodice had looked like it was just loose material but it fit snuggly around my ribcage, draping across my body in a close fit.

"It's too beautiful," I said, looking down. "I can't possibly borrow this."

"Of course it's beautiful; it's Elie Saab, and you *must* borrow it. Take a look in that mirror." She pointed at the full-length mirror on the other side of the room. "You look amazing."

I stood on my tiptoes to avoid trailing the skirt across the floor. "Oh wow, it has a slit," I said as the fabric parted, revealing my leg almost up to my hip.

"Just on one side," Darcy replied. "With your legs, it's the perfect dress for you."

I stood in front of the mirror—I looked so different. And I wasn't sure it was just the dress. *Things* were different in

London. *I* was different in London. The bravado I normally wore as a shield had been replaced with a genuine eagerness to learn and experience new things.

"If you've not found yourself some guy in London yet, you will in this dress," she said, grinning at me.

I'd never worn anything so beautiful and certainly nothing as expensive. I turned to the side. My waist looked half the size it really was, and the sweep of the fabric over my hips made me feel like I'd just stepped off the set of *High Society*. For a second, I imagined Alexander's face as he spotted me—that reluctant grin he had made me want to curl my hand around his neck and kiss him. I shook my head, trying to rid myself of the thought.

"Maybe," I said. There was no way I was going to be able to wear anything but this dress now. I'd fallen in love with it. But I wasn't so worried about finding a guy. I was just enjoying my life here in London.

"I'm glad you're going out, finally. You don't seem to be out as much as you are in New York. Are you sure you're having fun?"

In New York I went out as often as my tips would allow. Of course, I had fewer friends in London. I'd been asked to go to the pub a couple of times by the admin staff or the clerks, but I'd always found an excuse. For some reason, I didn't want to drink and flirt my evenings away. In London I looked forward to going to work in the morning instead of cursing each step I made on my way to the restaurant. I reveled in nights alone at home instead of finding random colleagues to go out drinking and hunting for boys with.

"I am having a lot of fun. It's just not my usual fun." It was the first time in a long time I'd felt as if I were in the right place. In New York, I'd worked so hard at living in the moment, not worrying about what was farther down the track, that I'd failed to make sure the moment was worth staying in. I'd just assumed that working toward something in the future was a waste of where you were, but I wasn't so sure anymore—in chambers I was surrounded by people working hard toward the future and it didn't seem so scary. I was beginning to see that maybe things could be different for me—I didn't have to be weighed down by my past. I could choose a new path.

"I'm so pleased that you are. It's so nice having you just down the road." Darcy and I stared into the mirror at my reflection.

"And you're sure you don't mind me borrowing it?"

"I insist you do. Now what about shoes? What size are you? Oh, and a bag!"

Darcy was possibly one of the most generous people I'd ever met.

We wandered back into her closet. "Try these," she said, handing me some silver, strappy heels.

"I can't. They're way too high."

"They look perfect with that dress, and you have a few days to practice. Wear socks at first to stop yourself from getting blisters." Darcy was clearly used to this world of fancy parties and London events, but I wasn't. I'd watched Scarlett get ready for these things a million times, but I'd never thought I'd ever want to attend one, let alone be a little excited about it. Which I was. Being in London, I felt freer than I could remember ever feeling. I'd never felt trapped in New York, but looking back, I had been. I might have worked in a hundred different restaurants with a thousand different people, but my days had all been the same. I'd been constrained in a way I wasn't here. In New York, my past trailed along behind me and it felt as though everyone kept glancing at it over my shoulder, reminding me it was still there. Here no one knew me.

"I don't know how to thank you, Darcy."

"I told you, it's no big deal. I'm pleased it's being worn—it's too pretty to keep in a cupboard."

"I don't just mean the dress. Thank you for suggesting I come to London, for letting me stay in this house. I can't tell you how much better I feel."

She grinned. "I'm happy you're happy. All we need is for you to find a knight in shining armor to rescue you and everything will be perfect."

I shook my head. "I don't need rescuing." I meant it. I always meant it when I said I didn't need a man, but normally I was fucking some random guy I knew would last no more than a month before I got bored with him. Now I wasn't fucking anyone and I was okay with that. I was more than okay with that. London was changing me.

FOURTEEN

Alexander

I checked my watch, then gripped the back of the chair as I stood and faced the round banqueting table where our chambers was seated. As I glanced around, I saw faces I recognized. Some I'd worked with. Others were familiar because they always came to these kinds of events.

I'd been one of the first to arrive at the table. The sooner we were all seated, the sooner the night could begin, and the sooner it would be over.

"Alex," a man called from my right. I turned to see Graham Ridley coming toward me, his arm outstretched.

We shook hands. "Graham. Good to see you."

"Thank you for your help with the United Streets case."

Graham was a managing partner at a law firm I worked with a lot. One of his partners had instructed me on some work last year.

"Thank you for the case."

"We won't be able to afford you soon. No doubt you'll be taking silk within a couple of years."

I was planning to go for silk as soon as I could, but it wouldn't be for a few years yet. Becoming a Q.C., or taking silk, as it was called, was the biggest promotion a barrister could get and didn't happen for at least a decade after being called to the bar and was more likely to be twenty years with the work I did. But my father had made it at eighteen years, and I didn't want to be even a year later. "We are some way off that," I replied. "What about you? How's business?"

After chatting for a few minutes, Graham moved toward his seat and another partner from a law firm came over, another in his wake. Arriving at the table early had clearly been a bad tactic. I should have waited until the last minute.

The chambers' table filled up with Lance, Craig, Jimmy, and others. There were only a couple of spaces left. "Who else is coming?" I asked, leaning across the table toward Craig.

"James will be here shortly," Lance said, then nodded toward the staircase. "And Violet King has just arrived."

Fuck. I glanced around the table. There was an open seat next to Jimmy and one seat next to me. So I'd either be facing her or next to her. If I'd know she was coming I would have made an excuse not to be here. We'd not seen each other for a few days and although the urge for her hadn't left me entirely, it was subsiding. Her presence here would surely reignite my desire for her, which was exactly what I was trying to avoid.

"I heard she's whipping you into shape," Lance said.

"Is that right?" I replied.

"Jolly good thing too," Lance said. "You know what I think about the state of your office."

Lance had made it clear on many occasions that he

thought my office needed to be sorted out. Lance had been my father's junior and when I first joined chambers he told me that if he could be half the mentor to me that my father had been to him, it was all he could hope for. He was the only one I listened to other than Craig and he was more of a mentor than I could ever have wished for. He had a sixth sense for when I was close to breaking point and always managed to talk me off the ledge without me even noticing. He had a big brain and a light touch and I respected him a great deal.

Lance and Craig began to discuss something, and I couldn't resist taking the opportunity to turn to see Violet. I spotted her instantly, halfway down the curved staircase, scanning the room for our table.

My heart began to thunder in my chest. Not seeing her for a few days had made things worse now she was here. She was breathtaking. Clearly, I'd always found something about her compelling, but I didn't think I'd ever realized how fucking beautiful she was. Her skin was luminous and her dark hair tumbled around her shoulders. As she took a few more steps down, the slit in her dress revealed one of her long, lithe legs. Shit. My pulse pounded in my ears and drowned out the chatter and music, leaving only her. I wanted to barrel over to the stairs and drag her away from this godforsaken evening. Take her back to my hotel and just stare at her for a while, then peel that beautiful dress off and worship her.

My breaths shortened the closer she got to the table and although I knew it was reckless, I wanted to ensure it was me she sat next to and not Jimmy.

I caught a glance of James coming through the crowd toward our table and deliberately shifted to conceal the empty chair next to mine, so he'd take the chair next to Jimmy. I wasn't sure if it was enough to put him off.

"Gordon," I said, shaking the hand of another barrister at a competing chambers. "Good to see you." I held his hand a little longer than was necessary, creating an additional barrier between James and the seat next to mine.

Gordon looked at me, eyes narrowed, forehead creased as if he might have slipped into an alternate universe. "Good to see you too, Alex. Good luck tonight."

In my peripheral vision, I saw James skirt around the human barrier I'd created with Gordon and take his position next to Jimmy. "Thanks." I grinned at Gordon. He'd probably never seen me smile. It didn't happen often, but I was pretty satisfied with the way I'd manipulated the seating.

And just in time, as Violet was just a few steps away.

Jimmy spotted her, and he offered her his seat, presumably so she'd be next to Craig and then he'd take the chair next to me. That wasn't going to fucking happen.

"This seat is free," I said, raising my voice to ensure the table heard me.

Violet declined Jimmy's offer—she couldn't do anything else without being impolite. She might not take any shit from me but she wasn't rude—no ruder than I deserved anyway. She made her way around the table, acknowledging each member of chambers she passed.

It seemed like she took forever to reach me.

She gave me a tentative smile as I held out her chair and she took a seat. I caught a whiff of jasmine and closed my eyes in a long blink. Maybe I should have let her sit next to Jimmy.

The table full, we all sat. My right leg was an inch from hers, her heat warming me, her breathing soothing me.

Fuck. I wasn't sure how I was going to get through the evening. Yet I wouldn't have it any other way.

I knew it was wrong to want her. Hell, I hardly knew her, but the way she was utterly unintimidated by me, the way she spoke to me, it was as if she'd unpeeled all my layers and saw the real me. I wasn't my father's son as far as she was concerned. Nor was I the future of the bar, a failed husband, or a brilliant lawyer. I was some guy who made her job difficult but made her come. She stripped away everything that wasn't relevant, and it only made me want her more. If it had just been her beauty I was drawn to, it would be easier to resist her.

To my dismay and relief, most of the dinner passed with Violet making conversation with the barrister to her right. I wasn't sure I'd ever spoken to him. I thought his name was Robert. What could he be saying that was so bloody fascinating?

As pudding was served, the emcee of the evening introduced himself and made a few less-than-funny jokes. Then he told us about the obligatory charity raffle and how we had to write our names on a twenty-pound note and put it in one of the gold envelopes that sat next to our centerpiece in the middle of the table.

I sighed and took out my wallet and pen from my inside jacket. I removed two twenty-pound notes and placed them flat on the table.

Violet's bag was on her lap and she was rummaging through it. I placed my hand over hers. "I have yours," I said.

She looked at me, her eyes a little wide. "I'm sure I have—"

"Violet, you don't pay for your own raffle ticket. There are many things about the bar that are old-fashioned and sexist, but this is just manners. Look," I said, nodding toward the other side of the table. "Lance is paying for Craig and Jimmy's ticket. This is how it works."

She sighed and closed her bag. "Thank you."

"It's just—"

"How it works. I know. I'm not taking it personally."

It wasn't personal, but for some reason I wished it could be. I'd like her to feel special, because she *was* special.

I pushed the purple notes into the envelope and passed it to my left. All around the table, everyone was talking, occupied and not looking at me or Violet. I ran my fingers over the knee exposed by the slit in her dress. "You look beautiful tonight." What was I doing?

She sucked in a breath. "Alexander. We agreed."

I nodded. We had, and it had been the right thing to do for a thousand reasons.

Still, I slid my fingers further up her leg. It was involuntary. I couldn't help myself. There were all these reasons to stop but they were powerless against this urge I had, the desire she created in me.

Violet placed her hand over mine. "Alexander."

"You don't want this?" I asked, trying my best to look as if we were just swapping small talk. "You don't feel this . . . energy between us?" Jesus, I sounded trite and pathetic. I'd just never felt this connection with a woman before, and having her this close to me was diluting all the reasons I had to keep away from her.

"I do. And that's a problem." She looked at me from under her lashes. "Let's quit while we're ahead." She glanced around the room as if she were looking for an exit. "Excuse me, I have to go to the ladies' room," she said, my hand drifting from her leg as she stood.

I ate my pudding as I watched her weave in and out of

tables before she met Jimmy coming toward her. They stopped and talked and she became more animated with him than she had been with me. Her smile was wide and a couple of times she threw her head back and laughed. Did she find him attractive? Was she flirting with him? No doubt he was flirting with her—he had a penis and from what I could tell was straight, and really, who the hell wouldn't flirt with Violet King? She was gorgeous.

The hair at the back of my neck bristled. Jimmy needed to let her go or I'd fire him, punch him, or otherwise make a fool of myself.

Eventually he came back to the table and my urge to connect my fist with his chin subsided.

I needed to get myself under control. I was all over the place. I was letting my dick rule my head. Violet had been clear—whatever had happened between us wasn't going to reoccur. It wasn't as if I was going to sit next to her at an awards ceremony every week. We'd arranged things so I wouldn't even have to see her in the office.

I stood, familiar self-control and discipline running through my veins. I rounded the table before stopping next to Lance. "I'm sorry, but I'm going to have to excuse myself. I've just had a call about an emergency injunction."

Lance turned. "Of course. Good luck, my boy."

"Thank you, Lance. See you in the morning."

I made my way out of the ballroom, staring straight ahead, determined not to seek out one last glance of Violet King.

Violet

I'd had to excuse myself from the table. Alexander's touch was like quicksand and I needed to escape before I gave in and he swallowed me up. I left the ladies' room braver and headed back to the table. Ordinarily, I'd have been more than encouraging of a man as tall, brooding, and sexy as Alexander coming on to me, even if he was an arrogant asshole. I wasn't in the habit of turning good sex down, but for the first time in my life a warning bell had gone off in my head when it came to Knightley, which was why I suggested we keep things professional. There were practical reasons around working with him, which meant it was a bad idea to continue our physical relationship, not least because I didn't want to cause Darcy any embarrassment but more than that, something instinctive was telling me to keep away. I was enjoying being in London—focusing on myself and considering my future. I didn't want anything to mess that up. And there was something in the way Knightley looked at me, touched me, in the way my body melted under his fingers, that told me he could be trouble. And I wouldn't allow a man to make trouble for me. Not again.

Alexander wasn't at the table. Had he come looking for me? I sat back down and twisted to face the stage as the emcee introduced the next category.

Fifteen minutes passed. Alexander hadn't come back to the table and listening to a bunch of people I didn't know win awards I didn't care about wasn't the most exciting thing I'd ever done. I wanted to fast forward to the Chambers of the Year category.

One of the other barristers who was sitting three seats down from me moved to Alexander's chair. "So, Violet, we've not met. I'm Charlie." There was a hint of camp to his voice, but I wasn't convinced he was gay. It could've been a British thing.

"Nice to meet you, Charlie."

"It's an absolute pleasure. You look fantastic this

evening. Elie Saab, is it?" he asked, staring down toward my cleavage.

Yes, definitely gay. A straight man wouldn't know the designer.

"Isn't it funny how whether we're gay or straight, men just love beautiful women?" he asked.

I laughed. "I'm not sure I can comment."

"Well, you are gorgeous," he said, unashamedly fixated. He sighed. "I hear you've tamed our Mr. Knightley."

Uncomfortable with his change in subject, I pursed my lips. I didn't often feel uncomfortable, but I felt loyalty toward Knightley and I didn't want Charlie to think I was going to sit here and bitch about him. At the same time, I didn't want to look like the stupid girl with a crush by saying he was a joy to work with. "I'm trying to get his billing up-to-date."

"And I hear you're doing a fine job." His eyes danced and he grinned at me as if he were up to no good. Was he insinuating something?

"I'm making progress. That's my job." I smiled tightly.

"I'm impressed. Many before you have tried and failed."

I reached for my wine glass, hoping he might be reminded to drink rather than talk.

"You two seem to have a certain chemistry, may I say," he continued.

I didn't know how to respond. I had only ever been polite to Alexander in public. We hadn't been flirting and no one would have seen his hand on my leg. I would hate for people to start talking and for it to get back to whoever Darcy's contact was.

"If anyone ever convinces Alex to come to one of these events, he rarely says a word to any of us. He was positively chatty this evening."

"Well, I imagine all that extra money I'm making him has cheered him up."

Charlie guffawed. "I'm pretty sure he's richer than the Queen. All that family money."

"He's from a wealthy family?" I asked. I would have guessed the opposite. I would have thought the way he worked, he'd known what it was like to have no money at all. More contradictions from him. Whenever I thought I had him pegged he surprised me again.

"Well, his dad was Alexander the Great," he said, as if I should know who that was.

"I'm pretty sure you don't mean the ancient Greek king," I responded.

Charlie laughed again. It was infectious and so loud that people at the next table glanced around. "No. But the greatest barrister ever to have been at the bar." He paused. "So they say."

"So he has a lot to live up to," I said, half to myself. Was that why he was so driven?

"With that lineage he doesn't have to try. All the judges love him because of his father. He gets away with murder in chambers—I mean, who else has a full-time assistant and his own office?"

Alexander was arrogant, yes, and moody and difficult, but I was surprised at the picture Charlie painted. Alexander wasn't some kind of shirker who was riding his father's coattails. He was the most hard-working person I'd ever come across. I admired his drive and his focus.

Before I got to ask Charlie more questions, the award we'd all be waiting for came around. Alexander was still nowhere to be seen. Where had he gone?

The nominees were read out and our table cheered at the mention of our chambers. The ballroom hushed as the gold envelope was opened. It was like the lawyer's version of the Oscars.

Despite only working at chambers a few weeks, a weird sense of loyalty I'd never felt before rose in my body. I wanted us to win. There were some fantastic people working in chambers, even if some of them were a little eccentric. I liked the place.

When the name of our chambers was read out, I jumped up and began clapping just as Charlie did beside me. Where was Alexander? Surely, even he'd get a kick out of this. Someone should call him or something.

Lance and Craig made their way up to the stage to accept the award. Of course, everyone was far too British to give speeches, and after photographs, they came back to the table. We were all beaming and took our turns inspecting the acrylic, miniature glacier of an award marked Chambers of the Year.

As the evening wore down, and people began to grow restless, the winners of the raffle were announced. Charlie was whispering to me, telling me bits of gossip that were travelling around chambers.

"Violet!" Lance boomed across the table. "You won!"

"Congratulations," said the young woman who approached me. "I really wanted this one." She handed me an envelope and turned away.

I didn't even know what I'd won.

"Charlie, you shouldn't have been distracting her. She won the second prize," Lance said. "We're a table of winners here tonight."

"Always," Charlie said, raising his glass, then downed his drink and excused himself.

I turned the envelope around and flipped open the back. I never won anything. Even if it was a balloon and a party hat, I'd be delighted. I pulled out a thick white card with gold writing on it.

Fortescue Hall Hotel and Spa.

Holy crap. A spa break? There was no way I could accept this. Alexander had paid for my ticket. I had to give it to him. I glanced around, hoping I'd spot him somewhere so I could tell him, but all I saw was Jimmy coming toward me.

He sat down in the seat Knightley had started the evening in and Charlie had just left. It was like musical chairs.

"Congratulations," he said.

"Thanks." I pushed the card back in the envelope and slid it into my bag.

"So given this table is on a winning streak . . ." Jimmy said.

My heart sank. Like a juggernaut bearing down on me, I knew what was coming.

"I wanted to know if I could take you for a drink. Or dinner. Whatever you'd like."

I took a breath before I responded. "A drink would be great—I don't have many friends in London." I emphasized the word *friends.*

"Friends?" he winced. "I'm not going to lie, I'm a little heartbroken." He smiled, defeated, and I was relieved he'd clearly got the message. "But I'll settle for friends."

I nodded. "I'm glad. I'm not in London for long," I said. "And I'm a way better friend than date."

It wasn't that I didn't like Jimmy—I did. He was attractive, thoughtful, and good-natured. And had this been a month ago in New York, I would have said yes. But I didn't have that urge to punch him in the face and kiss him at the same time. And after Knightley, anything less seemed like a compromise I shouldn't have to make. Anyway, dating Jimmy, however casually, seemed a bit wrong when I'd fucked Knightley. I didn't usually worry about shit like that, but there was something about what had passed between Knightley and me that deserved more. And if there was the slightest chance it might embarrass Alexander, I wouldn't risk it.

He deserved more.

FIFTEEN

Alexander

I often got told I was in a bad mood when I wasn't—I was simply focused or busy or both. But today there was no doubt that my mood was black. I stared at my laptop, though I wasn't absorbing anything on screen. I couldn't see through my rage.

I was angry at myself for making a pass at Violet last night. We'd both agreed to put a stop to whatever was between us. I wasn't sure what had happened last night to make me double back. Of course she'd looked stunning. But that was hardly a surprise—she was a beautiful girl. Having her close had been a temptation. But I was always able to resist temptation. Why was I so fixated on her?

Seeing her with Jimmy had been the final straw. As much as I didn't want anything from her, I couldn't think about the fact that someone else might have her. I wasn't sure that another man would appreciate her in the way that I did. She wasn't just some administrator with a pretty face and a phenomenal body.

Nothing about my reaction to Violet King made sense, but I knew one thing for sure—I never liked feeling as if I was giving anyone else power over my actions. So last night I'd left. "Come in," I barked at a knock on my office door. I clamped my jaw tight. I didn't need any interruptions today.

In my peripheral vision, Violet slipped inside and closed the door. Fuck. Why couldn't she stay away?

"You left last night," she said, walking toward my desk.

I wasn't interested in small talk. "What can I do for you, Violet?" I asked, turning to face her.

"I just came in to give you these." She tossed some papers on my desk. "This arrived by courier and is marked private and confidential. I thought it might be urgent."

"Thanks."

She turned to leave.

"Wait. What's this?" I asked, opening an additional envelope.

She stopped and glanced over her shoulder. "My raffle entry you paid for—it won. It's a two-day spa break thing." She shrugged. "Enjoy."

"I don't want it," I said. "And anyway, you were the winner, not me."

"But you paid for it, so I can't accept it."

I sighed. The woman was exasperating. "I explained to you how these things work. You take it." I turned back to my computer, hoping she'd leave.

"I'm sorry if I pissed you off last night. I didn't want you to leave."

"I had an urgent matter to deal with, which wasn't anything to do with you," I lied.

"I just think it's better, as we work together. It's not that I don't find you attractive," she said.

I snapped my head around. "Violet, please. I don't need your reassurance. You didn't piss me off, and it is precisely conversations like these that I'm trying to avoid." I ran my hands through my hair. "Let's just get back to work, shall we?"

"So, you're just in a normal, stick-up-your-ass, rude-to-everyone-not-Violet-in-particular kind of mood?"

I couldn't help but grin as I shook my head at her insolence. "It looks that way." I picked up the spa certificate and handed it to her. "Here, take this."

She shook her head. "I can't. It's for two, and my only friend in England is in New York that weekend."

I didn't know much about Violet other than how she felt under my fingers, how she made my cock jerk whenever she was around. I'd assumed she had roots of sorts here.

"Go on your own," I said. "As Jean-Paul Sartre said, 'Hell is other people'."

She laughed and I couldn't help but smile as her giggle took over her whole body. It didn't matter if she was in a ball gown or a skirt and blouse, she was still beautiful.

"If I didn't know better, I'd have attributed that quote to you. So, *you* go on your own," she said.

"You won. And anyway, I rarely take an evening off, let alone a full weekend."

"Jesus, do you ever just enjoy the moment?" she asked, raising her hands in the air and then taking the card from my hand.

I was enjoying *this* moment a little too much. "Close the door on your way out, please." I sat back in my chair and turned to the screen. She needed to leave before my willpower faltered and I did something I knew I shouldn't. I knew how soft her skin was, how wet I could get her pussy.

She had to get out of here. "Just one more thing before you go."

She glanced back over her shoulder and a memory of my hand up her skirt flashed into my mind. I swallowed it down. "It's none of my business and you don't need my permission, but if you were to date someone else in chambers, that wouldn't be a problem from my perspective."

"Someone else in chambers?" she asked, turning to face me again.

"You know, if you and Jimmy went out, whatever, that would be . . ." Fucking awful. For some reason, I felt some kind of ownership over Violet, but I wasn't going to tell her that.

"Well, you're right," she said, placing a hand on her hip. "It isn't any of your business, and I don't need your permission."

I turned back to my screen. I'd been trying to set her mind at rest, and convince myself that it really would be okay. I shouldn't have said anything.

"But I'm not going to date Jimmy." She cocked out her hip and tilted her head. "Ever."

I tried to keep my breathing steady. I wanted her to finish her sentence. I wanted her to fill in the gaps I had in my mind about what had happened between them.

"He asked," she said. "I said no. He's not my type."

I cleared my throat in an effort to disguise my smile as I mentally punched the air. I hated the thought of Jimmy's hands on Violet. "Not your type?" I repeated.

"Yeah. Apparently, I prefer assholes."

There was no way I could hold back my grin. "Good to know." She turned to go, and as I began typing, she closed the door behind her. The only chance I had of resisting the primal urge I had to pursue and claim this woman was if I kept a five-mile exclusion zone around her. For now, I had the space I needed, but how long would it last? Violet had picked at a thread in me and was pulling at it, slowly unravelling me.

I sank back into my chair and grabbed the courier package Violet had brought in. I tore off the sealed end and emptied the contents onto my desk. Papers. Legal papers. I wasn't expecting anything. I turned them over.

Decree Nisi.

My wife was divorcing me. Proof that I needed to stick with what I was good at and avoid any pretense at a relationship with a member of the opposite sex.

SIXTEEN

Violet

Over the last few days, I'd crossed all but the last few invoices off Knightley's spreadsheet. Just a couple of items to send to finance, and then he'd be up-to-date. I glanced up at the pile of filing that took up most of my desk. I'd been working hard on his filing and archiving, but his office still looked like a freaking war zone. At least I could completely focus on it now that his billing was done.

"Violet," Craig called out in the clerks' office.

He clearly still didn't know where I sat. "In here," I said, getting up and heading in his direction.

"Oh, there you are. Can I have a word in my office?"

I hadn't spoken to Craig in any detail about anything since my interview. Curious, I followed him.

"Have a seat, Violet," he said, indicating the chair opposite his desk as he sat down. "I've not had the opportunity to say what a fantastic job you've done. You've far exceeded my expectations."

I smiled. "I'm not sure if that's a compliment or not."

He chuckled. "Well, you're right, my expectations weren't high given our history with Mr. Knightley and the impossible task you had, but you've managed to bill over a million pounds. Some of it dates back five years. That's tremendous work." He slammed his hand on his desk, clearly delighted.

I hadn't been told I was good at anything since college. But then, I hadn't made an effort. I was proud I'd managed to do what I had here. Proud of the work everyone did. I was part of a team and it felt good. Craig was acting as if he'd given me the Gordian knot and told me I couldn't cut it. Instead, I'd meticulously unpicked it. "I'm really glad it worked out."

"So am I, my dear. So am I. And you've won Mr. Knightley's trust, which is no small feat. Most of the *barristers* around here haven't managed that, let alone the clerks and admin staff."

I shrugged. "He's not so bad. He's just not used to his fire being matched with fire."

"No, he's not." Craig chuckled. "And you've enjoyed it?"

"I have. More than I expected to, actually."

"I'm pleased to hear that, as I was hoping to extend your contract for another three months."

If he'd turned around, unzipped his trousers, and showed me his ass, I wouldn't have been more shocked. "Another three months?" I'd been planning to go back to New York after my time here had come to an end, even though I wasn't sure what I was heading back to.

"I don't know what your plans are or whether you've got something lined up—"

"But I'll have Mr. Knightley's archiving and filing done by the end of my contract. What will I do?"

"Well," he said, steepling his fingers, "something tells me that a woman as clever as you has been looking around our office and finding ways in which we could improve. Am I right?"

I thought about it for a few seconds. I'd wondered why they hadn't updated their document management systems and why admin staff couldn't raise invoices. There was also the way the meeting rooms were full, and people were complaining. I grimaced. "I might have noticed one or two things."

"As I thought. I think there would be plenty to keep you busy. Perhaps you could come to me with a list of your ideas and suggested improvements and together we can agree what you'll prioritize."

I couldn't believe what he was suggesting—he was giving me an opportunity to create a job for myself. "That sounds . . ." He trusted me. Believed in me. I chewed on the inside of my lip to distract myself from my rising emotion. "Unbelievable."

"Does that mean you'll stay another three months? I can arrange a visa for you."

"Can I take some time to think about it?" I asked. I had no idea whether or not Darcy would let me stay in her house.

It felt as if I was on the brink of finding what I'd been looking for when I'd first come to London. Part of me wanted to stay and see if it was what I was searching for. But the other part was nervous. What if I didn't like what I found out?

And what would Knightley think? What if he didn't want me to stick around? He probably didn't care either way. I wasn't quite sure why he was even part of my deliberations, but for whatever reason, he was.

"Of course. Produce a plan and then decide whether you want to execute it."

"You're putting a lot of faith in me."

He nodded. "You've earned it."

"Thank you, sir."

It had been a long time since I'd believed in the old adage "you reap what you sow." And even longer since I'd lost my belief in karma and the universe being a just and fair place. But right then, I felt that part of me begin to regenerate, and for the first time in a long time, I began to think about my future.

SEVENTEEN

Alexander

As I sat in my car at the end of the drive of my soon-to-be ex-wife's home, I knew I was risking a restraining order. It looked like I was staking her out. I wasn't. I was just putting off the final part of the journey. Despite being separated for three years, I hadn't been expecting the divorce proceedings. I guess we should have gotten around to it sooner but as always, I was busy. I hadn't thought about it—or her—much at all. I'd been buried in work before we got married, then fallen asleep during our wedding breakfast because I'd worked day and night for a week before the wedding so I could take my wedding day off. And I'd worked every day of our two short years together. Despite getting engaged, married, and then separated, nothing much in my world changed.

After the split, going to the hotel hadn't been the wrench it might have been for some people. I had no demands on my time other than from work. I didn't have to listen to Gabby scream at me because I was home late or because I'd spent an hour on the phone during a dinner party. My bed was made, my food cooked for me, and the commute short. If I was completely honest, when Gabby had told me to move out, it had been a relief.

I'd not seen her since. Even though our subsequent, infrequent phone calls had been amicable, I hadn't been back to the house. She'd told me she'd boxed my things up, but I'd never wanted to collect them. I wanted to concentrate on the future, not my past. I wanted to build the career I'd always dreamed of.

Getting the decree nisi was the first time I'd really felt anything about our separation. I had a gnawing in my gut that hadn't left me since I'd opened that envelope, but I couldn't put my finger on what was causing it. I'd called Gabby, and she'd told me she was going to donate all my things if I didn't come to collect them, so here I was at the end of the drive, stalling before I pulled up to the house and put a full stop at the end of the sentence that was Gabby and me.

What was I doing? I leaned my head back on the headrest. I was dredging up the past unnecessarily. I wasn't sure what was in the boxes she'd stored for the last three years, but it wasn't anything I'd missed. Maybe I shouldn't have come, but I wasn't about to turn around now she was expecting me. I just needed to get this over with. Perhaps what was in those boxes would rid me of this knot in my stomach that needed untying.

I started the engine and turned up the drive. She'd had it tarmacked. I'd driven this route every day for two years, but now it was as though I'd never been here.

The surrounding trees and shrubs had grown in the last few years, but the rest was the same. Just like my life had continued relatively unchanged, so had Gabby's. I turned and parked in front of the house. In the last few months before I left, I would often sit in the car, checking messages before I went in, bracing myself for the inevitable row about my hours or something I'd forgotten to do. Things had gotten so bad that it was a wonder I hadn't left long before Gabby had suggested it.

I opened the car and got out. I still had the house key on my key-chain. I should give it back.

I lifted the knocker, not knowing what reception I was going to encounter.

Gabby opened the door, her face blank of emotion. "Come in." She flounced up the hallway to the kitchen. She was thinner than when we were married. Her face a little more angular. As usual, she was immaculately dressed and looked like she'd come straight from the hair-dresser. That was the thing about Gabby—she was polished. In many ways, she really was the perfect wife. She'd just wanted more than I could give her. My behavior hadn't changed when we got married. I'd always worked hard. She'd had full disclosure, and she'd pushed for a wedding anyway. She'd pitched me on the whole thing, told me I needed a wife to support my work. But she'd changed the rules on me after we married, demanded more from me once we'd walked down the aisle.

"Thanks for keeping my things," I said as we stood in the kitchen. Gabby opened one of the drawers in the island and pulled out a bunch of keys. "I thought you might have burned them."

"I stopped with the effigy. The smoke was getting in my eyes." She folded her arms. "The boxes are in the garage."

I wanted to laugh but knew it was inappropriate.

She slung the keys across the work surface. "It's the

green one. They're in the far garage." She glanced at me and her eyes narrowed. "You look good," she said.

I smiled. "Thanks. So do you."

She sighed but didn't respond. "Do you want any furniture or anything else from the house?" she asked.

It hadn't occurred to me to want anything. She'd picked out every single thing in the place. There was nothing of me in there. "I don't think so." I picked up the keys and followed her as she opened the French windows and headed outside to the garage block. She stopped outside the door, her mouth turned down, her eyes dark with none of the sparkle I remembered. I wanted to do something, make things better.

"I'm really sorry," I said. "It was never my intention to hurt you."

"Of *course* it was intentional, Alex. You don't *unintentionally* work all the time." She took in a long, slow breath. "It's not like breathing. You have a choice, and you chose work over your marriage every time. It came before everything; nothing was more important to you."

"But that was the deal between us, wasn't it? You knew who I was going in."

She folded her arms and stared at the ground. "I know we didn't have some kind of grand love affair—that isn't who either of us are. We were both practical and straightforward, but I still thought it would work." She shook her head as if chastising herself for her own stupidity. "I thought when we got married, you'd want to spend more time with me. I thought you'd grow to love me." Her voice trailed off and she cleared her throat.

"I'm sorry." I hated that I'd hurt her. She didn't deserve that.

"It was all a long time ago."

For me, three years didn't feel all that long ago. It had passed in a blur. Gabby was the last woman I'd been out to dinner with. The last woman I'd taken a shower with. The last woman I'd spent Christmas with. Three years might have been a long time for her, but for me, it had felt like three weeks. Nothing had really changed in the intervening years except I was getting better quality work in chambers, and I was earning more money.

She snatched the keys from my hand and opened the lock on the garage. From what I remembered, we didn't keep anything in this space. She opened the door and switched on the light. There were half a dozen boxes in the middle of the concrete floor and my father's desk that looked like it had been wrapped up in cardboard and plastic. I'd forgotten it was here, but where else would it be? Christ, was this what comprised the history of my personal life? An ex-wife and a few cardboard boxes?

"Your sports trophies are in the one on top, I think. Most of the rest are the clothes you didn't take when you left."

"Thanks," I said, although it made me feel so uncomfortable. I wished she had burned the lot along with my effigy.

"Do you want to go through the house?" she asked. "You can have anything you like—I'll have to downsize when we sell anyway."

"You want to sell?" She'd found this house just after we'd become engaged, and I could still remember her face when she told me about it. I couldn't remember ever seeing her happier. For her, it had been love at first sight. A forever home, she'd said. But forever had only lasted two years.

"I'll have to. I won't be able to afford to buy you out."

It hadn't occurred to me that she would think I'd make her do such a thing. "Gabby, this is your home. I know how special it is to you. You found this place, furnished it, planted the garden, had it redecorated. I'll sign it over to you; you don't need to buy me out." She was right. I had been selfish during our marriage, but that didn't mean I had to be during our divorce.

"Don't do that," she said, shaking her head. "Don't try to do the right thing."

"I was trying to be nice." I was pretty sure I just conceded to something I didn't have to.

"Exactly. Don't be nice to me now it's too late."

"Okay," I said. Maybe this was why I'd not been back in three years. I'd been avoiding facing up to what I'd done to Gabby.

"You shouldn't have married me if you didn't want to be a husband."

Rightly or wrongly, I'd never considered whether I'd wanted to be a husband when I married Gabby. I hadn't been averse to the idea of marriage, but I hadn't really given it much thought, either. I'd gone in blind, assuming I'd just be able to continue as usual. "I mean it when I say I'm sorry." And I was. She was right; I should never have married her. I reached out and pulled her into a hug. "You deserved a better husband."

"I did. But we learn from our mistakes. I won't go into another marriage thinking things will improve once I've walked down the aisle." She pulled out of my arms.

I wished I could make it better for her.

"Will you?" she asked.

"What?"

"Learn from your mistakes?"

I frowned. There was no doubt I wouldn't marry again.

I wouldn't put someone through that again. Is that what she meant?

"Maybe start by getting rid of that bloody desk," she said.

I chuckled. "You think giving away my father's desk will be my salvation?"

"I wasn't kidding." She looked me straight in the eye. "It's a symbol. I never understood why you were so competitive with a dead man."

My spine stiffened. "Competitive?" What was she talking about?

"You have to be better, work harder, than Alexander the Great. I'm not sure if you're trying to prove to yourself that you're better or to everyone else. Maybe you're just trying to justify why he never turned up to a sports day or your university graduation." She shrugged. "Not my problem anymore."

I glanced at the desk my mother had given me when my father died. I'd never used it. It had sat in the study in this house, but I always ended up working at the dining room table. There was more space. And since I'd left here, I hadn't thought about it. She thought this was a symbol? Of what? The breakdown of our marriage? My failings? I almost asked her, but I wasn't sure I wanted her answer. I'd admired my father and been proud of him and the work he did, the career he had. Even now at the bar his was a name that was revered. He'd been the best at what he did. And I wanted the same thing—to be the best. What was wrong with that? I was driven and focused just as he'd been. And I didn't have children who needed me to turn up to sports days.

It was true I was following in my father's footsteps. But I hadn't considered that could be a bad thing. The thing I'd dreaded when I was first starting out was that people would compare us and I'd come up short. Perhaps that was what Gabby had meant—I was striving to have a career as successful as his. It was what I'd wanted since I'd been a child. I wasn't sure that put me in competition with a dead man, as she put it. To be the best at the bar took hard work. That's what it had required from my father. That's what it took from me. There was no point questioning it, looking at the right or wrongs. You couldn't be a great barrister without putting in the hours just like you couldn't be a Hollywood A-lister without being famous. Or a fisherman if you didn't like to spend time outside. I had no choice.

"As much as being married to you was painful," she said. "I want you to be happy."

Her words pulled the air from my lungs. I hated that our marriage pained her, when I'd barely noticed it. I should feel more at the end of a relationship that had been meant to last forever. I just didn't.

"I'm going to go and leave you to it. You can let yourself out," she said. "Can you make sure you send the papers back by the end of next week? I really want to have this wrapped up before my lawyer goes away the week after."

"Of course," I replied. There was no reason to prolong anything. "And you know I want you to be happy, too, Gabby," I said as she reached the exit.

"Thank you." She walked away without looking back, leaving me in a cold, dark room with six boxes that summed up my existence to date. And my father's desk.

EIGHTEEN

Violet

I glanced around and realized all the desks in the admin room were empty. Was everyone in a meeting? I spun my chair around and went into the clerks' room.

I checked the time. Oh my God, it was just before nine. How had everyone left without me realizing? And how had I worked four hours past my official finish time without noticing? When I was waitressing, I'd left my customers the moment my shift ended, even if there was food waiting to be delivered to my tables.

I grinned. Who would have thought I'd be happy to work overtime? I wandered out into the corridor to stretch my legs and go to the restroom.

I walked softly, almost tiptoeing past Alexander's office. It had been over a week since we'd had our conversation after the awards ceremony. I really wanted to talk to him about the three-month extension to my contract, but I didn't want to look like I was making a big deal about what had happened between us. It was just he was the only barrister I knew in chambers, and I wouldn't mind hearing what he thought about some of the ideas I had.

Just as I passed his door, the familiar squeak of his door handle echoed down the corridor as he opened it. I continued toward the restroom without turning around.

"Violet?" he asked after me.

I stopped and turned. "Hi," I replied. "Can I help you with something?"

He checked his watch. "What are you doing here so late?"

"Oh, just putting together something for Craig." I hadn't wanted to neglect Knightley's filing, so I'd been working on my suggestions for improvements in chambers after hours.

"I'm just about to order in some dinner. Can I get you something?"

I'd vowed to avoid Knightley. I didn't trust myself not to jump him, but it was late and I didn't have any food at home and despite not knowing him that well, I liked him. "That would be great."

"Come in, and you can choose what to order." He disappeared into his office and I followed him.

I was always so quick to dart in and out of his office when he wasn't around, I hadn't really taken the time to study the place for a while. It looked very different to how it had when I'd arrived. I could actually walk freely to Knightley's desk from the door without having to negotiate a labyrinth of paper. The room seemed much bigger.

"I couldn't believe it when I found that desk under there," I said, lifting my chin toward the desk across from the door.

"I know. I'd forgotten how big this room was. It will be useful to have an extra surface."

"I can get you a table to go over there," I said, indicating the wall he'd fucked me against, then wishing I hadn't mentioned it.

"Maybe," he said. "Sit down and see what you want." He indicated I should take a seat in his chair. I sat as he leaned on the desk next to me.

"There are too many choices," I said, looking at the online menu on his screen. "What are you having?"

"The steak," he replied.

"That figures."

"It does?"

I shrugged as I scrolled down to the fish. "Yeah. You're the type of guy who always orders the steak. Fillet, right? Rare. And a glass of merlot?"

He chuckled. "What, are you a food fortune teller?"

"No, I've just been waitressing a long time." I clicked on the sea bass. It was expensive and I couldn't really afford it, but if I took the contract extension and had another three months on this salary, I could.

"Putting that MIT degree to good use?"

I faced him and smiled. "It's a long story."

He looked at me as if he were waiting for me to continue. When I didn't, he frowned. "I have the merlot here in the office if you'd like to join me. I'm afraid I don't order wine by the glass."

I laughed. Of course he didn't. "Sure, why not?" I exhaled. Today had been a long day. Wine, especially wine that probably cost more than a week's salary, was just what I needed. And although I knew I should be keeping my distance from Alexander, I really didn't want to.

He stood and retrieved two glasses from the bottom drawer of his desk and a bottle of wine from the bottom shelf behind his desk and set about uncorking it. His fingers worked quickly and efficiently, and as he concentrated, I took in his sharp jaw and those lips that had whispered such dirty things to me. What was I doing sharing wine with this almost-irresistible man?

"Shall I move?" I leaned forward, about to stand up.

"No, stay there," he replied. "It suits you."

"What, sitting in your chair?"

He handed me a glass, his fingers brushing mine as he did. Our eyes met and my heartbeat scattered in my chest. I definitely shouldn't be doing this. Shouldn't this initial attraction to him have passed by now? Normally I'd have forgotten a guy's name if I hadn't spoken to him for a week.

He lifted his glass and dipped his head. "Cheers."

"Cheers," I said, raising my drink. We didn't clink. Was that a British thing?

He leaned against the edge of his desk, his long legs stretched out in front of him, and took a sip. I couldn't take my eyes off him as I put the glass to my lips. "Christ almighty," I said as the velvety wine slipped down my throat, stealing my attention. "I've never tasted anything like that." My brother had some pretty nice wine, but this was something else.

"Only forty bottles left in the world."

"Then why did you open it? You should have saved it for a special occasion."

He shook his head. "I think sharing a glass of wine with you is occasion enough."

I raised my eyebrows. "And I thought the wine was smooth."

A grin tugged at the corners of his mouth. "Too much?"

I tilted my head to one side. "Actually no. I like it."

His Adam's apple bobbed as he swallowed another mouthful of wine. How did he make drinking wine sexy?

"Did you hear that Craig wants to extend my contract by three months?" I asked. I wanted to gauge his reaction. Would he mind? Would he be pleased? I'd been the one to stop things between us, but now, as we shared a glass of wine—something I knew he didn't do with anyone else in chambers—things felt intimate, as if he saw me as an equal. For a man as brilliant as Knightley, it was more than flattering—it was intoxicating.

"I hadn't heard, but of course they want to extend your contract. You've made quite the impact."

"On you—I mean your billing."

"On me," he corrected me. "And because of the billing."

I couldn't imagine I'd had an impact on someone like Alexander. I didn't see how anyone would. If the building caught on fire, he was the sort of man who'd calmly stride toward the exit while everyone else ran screaming.

"Even after the awards? I thought you were angry at me?" I asked. Did that mean he still wanted me? Right now, I wanted to feel his lips skirt over mine, his tongue snaking its way into my mouth. It was a desire I was trying to fight—head over heart, mind over matter.

"You did the right thing. It wasn't like we could keep fucking in the office."

It was as if he'd doused me in cold water. I shifted in my seat, sitting up a little straighter.

"But maybe I could take you to dinner one night?" he asked.

Oh.

"One that doesn't involve a delivery guy on a motorbike and a plastic fork."

Knightley's cell buzzed on the desk, interrupting my response.

He was asking me out on a date. Away from the office.

I'd been on a thousand casual first dates, but something told me that dinner with Alexander would be anything but casual. I never went on a first date with any hope that it would go one way or the other, but if Knightley and I had dinner, I'd want him to enjoy my company. To kiss me afterward, fuck me like he had done the first time.

Alexander put the phone down. "Sorry, it was just—"

"Yes," I blurted. "Dinner sounds good." I was tired of resisting this thing between us. He was different from all those guys in New York. Complicated and confusing but challenging and desperately sexy. And I couldn't keep away. I didn't want to.

The way he tried to dampen his smile made me shiver.

"And we'll just keep us outside chambers," he said.

"Us?"

He sucked in a breath. "Our dinner and . . ." He shrugged.

I'd never seen him awkward before. It was beyond cute, and I wanted to sit on his lap, link my arms around his neck, and kiss his cheek. "Our dinner," I repeated, grinning.

"Food!" I jumped up when the front door buzzer went off. "I'll get it. You make a space." I nodded at his paper-filled desk.

I came back and unpacked the contents of the brown paper bag, letting him sit in his chair while I sat across from him.

We swapped containers, napkins, and plastic forks and began to eat.

"This is delicious," I said, closing my eyes as I took my first bite. "I can't believe it's takeout."

"Better, I didn't have to shop or cook to eat it."

"Do you ever cook?" I asked. Was he domesticated? I couldn't imagine him with an apron on.

"No. I live in a hotel."

"Wait, what? You don't own the bed you sleep on?"

He half choked as he put down his wine. "I never thought about it that way, but no. Or the sofa I sit on or the TV I don't watch. But you rent in London. Isn't it the same?"

"I'm staying at my . . . sister's sister-in-law's. I'm not sure what that makes her. Well, in her house anyway. Her main place is in the country."

"You own something back in America?"

I took another bite of my sea bass. I owned almost nothing I couldn't wear in America. I could fit my life in my car. "No. But I don't live in a hotel."

"It works for me."

"So this weekend you'll hang out at the hotel? Does it have a pool and stuff?" Did he have friends? Hobbies?

"I'll be in chambers this weekend," he said. "I work Saturdays and Sundays."

"Do you ever take time off?"

"You realize you're asking me these questions while you're eating dinner at work at ten in the evening?"

I laughed. "I know, but this is unusual for me."

"What about you? What are you doing this weekend?"

Before I could answer, I caught sight of the name of the company I founded with David on the edge of a folded, pink newspaper. I dropped my fork and grabbed the paper, unfolding the article so I could see.

Fuck. There was no escape. I'd not given David and the IPO a second thought in weeks. Why did I have to see this now?

This wasn't supposed to follow me to London.

I scanned the short article. There were a few details of the IPO and how it was all set for Monday.

"Violet?"

I glanced up and Knightley was looking at me, his brows pulled together.

"Yes, sorry. You were asking what I was doing this weekend. I don't know. I was going to that spa weekend. But . . ." The last thing I wanted to do was to be left alone with my thoughts all weekend knowing that David was preparing to make his fortune from my hard work come Monday morning.

"Is everything okay?"

I shrugged and sat back in my chair. "Yeah. Just some company I used to be involved with is going public on Monday."

"And that's a bad thing?"

It was supposed to be a great thing. It was what I'd spent so many hours working toward. And now it was someone else's future.

"Things ended badly. I left. It's just difficult for me . . ."

"I'm sorry about that," he said. "Maybe the spa is exactly what you need."

"If I don't drive myself crazy being on my own for two days, winding myself up while being massaged."

"I don't know what happened, but I do know you deserve a break. You've been working hard and making great progress here. Go to the spa. Try to forget about . . ." He glanced around his office. "Everything."

He was right. I shouldn't let what had happened ruin this weekend along with all the rest of the weekends it already had destroyed. I should go to the spa and try to relax. "I just wish Darcy was coming with me to distract me."

"Darcy?"

"My sister-in-law. Kind of. She's the only real friend I have in England."

"You have me."

I rolled my eyes. "Wanna come to the spa with me for the weekend?"

He chuckled.

"What am I thinking?" I gasped, dramatically. "You couldn't possibly take a day off work. That would be sacrilegious or something." I smiled and shrugged. "I don't know. I'll probably go. I wouldn't want to waste it, and I do want to see more of England outside London before I leave. I should make a list of things I want to do before I head back to the US."

"Good idea."

"What about you? Do you have a bucket list? Places you want to see, things you want to do before you hit your next big birthday—which is fifty, right?"

He raised an eyebrow as he dug his fork into his salad. "Be careful, Miss King."

I beamed at him, urging him to bring it on. I could handle whatever he could dish out.

"My next big milestone will be taking silk, but that's unlikely to happen before I turn forty. And no bucket list, no."

"Taking silk is when you become a Q.C., like with the longer wig and shit?"

He chuckled. "Yeah, I'm going all out for the longer wig."

"You all look a little silly if you don't mind me saying. I mean, we're in the twenty-first century and Prada exists."

He picked up his glass and swirled the wine around. "Which makes it more important than ever that the judge and jury aren't influenced by anything but the argument.

The wig and gown are there so as not to distract from the case. In your country, too much time is spent on what the lawyers are wearing and what they look like. We prefer to practice law."

He spoke with such authority and conviction that even if what he was saying didn't make sense, I would have believed him. "I like talking with you," I said, as I stared into his eyes. I didn't have a better response, and it was what I was thinking.

"I like talking with you, too."

I was damn pleased I wasn't in New York right now. Because of David and the IPO. Because of my lack of career and prospects, but also because there was no place I'd rather be, no moment I'd prefer to be having.

NINETEEN

Violet

I was either in the best place on earth or some weird, Stepford wives' holiday camp. The jury was still out. I tightened the belt to my robe and headed back to my bedroom from the pool, carrying my e-reader. When I'd come to England, I'd been looking for a fresh start, a flash of inspiration. The last thing I'd expected was to be alone at a spa, counting down until the company I'd co-founded went public without me having anything to do with it.

I'd thought my stay in England would be a lot like New York, just with different architecture and accents. But it had been completely different. There'd been fewer cocktails and less sex than I imagined—although what I'd lost in quantity I'd more than made up for in quality with Alexander, even if we'd only fucked once. Nothing was what I expected.

Back in New York, I'd known something wasn't right with my life but for the first time in a long time, I was actually giving thought to what that was and what I wanted after thirty. I hadn't come to any conclusions, but I was thinking further ahead than the end of next week.

I passed a couple in matching robes and smiled. Were matching robes in my future? I could move to Montana and live on a farm if I wanted—maybe go to the Cordon Bleu in Paris or move back to Connecticut. There was nothing stopping me going anywhere to do anything.

I let myself into my bedroom and began to get ready for dinner, but before I could step into the shower my phone rang.

"Scarlett, you will never guess where I am! I'm literally living your very privileged life," I told my sister.

"What, you're standing in your kitchen, covered in spit-up, deciding whether to clean up dog shit from the yard or change your baby's diaper?"

"Well, when you put it like that. Maybe for once, I have the better end of the bargain. I'm at the spa."

"I *wish* I were at the spa. How is it?"

"Oh, pretty perfect. I went on a hike this morning and then had a full body massage this afternoon. I'm just getting ready for dinner."

"A hike? You? Who are you? Tell me you haven't given up alcohol."

I lay on my bed and stared out at the huge pine tree outside my window as it became a black silhouette against the darkening sky.

"I was worried about you. I didn't know if you've seen the business pages at all."

"I don't want to talk about it." There was nothing to say. Scarlett knew the story. Talking about it wasn't going to change anything. I just wish she or Darcy were here to distract me. "Are you thinking you might come over to the UK while I'm in London?"

"I'll try but I can't promise anything. I just wish I could be there now. A massage is just what I need."

I missed my sister. Our lives couldn't have been more different, but she and my brother had been the few constants in my world. I hadn't realized until the last few weeks how much I relied on her as the anchor in my life.

"That's okay. I'll be home soon enough."

"You're not going to accept the extended contract?"

"Oh, I'm not sure yet. I'm going to see what Craig thinks of my ideas first. But even if I do stay, it's only another three months."

"And what about the man situation? It's so not like you to be man-free for this long."

I hadn't told her about Alexander—not that there was anything to tell. Even though he'd asked me to dinner, I was pretty sure he'd forget or be too busy with work. As he'd said, he rarely took an evening off. So even though he was the best sex I'd ever had, and I was completely attracted to him, there didn't seem any point in bringing it up with Scarlett.

Mini Scarlett, or Gwendoline, as my sister insisted on calling her daughter, began to cry in the background. Scarlett groaned. "I'm going to have to go. I thought she'd sleep for longer. I'm sorry."

I wanted to talk longer, but I understood that being responsible for a tiny human was more important. "That's okay. Call me again soon, right?"

"I promise. I love you."

I slung the phone on my bed and went into the bathroom to turn on the shower. Scarlett might not be here to keep me company at dinner, but that didn't mean I wouldn't blow-dry my hair and do my makeup as if I had a date with Ryan Gosling.

Last week I'd bought a super-cute black cocktail dress from a shop in Covent Garden. I'd seen it in the window when I'd first arrived and almost pressed my nose against the glass I wanted it so badly. It had taken three weeks of paychecks, putting a little bit of money aside each week, and I'd finally been able to afford it. I couldn't remember the last time I saved up for anything, but as I'd got it home and slipped it on, I knew it had been worth it. I wasn't one to show off my boobs but with the neckline on this dress there was no choice, and the V thinned toward the bottom so that it hinted at something rather than shouting it to the world. The black fabric had a shimmer to it and the loose skirt and the spaghetti belt all added up to casual glam.

London had been all about new experiences. Tonight I had a date with myself.

Alexander

This was either one of my better ideas or one of my worst. Violet had told me she was coming to the spa by herself, but that could have changed—she'd have no reason to update me. I didn't know the whole story about the company she'd been involved with, but after she left I'd read the article she'd poured over in my copy of the *Financial Times*. It was an IT company founded by some guy at MIT. She'd said she'd been involved with the company, but the defeated look in her eye and her slumped shoulders after she'd seen the piece made me think that there was more to the story. What had happened that she was involved with a company about to float for a hundred million dollars, but she'd been working as a waitress? She'd said she needed distraction this weekend, and she'd seemed so unlike herself that I wanted to do something. And she had invited me, even if she'd been clearly joking. I'd thought that my turning up might be a good idea. My encounter with Gabby last weekend had been swirling around my brain all week. The things she'd said about my relationship with my father had been off base, but the fact was that three years had gone by and I'd barely noticed, hardly looked up from my desk. I didn't think I'd left London once since I'd moved into the hotel, and I certainly had no memories of doing anything that wasn't connected to work since my time with Gabby. Taking the evening off to have dinner with a beautiful woman seemed overdue. Now I was here, waiting for Violet, it felt like a ridiculous thing to have done. I should have at least called her to ask if it was okay. It wasn't like we were dating. Or even fucking. It was just that I'd felt something shift between us as we shared dinner in my office together. Like maybe we *were* friends as I'd jokingly said to her. I didn't have many benchmarks to measure friendship by, but I liked Violet.

I shifted in my chair at the bottom of the staircase of the hotel, clasping my hands on the arms and then linking them in my lap. My plan was to intercept her on the way to the dining room and ask her whether or not she wanted to move up our date. Hopefully she wouldn't think I was an idiot. If she did, I was pretty sure she'd tell me. I chuckled at the thought.

Who the fuck was I becoming? I'd taken the night off work when I was already behind on my preparation for court next week, and I'd worn a Prada suit for her. I should probably head off before I made a complete fool of myself. I stood, thrust my hands into my pocket, and headed toward the door.

"Knightley?" Violet called from behind me.

I was too late.

I turned and glanced up the stairs.

"Alexander, is that you?" she asked, grinning as she came downstairs, her long legs moving elegantly, her skirt hitting her mid-thigh in a teasing, tempting way.

This woman.

Her smile grew as she came toward me and I couldn't help but smile back, her infectious positivity relaxing me.

"What are you doing here?"

The curve of her neck, just visible beneath her wavy hair, and the subtle scent of jasmine left me breathless.

She was the most beautiful woman I'd ever seen.

"You said you needed distraction, so I'm here to take you to dinner—unless you have other plans. You agreed to a date, after all."

She grabbed my wrist as her eyes widened. "Brilliant! As you'd say in England."

I offered her my arm and we headed toward the dining room.

"You came all the way to have dinner? That's so nice of you."

"I think you might just be worth it," I said. I couldn't ever remember thinking that about a woman before. Even with my wife I didn't remember doing anything just because I wanted to make her happy.

Violet stopped abruptly and I turned to look at her.

"I just want to say that you being here, it's really thoughtful. Thank you."

She didn't think I was a lunatic. It was good to know my judgment wasn't entirely off. "I'm looking forward to having dinner with you. As I said, I like talking with you."

She grinned and squeezed my arm and we continued to the dining room.

"Isn't this incredible?" she asked, glancing around as we

took our seats. "I hardly read a page at dinner last night, I was so taken with this little hobbit house."

The ceiling of the dining room was low and, like the walls, was beamed and uneven. Most likely, the building was still the original wattle and daub. To me it looked like a thousand places I'd been to before, but it was nice that Violet was enjoying it.

"Is the food good?" I asked.

"Sure. I mean, if I don't have to serve it, food always tastes better."

"Were you really a waitress back in New York?" I asked as I placed the napkin in my lap and took the wine list and menu from the waiter.

"You don't believe me?"

"I believe you. I just don't understand it."

"For four years." She shrugged and scanned the menu, her hair tumbling over her shoulders. "I wanted a job where I could enjoy my life."

It seemed so strange to me that a woman as clever and charming as Violet could be happy waiting tables. "And waitressing allows you to enjoy life?" I asked.

She put her menu down and looked at me as if she were really considering the question. "Yes and . . . no. I guess I thought it would."

There were a thousand things she wasn't saying that were hidden just beneath the surface of her words. But I was used to getting people to tell me the truth of a situation. I wanted to uncover all those secrets.

"What did you want to do when you started college?"

"I wanted to have my own business. I majored in computer science, so it gave me a lot of options."

"Are you ready?" I asked Violet as the waiter

approached. "And of course, you're going to pre-empt my order, don't forget."

Violet didn't even look up. "Oh, you'll go for the venison, for sure."

I turned to the waiter. "Apparently, I'll have the venison."

"I think I might have that as well. I've never tried it. Is it good?"

"It depends."

Violet shook her head at me. "Don't be too enthusiastic." She turned to the waiter. "I'll have the same. When in Rome and all that."

"And you'll have some red wine?"

"Only if you get a bottle. I don't drink it by the glass," she said, in a put-on English accent.

I tried not to give her the satisfaction of a smile and instead ordered something that looked like it might be halfway decent. The wine list wasn't great, but the company more than made up for it.

"So you were telling me about what you wanted to do when you were at university."

She shook her head. "Nothing more to tell."

"You just decided to change ambitions from computer whiz to waitress?"

"Sure." She reached out and shifted the salt and pepper so they were touching each other. "What did you want to do at college?"

"Become a lawyer."

She rolled her eyes. "Of course you did. Because your dad was a lawyer?"

I hadn't mentioned my father before, which made me wonder who'd told her about him. "I always enjoyed advocacy," I said, evading the question.

"I heard he was like the world's best barrister or something. He had a nickname . . ."

"Alexander the Great," I filled in for her.

"That's the one. How's that, following in the footsteps of a man who was nicknamed after a Greek king who conquered the world before he was thirty?"

I couldn't help but laugh. She'd summed it up perfectly, getting to the heart of an issue as she always did. "It was how you would expect it might be."

"Well, that's an answer from a lawyer if ever I heard one."

The waiter came over and poured our wine. Violet and I didn't take our eyes off each other, as if we both wanted to maintain the moment before we were interrupted.

"Takes one to know one," I said once he'd left us.

She frowned. "I'm not a lawyer."

"Yes, but you answer questions like one."

"I do not." She took a sip. "This is good." She lifted her chin to indicate the wine.

"It's only okay, and you're evading again. What happened at college that made you think that you couldn't enjoy your life doing anything but waitressing?"

"What makes you think something happened? People can change their minds about things."

I didn't respond. She was talking bollocks and I wanted to know the truth. For the first time since I'd met her, Violet was something other than confident and sure of herself when she'd seen that newspaper. I wanted to know what could shake her like that.

"If you must know, my boyfriend and I developed some software. We put together a business plan in our final year and after graduation we worked hard for two years to get it to market. We were just about to start talking to investors.

We had the next three years of our lives planned out and all these ideas of where we were going to take our business and how much it was going to grow. We were going to get engaged after graduation and married once turnover reached a certain level. I had *a lot* of plans."

"And?"

"And I found out he was fucking my roommate and the business I thought we'd set up together was only in his name."

I seethed. "He stole from you?"

"And he cheated on me."

I balled my hands into fists. "That's stealing, too. I'm so sorry, Violet."

She shrugged as if she didn't care, but I could tell by the way her glance sank to her lap that she still felt betrayed by it.

"And that company that you founded. That's the one that's floating on Monday."

She looked up at me, frowning.

"I read the article once you left."

She took a deep breath and nodded. "Yeah. On Monday when the bell strikes he'll be a multi-millionaire."

I sat forward in my chair. "Jesus, Violet. It's not right. You didn't take legal action?"

"No. I was so blindsided I just walked away. I abandoned every plan I've ever had. I didn't want to think about the level of betrayal, let alone live it again through some protracted legal case."

"So you stopped planning and became a waitress."

"I needed a new place to live and to earn some money right away. I had nothing. And waitressing was fun." She paused and tilted her head. "At first. And the people were all about the here and now. College is supposed to be about drinking and partying and getting laid, but I'd been too busy working toward my future. Focusing on my boyfriend. I wanted to live in the moment, to bask in the sun when it was out."

"But eventually, you didn't want to put your degree to good use?"

"I didn't want anything to do with MIT. It felt toxic. Cursed. And I had no other skills. All that time and effort I'd put into the business had been wasted. I didn't want to make that mistake again."

"I can understand that." It all made sense—why this clever, charming girl was meandering through life. I wanted to pull her onto my lap and tell her I'd fix it for her—I'd sue the guy and then have him killed.

"You would never be so reckless, of course. You're a planner, right?" She adjusted her cutlery, making sure it was all set in a straight line.

Part of me wished I hadn't brought up college, she was clearly distressed about it, but another part of me was pleased that I had—I wanted to know what drove Violet. I didn't just want to know the woman everyone else saw. I liked the one who lay just beneath the surface even better. I enjoyed understanding why she did what she did and said what she said.

"I'm not so good at living for the moment. Not so good at basking in the sun."

"Is there a pot at the end of the rainbow that you're looking for? An end goal? Or is the work itself the aim?"

I didn't have a clever answer. Perhaps an honest one would do. "I don't know. I guess the goal is to be the best at the bar."

"Do you enjoy the work at all?"

"Absolutely. I love my job and can't imagine wanting to

do anything else."

"But you're doomed to never be satisfied with yourself."

Nausea churned in my gut. "What makes you say that?"

She paused, clearly thinking carefully about what she was going to say. "Because being 'the best' is subjective and your dissatisfaction with yourself drives you. You'll always think you can be better because you always can be. No one's perfect."

She'd left me speechless and I could do nothing but stare at her.

"You ever thought that if you lowered the bar—no pun intended—you'd be happier? Change up your goals?"

She said it like it was easy. Like I could just click my fingers and be satisfied with mediocrity. "Mediocrity was a sin in our house when I was growing up. I was expected not just to get good grades but to be the top of my class. If I took on a sport, I had to be the best or I had to endure my father's disdain. Perhaps I'm just programmed to want to do better —to keep that bar as high as it will go."

"Whatever the cost?" she asked.

"I focus on the reward," I replied.

She shook her head. "Do you ever reexamine the reward? Ask yourself if it's worth it? I've seen how hard you work."

I shuddered. I'd never thought about it. I'd just had a goal and gone after it—whatever it took. I'd made up my mind what I wanted to do when I was still a child and from watching my father, I knew what it took. I didn't have a choice if I wanted what he'd had. I'd never once since questioned the goal itself or considered the sacrifice. I glanced up and Violet was grinning at me and her smile overrode the chill that had run down my spine.

"I'm here," I replied. "Doesn't that count for anything?

You can poke fun at me, but taking the whole night off is a big deal for me."

She didn't laugh as I expected her to. She just nodded. "I know, which is why I'm taking it as a compliment."

I grinned at her. "You should. I wanted to come tonight. To spend the evening with you. And it takes more than it should to draw my attention away from work."

"Well then I'd better be entertaining," she replied, her eyes sparkling.

"You could never be anything but."

She laughed. "You are crazy. Crazy handsome, yes, but crazy nonetheless."

Violet

"Shall I order another bottle of wine?" Alexander asked as I set my glass back down. He was looking at me as if he wanted to uncover my deepest secrets, but he'd already managed to do that tonight. I hadn't talked about MIT or David for a long time. I'd locked away the whole experience in a waterproof chest and dropped it into my memory's ocean. But recently it had bobbed to the surface, and tonight Alexander had retrieved it and smashed it open. For a few months now, maybe even longer, there'd been a gnawing in my gut that had told me things weren't right, that I needed a change. Maybe it had been the news about the IPO or losing my job, or maybe it had started before that. Whatever the reason, it had brought me to England. It wasn't that I wanted to do clerical work forever, but my job in chambers was giving me confidence to think about what I really wanted in my career, in my life. I just hadn't quite figured that out yet.

"Before we decide, I need to tell you that I'm going to

say yes to the extension of my contract."

He leaned back in his chair and stretched out his legs. "Does that mean you want another bottle to celebrate?"

"Are you okay with me saying yes?" I didn't expect him to say no. But I wanted to know what he thought.

He looked at me the way he always did when he was trying to elicit more information from me than I was giving him. "Of course, you're doing an excellent job."

"So it's no big deal that we're sitting here, but will be working together?" He was clearly a private man. I wasn't sure he'd want anything personal with someone he worked with, but I kinda did. I didn't think I'd ever wanted a man as much as I wanted Alexander Knightley.

"Not unless we make it a big deal."

"In that case, can we get the wine to take back to the room?" I asked.

"Oh, yes, of course. I should get going anyway. I'll order a cab." He glanced around as if trying to find a waiter.

My heart sank. He was leaving? "You're going back to London?"

"You're ready to go, right?"

"Back to my room—with you, I'd hoped."

His eyes widened and the corner of his mouth twitched. "I was trying to be a gentleman."

I tilted my head and smiled. "I don't want you to be too gentle."

Alexander groaned. "You're sure?"

I nodded. "Let's stay up all night and talk and drink wine, get naked, fuck, and talk some more. We can spend the whole night enjoying the moment."

"Another bottle of wine to go," Alexander told a passing waiter, "and the bill, please."

As we walked up the wide staircase, I slipped my hand

into Alexander's. I couldn't remember the last time I'd shared so much of myself with a man. I got physically naked with men all too often but rarely did I allow them to see as much of me as I'd revealed to Knightley. I didn't even talk to Scarlett about David anymore. She often scolded me for being flighty and unfocused, but the truth was she'd never understood why. In one conversation Alexander knew more about me than people who'd been in my life for decades.

Alexander took my key and slid it into the lock, then held the door open as I stepped inside.

I set down the wine glasses I'd carried up and Alexander poured our drinks.

"I like your suit," I said. "It's better than a gown."

He handed me a glass. "It's Prada. Because, you know, that's what all barristers should be wearing."

"I approve," I said, smoothing my hand up his lapel and cupping the back of his neck.

"Thank goodness."

I grinned at his sarcasm. Somehow he managed to be charming without being too much. He got the balance just right.

He dipped his head and pressed his lips to mine and that light, heady feeling I got when he kissed me in his office enveloped me. Too soon, he pulled back. I was impatient. I wanted more. I had to get to the part where his hands were on me, his tongue was over me and his cock was in me. I needed to understand whether it was as good as I remembered it was.

"Hang on," he said, taking my wine and placing it on the nightstand alongside his. Then he shrugged off his jacket, arranged it on the back of the chair, and kicked off his shoes.

"Come here," he said, circling his hands around my

waist before lifting me up onto the mattress. "A bed's a novelty for us."

I laughed. "I guess."

Fully clothed, he lay down next to me, his head propped up on one hand while he trailed his free fingers over my ass. He was in no rush and although I was, I knew he was setting the pace and he wouldn't give in to me.

"Do you make time for fucking?" I asked. He was so focused on work, I wondered if he had many women, girl-friends.

"Fucking you? Yes." He pulled me closer, the length of our bodies touching.

I traced the contours of his face with my fingers. He was all angles and his beard was rough. I hoped I'd find out how it felt between my thighs before long. "Who was before me?"

He exhaled and turned on his back. "Some girl I met in a bar."

"You go to bars?"

He chuckled. "From time to time I do things that normal people do. I stopped in for a whiskey one night. It was late. She approached me. I went back to her place. I didn't stay the night."

It was the kind of sex that made sense for Knightley—convenient, fleeting, and something he didn't spend time focusing on. He wasn't like that with me. Not here tonight but not even in his office. It was as if I were the only thing in his mind when he fucked me and for a man who thought about so much, it was the ultimate compliment. To have that attention and intensity targeted on me made me heady, filled me right up to the top.

I undid the buttons on his shirt, and he reached beneath my dress, cupping my ass.

"I've wondered what you'd look like completely naked," he said, dipping his head to my neck and pressing his lips to my skin. "Fantasized about it."

I pushed my hand down to his pants and found him straining against the material—a perfect fit for my palm. He pushed against me and groaned. "What did you imagine?"

"Smooth skin." He swept his hand up and down the back of my thigh. "Breasts that make me salivate." He slid his hand between my breasts, reaching into the lace of my bra. "Just like this." He groaned and pushed me to my back. "I'm going to have to change the order of things tonight," he said.

"You are?"

He pressed his thumb against my bottom lip, as though he wanted me to know he was going to kiss me soon. "We're going to fuck, then drink, then fuck, then talk. Then we're going to hit repeat." Pressing his lips against the corner of mine, he lay on top of me. "And we're not going to rush any step." He kissed me again. "I want to make sure that I know your body and mind better than anyone ever has by the time we finally leave this room."

I shivered at the thought because I believed him. I knew by now that Alexander Knightley didn't say things he didn't mean.

Alexander

After what seemed like hours of kissing like teenagers, I couldn't wait any longer—I had to get her naked, wanted to see every inch of her, choose which part to touch, rub, kiss, suck, plunder. I kneeled on the bed and peeled off her dress, revealing each part of her, allowing myself to soak into the wonder of her body. As if she were a painting, the oil still fresh, every line, every curve, was perfect and smooth. I slid my gaze to her firm, pert breasts, her rosy nipples jutting out, pointing at me as if they were begging for my particular attention. I'd get to them. Soon.

After I removed her dress, I pulled down her underwear and she was left entirely naked. Her lack of embarrassment fed my need, urging me to take the time to look, to think about what I would do to her. I pulled my shirt out of my trousers and stripped it off. "You have a beautiful body," I said.

"Thank you," she said, her chest heaving as she smiled.

I didn't want to move away but I needed her skin against mine. I quickly stood, kicked off my trousers, and found the condoms in my wallet.

"You have a great body," she said as I got back on the bed. "You must make time for the gym."

"My mind doesn't work well without the exercise. It sets me up for the day."

"Thank you for that."

I chuckled. "You're welcome." I kissed her on the lips, intending for it to be a quick peck, but I couldn't pull away. I deepened the kiss, my tongue pressing against hers, her fingers in the back of my hair sending shockwaves down my body.

Every kiss with Violet felt like my first kiss. I didn't have any memories of women before. Violet had wiped my mind free of everything in the past. I smoothed her hair back from her face as her legs slid against mine, urging me on.

She groaned and I pulled back. "You're a really great kisser," I said.

"Back at you."

I pressed my lips to her taut belly, then licked my way up to the space between her breasts. "This feels decadent."

There were no other words to explain the indulgence I felt being here with her.

"Sex?"

"Having you naked. Spending time in your company." There wasn't much I enjoyed outside of work but being right here was exactly where I wanted to be.

"It does?"

"Yeah, better than your skirt around your waist and my trousers pooled at my feet." She deserved more than some quick fuck against the wall, however good it was. However hard she'd come.

She laughed. "Well, that was fun, too."

"I like being able to take my time. To savor you."

She traced her finger over my eyebrow and smiled. "That's a nice thing to say."

"I mean it."

"And you don't say things you don't mean—that's why it means more."

She was right. I enjoyed spending time with this woman —naked or with clothes on—and I liked that she knew me well enough to know it wasn't a line.

I sighed as I glanced down her body. "I don't know where to start."

She opened her legs in response.

I chuckled. "Oh yeah?" I asked and she just smiled. She was confident enough to ask for what she wanted but I knew she understood that I had the control where it counted. I decided how hard, how deep, how long.

I moved between her legs and pressed her thighs wide. I glanced up and she was watching me, and my fascination with her pussy. I was prolonging the build up to when I would taste her. I sucked in a breath and I lay my tongue flat against her so the tip nudged at her opening. She smelled of jasmine everywhere—it was the perfect combination of sweet and sexy.

Her hands flew to the back of my head as I swept my tongue up and began to explore her folds. Her arching back and loud groan had blood rushing to my cock. I closed my eyes, trying to block out the curves of her body and the warmth of her skin so I could get her good and wet. When I slid my cock into her, I wanted her to be so desperate she'd do anything I demanded.

She tried to roll her hips up, but I held her in place as she bucked under me. "Alexander," she moaned. "Alexander."

I'd never heard anyone say my full name without flinching, but Violet owned it, made it impossible for me to feel like anything but the king of kings.

I circled and flicked her clit before delving down and then back up. I needed her to be hungry for me to focus on each and every part of her pussy. I wanted her to be needy for my tongue to arrive and desperate when it left.

Her sounds grew louder as her clit became harder against my tongue and I had to grip her hips tight as sensation overcame her. Her hands left my hair to fist the sheets, and she arched her back and screamed my name again and again and again.

Her body melted against the mattress and the aftershocks of her orgasm pulsed against my tongue.

"Jesus," she said.

I wiped my mouth on the back of my hand and crawled up her body. "One down."

"I've never come like that. Not with a man going down on me."

It didn't surprise me. There was something that happened when we were together that I was certain wasn't normal. Wasn't ordinary. "That's because I've never done it."

She sighed. "Apparently."

I kissed her on the lips and she pushed her tongue into my mouth, wanting to taste herself, as she wrapped her arms around my neck.

"I want your dick inside me so badly," she said as I pulled away.

Jesus, those words from her were almost too much—it was as if she knew the exact right thing to say but I understood by the hunger in her eyes and her breathless delivery that it wasn't why she said it. It was how she felt. I didn't say things I didn't mean but Violet wasn't so different.

"So impatient."

"It's been weeks," she whined.

My straining cock agreed with her. "Flip over onto your stomach." I reached across and grabbed one of the condoms I'd left on the nightstand, tearing the packet open and covering my dick.

She'd positioned herself on all fours but that wasn't how we were going to start out. "On your stomach," I said.

She glanced over her shoulder and frowned, but obediently did as I asked. Fuck, I liked this woman.

I straddled her, my weight on my elbows and forearms. I pushed inside on an achingly slow thrust, trying to tune out her whimpering, until I got as deep as I could get—she was every pleasure I'd ever denied myself all at once.

I paused, trying to get myself together, trying to steady my breathing. With each heaving breath I sucked in the scent of jasmine, and it became a part of me. I closed my eyes, taking in her heat, her intense pressure surrounding my dick, the way my fingertips seemed to find home when they pressed into her skin.

"See how perfect my cock is for you?"

She wasn't coherent enough to form words but I enjoyed the cries, the whimpers, the moans. They told me everything I needed to know. I understood that she felt this too—this connection, this perfection. I'd thought she was the fuck of the decade when she was against the wall in my office but this was better than I remembered.

I dipped and grazed my teeth against her shoulder—I wanted her to feel me everywhere.

Pushing up on my hands, she cried out from where she was pinned beneath me at the change in angle. "It's too good." The vibration of her voice reverberated along my spine and down my cock. This woman only had to speak to get me to the edge.

I pulled out almost all the way and thrust again, breathless with lust. "This way, I can hear when your breathing changes. I can whisper in your ear how good it feels." I pushed in again, sharp and determined. "And I can tell you how hard I'm going to fuck you."

She moaned and I picked up the pace, wanting to pull another orgasm from her before I gave in to mine. She tried to move, tried to push up on her hands, but she had no hope. She was where I wanted her—completely under my control, tamed and conquered. As I pulled her arms back down beside her body, she shuddered, turned her face into the mattress, and screamed.

I continued to thrust, knowing I couldn't last long as she spasmed around me. "Fuuuck," I cried out as I came on the tails of her orgasm, pushing her into the mattress with every move.

I collapsed on top of her, then rolled to my back and discarded the condom. My heart was hammering through my chest and my pulse boomed in my ears.

"Violet?" She hadn't moved a muscle.

She turned her head, still on her stomach, her arms by her side.

"Are you okay?" I asked.

She blinked as if she'd just been let out into the sun after hours in darkness. "I think so. It was . . . intense."

I reached out and she shifted to my side. "It's been building between us for a while."

"Maybe that's it," she said, trailing her fingers over my chest. "But I think it's more than that. I don't know what it is, exactly, but it felt bigger than sex."

I knew what she meant. I might dismiss it as being good sex but she was right, it was more than that. Maybe it was the things we'd shared at dinner, but it wasn't *just* lust. I knew we had an extraordinary connection the first time in my office but tonight hadn't been just physical. It was more intense. More connected. More profound. I'd never had this before and now that I had I wondered if I could ever get enough. Would I ever be able to let Violet go?

She stroked up my chest and tipped her body toward me, her leg falling between mine, her hot, pussy against my thigh. "I *need* it again," she whispered.

The way she lingered over the word need. I knew it was more than a craving. She pushed up on her hands and straddled my body, my dick heated by her sex and she gazed at me, creating a stirring in my cock. I trailed my hands over her breasts, catching her nipples between my thumb and forefinger, lazily pinching and releasing as they swayed in front of me. Enjoying every bob and quiver. She began to move. Shit, it had only been a few minutes since I'd come and I knew it would only be a few more until I was hard again. She placed her palms flat against my chest, squeezing together her breasts—my cock appreciated it and I grabbed onto her hips, my fingertips sinking into her skin where they belonged as I encouraged the slide of her wet pussy over my growing erection.

She began to pant and her head fell forward, her glossy, black hair falling around her shoulders and over my arms, connecting us further as she moved faster and faster, urged on by my firm grip.

"You feel so fucking good," I growled.

"I want you to fuck me," she cried as she stopped and collapsed on my chest. "I need it, *please.*"

This feisty, sexy woman was begging for my dick. It couldn't get better. Blood rushed to my cock and I flipped her over to her back in one swift movement. I kneeled and covered my dick with a condom. I needed to be inside her like I hadn't come for Britain already this evening.

As I entered her we both cried out.

She was still so tight, like a bloody fist around me. I was going to have to work hard not to come within seconds.

Face to face I began to thrust, she was slippery wet and the drag was so fucking perfect that I had to focus on something else. But everywhere I looked it was Violet. I dipped forward to press my lips to hers, sloppily plundering her mouth and then pressing my forehead against hers, sharing breath, words, and pleasure.

Underneath me her sounds got louder, the sentences disappearing into fractured words and syllables.

I pulled up her thigh, needing to get more of her, to get deeper in her, wanting us to merge into one. She was so close and so was I—we were about to reach the peak, the rope was about to snap and release us both. One last push and the first quiver of her orgasm severed the final cord for me and we both came silently, our mouths open, our bodies connected as we stared into each other's eyes, unable to comprehend what was happening and how anything could feel so good.

In that instant I knew I was changed. I understood everything would be different after Violet King.

Violet

"If you open those drapes, I swear I'll find the nearest fork and stab you in the eye with it," I said as Alexander stood totally naked in front of the window, his hands poised to welcome in the morning.

"It's nearly half past seven." His accent seemed more British this morning, but maybe that was just my lack of sleep.

"Which means I've had three hours sleep. Come back to bed and be still." I pulled the covers up over my head.

"You want me to wake you up?" he asked as the mattress dipped.

"You kept me awake all night. I need to sleep."

"We should go to the gym. You can't be here naked and expect me to just lie next to you."

I squeezed my thighs together, whimpering as the effects of his body on, over, and in mine all night came back to me. "I think I'm broken."

"You're perfect. Let's go and work out. You said there's a pool here?"

"How do you have this much energy? It's annoying. You should be exhausted with all the hours in chambers and all the fucking last night."

"If you don't want more of the fucking then we need to get to the gym."

I groaned and pushed myself up. My body couldn't take any more. I needed at least a few hours off. I watched him for a couple of seconds. The sight of his tousled bedhead when he was always so put together in chambers was adorable. I tried to hide my grin as he began to dress.

"Hey, where did the sportswear come from?"

He glanced over at me, his eyes gleaming. "You're too sexy."

I frowned when he didn't answer my question.

"My car. Where do you think?"

I stumbled across the room and shut the door to the bathroom. Nothing about last night had been expected. Not Alexander showing up. Not the conversation. And not the sex. Had it really been how I remembered? I grinned around my toothbrush as I remembered the first orgasm, then the second. The way he was so powerful and in control of my body. The third and then the fourth. I'd loved the way he'd revealed a different side of himself last night—he'd removed the stick from his ass and focused on making me come in the best possible ways.

"Come on," he yelled from the bedroom. "Checkout's at ten."

I rinsed my mouth and swung open the door. "Are you always this chirpy in the morning?" I put my hand on my hip and narrowed my eyes at him.

"Are you always so irritable?"

"I'm charming," I corrected him. "At all times."

He chuckled. "I'll try to remember that." He pulled me close and took my face in his hands. "Did I tell you that you're also completely beautiful?"

"What has happened to you? Is this weekend Knightley?"

He kissed me lightly on the lips and then released me. "Are you ready?" he asked, ignoring my question. His lightness had caught me off guard. Last night we'd escaped the world for a few short hours and existed outside reality. I'd fully expected to land back on earth with a thud this morning and be embarrassed by how open I'd been, by what I'd shared. But instead of feeling awkward, I wanted more of the same. More of Alexander Knightley.

I dressed in my running gear and pulled out my sneakers from the closet. "So what happens now?" I asked. "With you and me?"

"I thought you were all about living in the moment."

I followed him out of the bedroom. How was I going to the gym this early? "I thought you were all about the plan. Working toward something that's so far away you can't see it."

He grabbed my hand and picked up the pace.

"We're going to go to the gym, then come back to the room to shower and fuck. Then I'm going to drive you home." He stopped. "Where do you live?"

"Mayfair. Hill Street."

He scowled. "Really?"

"My sister's sister-in-law's place. I told you."

He nodded and started down the stairs, pulling me after him. "And then I'm going back home—"

"To the hotel?"

"Where I live," he agreed. "Then I'll try to make up for all the time I lost last night and today."

I wanted to ask him about us. Would I see him again outside chambers? Were we still going for dinner this week?

Where the fuck had Violet gone and could someone please bring her back?

Maybe a run would do me good, get me to focus on right now, today, and let go of what may or may not come next week.

TWENTY

Violet

As I turned right into the clerks' office, I glanced over at Alexander's closed door and smiled. He was probably busy working away in there, doing that cute little frown thing he thought made him look ferocious but actually made him look sexy.

Yesterday had gone exactly the way he'd said it would, although we made out in his car for ten minutes before he dropped me off. He was an incredible kisser. I bet he could make more money kissing for a living than he did from the law.

"Hi, Jimmy," I said as I passed his desk.

"Violet. How was the spa?"

I pressed my lips together to smother a smile. "Good. Relaxing." I'd returned to London boneless and ready for bed, but I wasn't sure the spa had been responsible for that. "How was your weekend?"

"Great. United won."

I wasn't sure what he meant but I high-fived him

anyway and made my way to my desk. On top was another familiar, shiny black box like the one that had contained my skirt. I'd never had a man buy me gifts before. Hell, I could count the number of times a guy had bought me dinner on one hand.

I took my coat off, dumping it on the chair, and pulled the ribbon off. I'd have to be quick. The others would start arriving soon. Reaching into the tissue paper, I pulled out some fabric—it was fine and delicate and as I held it up, I realized it was a sheer, black blouse. God, it was beautiful and would go perfectly with the skirt he'd bought. Voices drifted in from next door and quickly I folded the blouse, put the lid back on the box, and stuffed it into the bottom drawer of my desk.

I checked the time on my phone. I had a meeting with Craig at nine to go through my proposal and didn't want to be late. I just had a couple of things to print off and then I'd be done. I'd worked hard on the presentation. What he'd asked me to do was far more than just clerical work. He'd trusted me to make improvements in his business. He'd had faith that I'd be able to really make a difference. Nothing I'd done since I'd walked away from the start-up had felt as important, and I didn't want to screw this up.

Alexander and I had swapped numbers last night, and I sent him a quick thank-you. I'd messaged him last night to wish him sweet dreams, and I woke up to a reply telling me he'd dreamed of me. I couldn't remember the last time I had butterflies at just the thought of a man.

I felt as if I were floating. I wasn't used to being giddy, particularly over a man. Bored, yes. Irritated, for sure. But Knightley was everything every other man had failed to be. Alexander was moody and demanding. He was ill-tempered and mercurial, but he was anything but boring.

I printed off the final few things for my informal presentation and headed to Craig's office.

I knocked on the open door.

"Violet. Excellent. Come in and have a seat. I'm excited to see what you have for us."

I sat down at the small conference table and pulled out a pack of papers for each of us.

"So, I've broken down the areas for improvement into four categories: Billing, cash flow, real estate, and communications. Realistically I think we should focus on the first three because communications feeds into each of them."

Craig was nodding as he opened his pack of materials. "Excellent."

I took him through my report page by page, explaining where the issues were, backing up my findings with evidence and then telling him how I thought we could solve the problems. Some were simple operational solutions, but the overarching recommendation was for a new document management system that would link into the billing system and would improve cash flow.

"It's an ambitious plan," he said, closing the presentation and leaning back in his chair. "But there's nothing in here I disagree with. In fact, if paid consultants had come in and made the same recommendations, I wouldn't be surprised. Have you ever thought about doing this kind of thing as a living?"

"Like as a consultant?"

"Exactly. You've pinpointed our issues as if you've been here for years, and your solutions are practical and workable. I'm impressed."

I wrung my hands under the table. He couldn't have said anything that would have made me feel any better. To compare my work with a professional consultant was nothing short of jaw dropping. Not only had I not let *him* down—I'd not let *me* down. I'd proven I was capable of more. Working here, being in London, I'd discovered that I wanted something bigger than what I was doing in my life in New York.

"The only issue we have is the cost of the software and implementation."

"I've only done some high-level research—we'd definitely need to have an expert come in and provide a quote."

"And we'd need to find cost savings from elsewhere. There's no way I'll get the barristers to increase their contribution to pay for it. We're not the cheapest chambers as it is."

"I understand. And I can look into it. My real estate recommendation might help. If you were to move into new offices, running costs would come down because you could use a purpose-built office more efficiently."

He nodded as he stroked his chin. "Look into it, will you? And let's get the actual figure on how much the software would cost." He closed the presentation pack and patted it with his hand. "This is excellent work, Violet."

"Thank you."

"I trust you'll be with us a few more months? I think officially you're due to finish at the end of the week otherwise."

"I would love to stay if you'll have me."

"That's agreed then."

Our meeting over, we left the table, and Craig opened the door to his office to the sound of a woman shouting. "Where is he?"

Craig frowned as he followed me out into the corridor.

"Craig," said a tall, glamorous, blonde woman who looked nothing like the few female barristers in chambers but seemed to know her way around. "I'm looking for my husband."

"Mrs. Knightley, how marvelous to see you."

Mrs. Knightley? The walls of the corridor began to bend and curve as if they were about to collapse. I tried to think of possible explanations as to why Craig was calling this woman Mrs. Knightley and why she wanted to see her husband. Was there someone else in chambers with the same name? Was she Alexander's mother? Of course I came up empty. I knew the answer. I just didn't want to believe it.

Alexander was married.

"Craig, you're very sweet, but I just want to speak to Alex. Is he in his office?"

The familiar rattle of Alexander's doorknob echoed down the corridor, and I watched as the man I'd had butter-flies about this morning fill the frame of the door. "Gabby?" His eyes slid from his wife to me, then back to her. "What are you doing here?"

She marched up the corridor and pushed past him into his office and shut the door.

I turned to Craig, who said nothing, so I followed his lead, forced my mouth into a shape I hoped resembled a smile and headed back to my desk, clutching my presentation to my chest.

Knightley was married?

Was I the other woman?

My stomach churned and my hands went slick with sweat. I wanted to be back in Connecticut with my sister, sitting in bed and watching reruns of the *Golden Girls*. I knew what being cheated on felt like. I understood what it was like to be in love with a man who didn't respect me enough to keep it in his pants. How had I misjudged Knightley so badly? How had I become a woman I vowed never to be? I would never knowingly have sex with a man who had a wife or girlfriend, let alone share the things—the personal things—I had with Alexander. I'd thought I had learned my lesson with men already. I knew they were fundamentally untrustworthy—that's why I never let myself get involved. I *had* proof. I didn't need more evidence. How could I have been so stupid to be taken in by his taciturn charm? He was just like the rest of them—driven by their dicks and their egos. He better keep away from me because if he came within three yards, I'd punch him in the balls.

Alexander

"What are you doing here?" I asked, stalking back to my desk. It had been a long time since Gabby had turned up to chambers.

"You promised me that you'd let me have the signed papers by the end of last week."

Shit. I'd totally forgotten. So much had happened last week and this weekend with Violet that it had completely slipped my mind. Gabby deserved better.

"You promised me, Alex." She looked dejected, beaten almost. "I need to move on."

I was used to Gabby angry, but I wasn't used to seeing her upset. Yet this was the second time in just over a week that I'd seen her so vulnerable. It didn't suit her, and I seemed to be the cause of her pain, which I hated myself for.

"I bet you've been working all weekend and not given those papers a second thought." Her gaze flitted over my desk.

Guilt tugged at my chest. I'd not worked enough and I was paying the price today. It had been worth it though.

There weren't many times in my life I'd thought anything was more important than work, but spending the night and the next morning with Violet had been. It felt like being plugged into the mains after being on a fading generator for too long. My mind was clearer, sharper, even if my muscles ached from the hours we spent in bed together.

"I'm sorry," I said.

She shook her head. "I've had enough of your apologies to last me a lifetime. Just sign the bloody papers. You promised."

I headed over to my desk and pulled out the manila envelope that had arrived a couple of weeks ago. I'd meant to look at it this weekend, but I'd been selfish, again. Neglected Gabby's needs, again.

I signed the last page, then worked my way page by page to the front of the document, initialing as I went. It was a standard document. Nothing contentious about it.

"You see?" Gabby said. "It took you five seconds, and I've had to waste half a day coming out here."

"I know. I should have done it."

"I'd feel better if you'd have been having the weekend off. Doing something other than working. Have you thought that it might do you good to not spend every waking hour in chambers?"

This weekend I'd taken the whole of Saturday night off and almost all of Sunday and although it had been worth it, I couldn't do that regularly. It had left Gabby angry and me behind in my work. "I get the message Gabby—you think I work too much."

"Look, I never wanted to be the wife screaming at her husband. I used to hate myself after we'd argue." She leaned against my desk. "As much as I wanted your attention, I also wanted you to be happy and have a good life. You're a decent man and you deserve to do more than spend your whole life working."

I'd forgotten the good parts about Gabby in all the shouting. She was kind and compassionate and wanted the best for people.

"Thank you," I said. "But I'm doing what I always set out to do, Gabby," I replied. "You don't need to worry about me. I've chosen this life."

"I know." She closed her eyes.

"But I did take Saturday night off this weekend after our conversation in the garage."

"Wonders will never cease. Sometime in the next decade you might have worked yourself up to a whole week-end. You know, I just booked a holiday. I'm going to Sri Lanka. Did you ever go in the end?"

I couldn't remember going anywhere since I'd been to India during university. "No, never. Was I meant to?"

"I remember you saying you always wanted to."

I squinted. "I did?"

"Yeah. Before we were married you said it was next on your list—we even talked about it as a potential honeymoon before your workload meant we had a three-day trip to Wales instead. I guess you've still not made much progress on that list."

I had no memory of wanting to go to Sri Lanka. No memory of having a list of things I wanted to do or places I wanted to go. I'd thought law had always been my sole focus, but perhaps at some point I'd had other goals as well. "I guess not."

She shook her head. "I'll send you a postcard—at least you'll have a picture to show you what it's like. I hope one day you figure it out yourself or meet a woman who can get through to you better than I ever did."

Perhaps I should try to organize my work to have a few more evenings off. I'd enjoyed the night I'd spent with Violet. Talking with someone about something that wasn't work had been surprisingly fun and the sex had been phenomenal as well.

Gabby stuffed the papers into her bag, and we both walked across my office to the door.

"Take care," I said. I wanted to give her a hug. It seemed such a weird way to end things. "Enjoy Sri Lanka. I'll be waiting for my postcard."

"Good luck," she replied and gave me a half smile before heading down the corridor.

As I went to shut my door, Violet passed by. I smiled at her but she just looked away and kept on walking.

TWENTY-ONE

Violet

My phone buzzed. Alexander. Again. I flipped the phone face down on the duvet and sat back against the headboard.

"Was that him?" Scarlett asked from the screen of my iPad. After spending most of the evening pouting, I'd finally called her for a video chat and told her about Alexander.

"Yes, the lying, cheating asshole. I should have known better." I pulled the arms of my soft gray sweater over my hands and crossed my arms.

"I'm glad you opened up to someone," she said, chopping some unidentified vegetable on the other side of the Atlantic.

"Ha! You've got to be kidding, right?"

"I know this is a setback but—"

"A setback? Are you shitting me? I didn't know he was *married*. He cheated on his *wife*. With *me*. I'm complicit in adultery and it's all that asshole's fault."

More chopping and slicing, for a salad, by the look of it. "I don't know, Violet. I think you need to give him a chance to explain. Are you sure it was his wife? Maybe they're divorced."

"You are so irritating when you're doing this cup-half-full thing. Don't you get it? I'm a cheater attractor."

"Don't be ridiculous. You've had a hundred boyfriends." She paused. Boyfriends wasn't what I'd call them and Scarlett knew that. "Kinda, since David, and none of them have cheated on you."

I didn't want to tell her that I hadn't given them the chance, that I'd tossed them to the curb before they had a chance to get bored with me and find someone else more interesting. "I'm the only one talking sense in this conversation. David was a cheater. Now Alexander. I just want to come home. At least in New York I could attract cheaters *and* drink diet Dr. Pepper. And it's Thanksgiving in a few weeks. I could help decorate Mom and Dad's place."

"Mom and Dad are in Hawaii for the holiday."

"Are you freaking kidding me? Do they know they have kids?"

"They know they have grown children who are happy for them to take a well-deserved vacation to one of the most beautiful places on Earth."

I growled but I couldn't argue with her. As far as my parents knew, I was going to be in London for Thanksgiving.

"I was going to suggest we all have Thanksgiving at Woolton."

I sat up straight. Woolton was Darcy's place in the country. "You were going to fly over?"

"Yes. And I'll do Mom's candied yams if you behave."

I grinned. All wasn't lost in the world. "I would really like that."

"Perfect. I'll make it happen."

She really could be a great big sister when she wanted to be. "Also, I wanted to talk to you about something I'm thinking about, so it will be good if you come across for Thanksgiving." I knew Scarlett thought it was a good idea to go back to college, and the longer I spent away from New York, the more it didn't seem such a ridiculous prospect—more like an opportunity for a do-over.

"What kind of thing?"

I'd prefer to talk to her in person. "Just some stuff I'm thinking about."

She stopped what she was doing and faced the camera.

"I've not decided on anything. I'm looking at all the options, but one of them is going back to school."

She stayed silent but broke out into a huge grin.

"Columbia, maybe. But I'd need a place to stay and . . ."

"Well, you could stay with us, of course. We're hardly ever there and if you needed me to lend you course fees—"

"Seriously, Scarlett. I don't want you to assume this is a done deal. I'm only thinking about it." I should never have brought it up, except that I wanted to gauge her reaction—see if she thought I was nuts.

"I promise I won't mention it again until I see you." With her finger she made a cross on her chest. "And you promise me that you'll listen to what Alexander has to say."

I rolled my eyes and edged down the bed, farther under the duvet. "I'm not going to be made a fool of."

"Of course not, but don't cut him off without listening—try to stay objective." She glanced over her shoulder. "I have to go. Gwendoline needs a drink. Just don't do anything rash without telling me, okay? No quitting your job, you hear me?"

"I promise I won't resign without telling you first. I love you."

The screen went dark and I couldn't help but wish I was with her in Connecticut rather than here in London. How on Earth had I managed to have another guy shit on me after so many years of shit dodging?

The doorbell rang. I flipped my cell over; it was after eleven. The bell sounded again as I forced myself out of bed and my fluffy-sock-covered feet hit the floor.

"Violet," Alexander bellowed through the letterbox.

I stomped down the stairs and opened the door a fraction. "You're going to wake the neighborhood."

"If you'd just answer your phone, I wouldn't have to be calling through the letterbox."

I folded my arms across the cardigan I was wearing over my pajamas. "What do you want, Alexander? I'm trying to sleep."

He frowned. "Can I come in?"

"Of course you can't come in. I suggest you go home to your wife."

He drew back as if I'd punched him in the face. "What? No." The door flew wide open as Alexander pushed his way into the house.

"Get out!" I screamed, stumbling back. "Get out of this house."

Calmly, he closed the front door and faced me. "Calm down, Violet. I don't know what the hell you're thinking or how much you've wound yourself up, but you need to hear me when I say that I've not been home to my wife in three years." His voice was deep and even, as if he were trying to talk someone off a ledge. Which maybe he was.

"Whatever. I'm not interested." I flounced into the living room.

He was right behind me. "I've seen her twice since we

split up three years ago and both times were about our divorce."

I put my hand on my hip. "Who the fuck waits three years to get divorced?"

He sighed and looked around as if he were trying to find something tangible to back up his story. "I don't know what to say to you, but you said it yourself—I don't say things I don't mean. I'm not lying to you."

"Even if that's true, which I *very* much doubt, why didn't you tell me you were married? That's not a small thing, Alexander. It's not as if you failed to mention you had a Labrador as a kid or you don't eat chicken. You are someone's *husband*. I fucking poured out my heart to you this weekend and you don't mention the fact that you have a wife?"

As I stopped yelling, my voice echoed around the room. I hadn't realized I'd been shouting.

He looked at me as if he was about to say something and then turned away. "Fuck," he spat, thrusting his hands into his hair. "Fuck, fuck, fuck."

"Just go," I said, resigned. He had no defense. Nothing to say.

"No," he boomed. "I'm not leaving. Sit, please."

I don't know whether it was out of shock or exasperation, but I fell back onto the sofa.

"Gabby and I split three years ago. I probably should have mentioned it."

I went to speak but he lifted up his finger to shush me. I looked away; how the hell did this man have me doing whatever he asked?

"But honestly, rightly or wrongly, I don't think of myself as married. I don't think I ever did." He paced in front of me, talking to the ground. "When I left, Gabby and I spoke on the phone a couple of times, but there was never any hope of reconciliation. We spoke to sort out the practicalities of bank accounts and mortgage payments." He glanced over at me as if to see if I was listening.

I was. I wished I could block out my ears. Pack up my heart.

"I saw Gabby last week for the first time in three years."

"And she wants you back?"

"No." He stopped and looked at me as if I'd just said the most ludicrous thing he'd ever heard. "She wants a divorce."

"And you won't give her one because you're still in love with her," I said.

"For crying out quietly, Violet, why on earth are you jumping to all these wild conclusions?"

"Oh, I don't know—maybe because you forgot to tell me you were *married*."

"It didn't come up."

"So if I had three kids stashed in the States, you think it would be okay for me to fail to mention them? You can't give me that it-didn't-come-up shit."

"Look, I know it looks bad—"

"Looks bad? It *is* bad."

"I swear to God, woman, do you have an off switch?"

"Yeah, it turns on when you leave."

"Just listen to me. I've not seen Gabby for three years. She's not relevant to my current life. You and I haven't had time to share everything about our past yet. But I can guarantee you that Gabby doesn't love me anymore. Maybe I loved her at some point in my own fucked-up way, but whatever was between us died a long time ago. A divorce is just a piece of paper, Violet. Two people who haven't seen each other in three years aren't married, whatever else it might say on the public record."

My judgment of men was so off, I didn't know what to think. He sounded genuine, but if I'd learned anything in my life it was that I couldn't spot a cheater.

"I got the divorce papers last week, then went over to the house to collect my things."

"In three years you hadn't been back to get your stuff? That's bullshit."

"That's the truth. When we first split, she emailed me that she'd boxed some stuff up and left it in the garage, but I never found the time. I didn't think she'd kept them."

"So why did she come to chambers today?"

"I don't want you to freak out."

This was the part where he dropped a bombshell, I just knew it. "Just tell me."

"I hadn't signed the divorce papers—I'd planned to go through them over the weekend but . . ."

"Because subconsciously you didn't want to?"

"Because I was enjoying my time with you. And then I was behind with work and as Gabby rightly points out, work has always come before her."

"She's mad at you?"

The cushions of the sofa tipped as he sat down next to me. "All the women in my life are mad at me."

I shrugged. It was no more than he deserved, but still, I believed him. No one at chambers had ever mentioned Alexander was married, and I'd heard a lot of shit about a lot of barristers and their wives and who was cheating and who was being cheated on. No one had ever mentioned Knightley. But more than that, now he was here in front of me, telling me the details of his marriage, I believed him. He wouldn't lie. Not to me and not to anyone. He wasn't a man who ever thought he needed to.

"Ironically, seeing her gave me the idea of coming to the spa."

"What, she told you to go and meet some random woman, take her to dinner, then fuck her into next year?"

"Not quite, but seeing her did make me realize I haven't done much other than work since I moved out. I was hoping you were going to help me exercise that particular non-work muscle." He reached around my waist, and I didn't try to stop him when he pulled me close.

"Am I forgiven?" He lifted me onto his lap, but I didn't respond.

"It's late," I muttered.

"Time for bed?" he asked, as he kissed my neck.

I shook my head. "I don't think so. I need to know what else 'hasn't come up' before we resume . . . whatever this is."

I pulled back but he held me tightly. My stiff body softened against his hard chest.

"I'm not deliberately keeping anything from you. You know what my life's like; I don't have time to get up to anything interesting."

"No kids?"

"You think I'm hiding them under my desk?"

"What about girlfriends since Gabby?"

"I can't say I've been celibate, but girlfriends, no. I don't have bandwidth."

For the first time since college, I wanted to feel like the exception to someone's rule. I'd accepted the cold hard facts in my relationships with men after David—I'd been using them as distraction, for sex, or to make myself feel better. But I wanted Alexander to tell me how I was different, that he wanted to make time for me.

"I enjoy spending time with you, Violet. And I'm not deliberately hiding anything. My life, or lack of it, is an open book, but that doesn't mean you know everything about me. We're just not there yet."

The longer he held me the more I wanted to believe that one day I would know everything about him. I hadn't felt this way about anyone in a long time. It was scary, but at the same time it felt right, as if this was part of why I was here in England.

"So how about we have a few more moments together? What do you think?" he asked.

I swept my fingers over his cheekbone. "Don't hurt me." It was the first time since David that I'd been close enough to a man to allow them to wound me. The first time I hadn't hurt them or run before I got too close. But with Alexander, I didn't have a choice. I was being swept up on his wave and for the moment, I was happy with that.

"I'll really try hard not to."

I wanted something more than he'd *try* not to hurt me. I wanted his promise in blood. "That's not very convincing."

"It's honest. There are no guarantees, Violet. But I won't lie to you."

I nodded. It was an adult response—a man's answer.

Alexander might be the first *man* I'd ever dated.

TWENTY-TWO

Alexander

Everything in the world was conspiring against my getting these amended pleadings out. If I started working with a junior barrister more often, they could probably handle them, but as Lance liked to point out, I was a control freak.

"Come in," I answered the knock on the door. My office had turned into Piccadilly Circus today. It had been one thing after another, but I happily closed my laptop as Violet's legs came into view.

"You're a sight for sore eyes," I said, beckoning her over.

"Why sore? You're the talk of chambers this morning."

After the incident with Gabby last week, things had settled down between us. We'd had dinner at my hotel late last Thursday and I'd taken another Saturday night off to take her to my favorite restaurant in London. Two Saturday nights in a row—no one would believe it.

"I can imagine. Presumably not just because of my divorce."

"No, because of this huge case—Bar Humbug or whatever."

"It's the Crown against Hummingbird Motors, but Bar Humbug will do."

She jumped up onto my desk next to me, crossing her long legs so I couldn't see up her skirt.

"Have you come to tell me that chambers is gossiping about me?"

"Nope. I've come to take you to lunch."

"Violet, there's no way I can—"

She pressed her finger against my lips. "You have an hour. I know you're working on those amended pleadings, but they don't have to be filed until tomorrow."

I grabbed her wrist and laced my fingers in hers. "No, they have to be in today."

"I checked—it's tomorrow." She nodded at my laptop. "Take a look."

I opened the computer and began to check through the emails and my calendar. "Yeah, you're right. The solicitors had it wrong."

She shrugged. "So you have an hour. Meet me in Lincoln's Inn Fields at the back of the tennis court—there's a little pavilion to keep us dry if it's raining." She hopped off my desk and headed to the door. "Wrap up warm and don't leave for ten minutes."

Before I had a chance to argue, she'd gone.

Even though I had an extra day to file the pleadings, it didn't leave me with free time. I had a million things to do tomorrow that couldn't wait.

But I wanted to stare at Violet's beautiful face for an hour. I wanted to be amused by her quirky take on the world and be bowled over by that brain of hers.

I could find an hour.

Even if it meant that I'd have to stay later tonight. Spending sixty minutes with Violet King was worth it.

I pulled on my coat, scarf, and gloves and headed out just like I always did to collect my lunch. I nodded at someone who I'd been to school with as I headed out of New Square and across to Lincoln's Inn Fields. The yellowing leaves on the trees contrasted beautifully with the bright blue sky. I rarely noticed the changing seasons. I often arrived at work before it was light and left after dark, no matter the time of year. But today was a perfect autumn day.

It was less than a two-minute walk to the spot she'd described. Pavilion was probably too grand a name for the place Violet wanted us to meet, but I knew where she was. I'd walked by it a few times, but it was off my main route through the Fields.

Violet waved, her smile infectious. "You've come out of your cave and haven't been struck down by lightning. Who would have thought?" She put her arms around my neck, and I dipped to kiss her on the lips. The cool air had added color to her cheeks and the light had turned her eyes the brightest of blues.

"You're beautiful."

"Come on. We're over here." She took me by the hand and dragged me under some trees.

"What's this?" I asked, taking in the two fishing chairs covered in blankets and a cooler.

"Lunch," she said, grinning at me. "I wanted to say thank you for coming to the spa."

"There's nothing to thank me for. I had a good time." We both took a seat and arranged the blankets.

"I know, but it was a big deal for me. And after, because of . . ."

"Gabby."

She nodded "Anyway, I thought it might be nice to get you out of chambers and to say thank you."

I leaned forward and swept Violet's hair off her face, tucking it behind her ear. "I should be saying thank you to you. This is . . . nice." As much as Gabby hated me for the time I spent working, I couldn't remember her ever having done anything like this for me. I couldn't imagine saying no if she'd turned up to London with a picnic and asked for an hour of my time.

"So, first thing's first: hot chocolate." Violet pulled out a flask from the bag beside her and produced two mugs. She handed me the hot chocolate and held the cups steady as I poured.

"What shall we toast to?" she asked.

Right then I wanted to toast to her, to tell her that no one had ever done anything this thoughtful just so they could spend a few minutes with me. "Autumn picnics?" I suggested.

The corners of her mouth dropped. "Is this a terrible idea?"

"No." I reached across and grabbed her hand. "Quite the opposite. It would never have occurred to me."

"Not as fancy as you're used to, I guess."

"Better." I'd pick an hour in the November chill with Violet over a stuffy dinner with anyone else every day of the week.

"Really?"

I paused, waiting for her to correct herself.

"I know, I know. You don't say things you don't mean."

"I'm ravenous, what are we eating?" She'd brought a veritable feast. And everything was boxed up in containers as if she'd brought it from home.

"You make this yourself?"

"You sound surprised."

"You like to cook?"

"Yeah, when I get the chance. My kitchen in my last place in New York was too tiny to do anything other than open a can of soup, but the one here is just incredible. I could spend days in that place without sleeping."

"Is that cold macaroni?" I asked, poking into one of the containers. "It's my favorite food."

"Really? I'm surprised it's not venison or caviar."

"This reminds me of boarding school, and anyway, you're the one living in central Mayfair." I dug my fork in and took a mouthful, straight out of my childhood.

"Yes, but that's my sister's sister-in-law's place. I'm just a guest."

"You're not interested in money, are you?"

She paused, staring at the unopened plastic box on her lap. "After college I rejected anything that I'd previously wanted. So, it's not that I'd wanted to make money before, but I'd wanted to be successful. You know, with the company, and it really looked like it was going to happen but then—" She snapped her fingers. "Just like that, it was taken away from me, and I realized how fragile our dreams were."

"Fragile, but still worth having, right?"

She shrugged. "I don't really think about it . . . or talk about it."

"Because you're just living in the moment," I stated.

"What about you, how did you end up getting married?"

She was deflecting, but I would let her. I wanted her to feel comfortable asking me questions. She should know that I wouldn't deliberately keep stuff from her. "I'd known

Gabby a long time. Our parents were friends. We had a very casual thing. And then one evening, she pitched me on getting married."

"Pitched you?"

"You know, told me how she thought we'd be a good couple and how she'd be a good wife and that being married could only help my career." I couldn't remember now when it had come up. It must have been a morning after I'd stayed at her place.

I glanced at Violet when she didn't say anything. "What?"

"Sounds romantic," she muttered.

"It was anything but—but that wasn't what I was looking for."

"And you said yes because?"

"What she was saying made sense. We both came from the same circles, knew the same people. She was an excellent hostess."

"Christ, it sounds like you were hiring a car." She took a bite of the barbequed chicken.

"I think she was looking at the kind of relationship her parents had—the kind mine had. It was a bargain, not a love match." I was sure that many of my peers had similar arrangements.

"Who broke the deal?"

"I gave her less than she wanted." That was the simplest way to explain it. Our expectations had been uneven.

"Because you're so fixated on work?"

I nodded. "She wanted to start a family, but that was the last thing I wanted. I knew it wasn't right between us, our relationship not strong enough to bring children into the world. I pulled away even more and eventually she'd had enough."

"What was the sex like?"

I almost choked on my hot chocolate. "You didn't just ask me that."

She shrugged as if I was making a huge deal out of nothing. "Sex is an important indicator in a relationship."

"It was fine."

"Fine? Wow, there's condemnation, right there."

"I'm not condemning anything. I just don't want to talk about it. How would you like it if I asked you about your sex life back in New York?"

She put her thumb in her mouth, her cheeks sinking around her finger. "It was sex—"

I lifted my hand to stop her but she continued.

"It wasn't like it is with you," she said defiantly.

A warmth in my stomach bloomed. Now I wanted her to keep talking and was irritated at myself for cutting her off.

"Here," she said, reaching toward me and wiping her thumb across my bottom lip. "Sauce," she said and popped her thumb in her mouth again.

Christ, she was mesmerizing. I grabbed her wrist and pulled her onto my lap. "What do I get for pudding?"

She pressed her hand against my chest. "What if someone from chambers sees?"

"I don't care. Do you?"

"It's okay for you—you're earning chambers money. I'm expendable."

I sighed dramatically. "Come on, Violet. Live in the moment. You're so concerned about your career. Carpe diem."

She laughed and tipped her head back, exposing her throat, her hair trailing over my arm. This was the best lunch I'd ever had in my life.

"Stop taking the piss out of me," she said in her best British accent. She pressed her palms against my cheeks and kissed me. We could have been in the arctic and I wouldn't have cared.

She was my own personal sun.

She pulled back, grabbed at my hand, and looked at my watch. "Shit, we gotta go."

"Hey, let's stay just a little longer." My hour was almost up, but I wasn't ready to leave yet.

She jumped off my knee. "No way. I don't want you turning into a pumpkin."

"It can wait," I said, pulling at her arm.

She twisted away. "Seriously, get up." She started packing up the uneaten food and folding the blankets. "I want you to agree the next time I ask you to lunch, but you won't if I say it's going to be an hour and it turns out to be two. I want to carpe another diem with you some other time."

I groaned. "I wish you'd been my Latin teacher."

"With your terrible manners, you would have been in line for a caning."

"Promises, promises."

"Help me take this to that entrance?" She pointed to the exit on the south side of the Fields.

"I'll carry it back to chambers," I said.

"I have a friendly cab driver who's going to drop it off at home for me."

"You've thought of everything. Who said you weren't a planner?"

"I like my job, and I think I'm good at it. I don't want people to think I'm getting special treatment because we're . . . because I'm . . . you know."

I spun her around and pressed my forehead against hers. "Because you're my girlfriend?"

"Whatever." She rolled her eyes.

I wasn't sure if she wasn't ready for the title, or if she was just embarrassed. I chuckled. "Because I'm your boyfriend?"

"Well, if you're my boyfriend, you'll help me get these things to the cab."

There was nothing she could ask me to do that I'd say no to. For the first time ever in my life I wanted more from a woman. I wanted Violet to be my girlfriend. I wanted to be her boyfriend. I wanted to make her happy because that's what she made me whenever I was with her.

TWENTY-THREE

Violet

I had a boyfriend.

Not only did I have a boyfriend but I was *excited* about it.

Normally, when men started referring to me as their girlfriend or started talking about plans three months out, it set off alarm bells. But when Alexander had said it last week in the park, I didn't take it as a signal to run. It felt completely natural. I thought of him as my boyfriend. More, I wanted him to think of me as his girlfriend. I couldn't remember ever feeling like that.

I slotted in the last files I had on my desk and finished taping up the cardboard box. The more recent the cases, the more paper they seemed to consume.

"How are you doing?" Jimmy asked as he strolled into the admin room.

"Good. Another five boxes to go off to archives."

"Great job. Surely you can see carpet on the floor of Knightley's office now?"

"Well, half a carpet anyway."

"And he doesn't mind?"

"I don't give him a choice."

Jimmy chuckled. "Well, whatever works. I don't know how you've managed to get away with it."

"Fire with fire," I said, passing him as I headed out. "And now I need more files." I turned right up the corridor and knocked on Alexander's door.

"Come in," he yelled. He was so moody at work. We didn't often see each other during the day. I wasn't complaining. So many men were too needy, but finding time to be with Alexander was a challenge. I felt special if I got him for more than an hour before bed. Maybe it was a touch of masochist in me, but I liked the fact that he had other demands on his attention. He was busy being brilliant, and I was okay with that.

I shut the door behind me and Alexander looked up. He grinned, which was a good sign.

"Hello, handsome. I'm just going to collect some files. I'll be two minutes."

"Come over here." He coaxed me over to his desk. "I could do with a break."

"You working on your Bar Humbug case?" I hitched myself up onto his desk, settling next to his laptop. "With that name, it suits you perfectly."

"Something like that. I think I'm going to have to bring in a junior earlier than I'd hoped." He swiveled his chair around and smoothed his palm up the inside of my thigh.

"Why don't you like working with other people? Because you're a control freak?"

"You noticed?"

His hand slipped higher and I squeezed my legs

together to stop him going any farther. "Knightley. We agreed—no fucking in the office."

"I didn't mean it," he said, shifting me into the center of his desk.

"You don't say things you don't mean, remember?"

"You shouldn't be so irresistible."

"Speaking of irresistible, thank you for my gift this morning." I'd arrived in the office this morning to find another shiny black box on my desk. Thank goodness I'd been the first one in because even without an audience, the underwear he'd bought me had made me blush.

"I'm not sure if that gift was for me or for you."

"A joint gift, then."

"Are you wearing them?" He lifted my skirt and took a peek before I smacked his hands away.

"You'll have to wait. Can you come over tonight?" Alexander rarely stayed at my place. Most of the time he came in, we made out, and then he'd leave because he had to be up early or because he still had work to do.

He sighed. "I want to. I really do. I'll have to see how things go, but I've carved out some time on Saturday afternoon because I have a late afternoon appointment with a real estate agent. We could have dinner after that?"

I narrowed my eyes at him. "A real estate agent?"

"The divorce got me thinking—I've been in that bloody hotel too long. It's a much better long-term investment for me to buy something."

"And because normal people don't live in hotels for three years." I poked him in the chest. "You're not Lindsey Lohan, just saying."

"Who?" he asked, grimacing.

I shook my head. "Never mind." Chambers was full of eccentric characters, so I never knew what to expect, but popular culture wasn't something that the barristers were typically up on—even the ones straight out of school. They all seemed to live in a world without celebrities, reality TV, or rap.

"So, dinner?"

"I'll check my calendar." Of course, I'd say yes, but he didn't have to be so sure.

"You can come meet the agent with me if you like, although I'm sure you have better things to do."

I looked at him, checking to see if I'd heard him correctly—we never made plans during the day at the weekend. "I totally want to do that."

"Really?"

"What, poke about in strangers' houses? Of course. I'll do some research. No doubt you don't have any clue about what market prices are."

He chuckled. "You have that right."

"Where do you want to live?"

"I like where I am—Mayfair."

"On it." I slid off his desk. "I'll just get a few files and leave you in peace." I headed toward the current pile I was working on dismantling, passing the now clear desk in the corner.

I turned back to Alexander, who had his head buried in his laptop. "You know, if you let a junior sit at that desk, you could stay on top of their work more easily, listen in to their phone calls—train them exactly the way you want them to work."

"I don't share my office, Violet," he mumbled at the screen.

"Everyone wins in that situation—you're less stressed and have more time. Which means more sexy underwear. More nights I can keep you awake."

He looked up at me. "Tempting as that might be, I need silence to work."

"But Lance has told you that if you're going to progress, you have to work better with juniors, and Craig has told me that if we're to implement this new document management system, I need to find cost savings. This desk in your office is worth about fifty grand a year."

Why hadn't I thought about it before? It was the perfect solution.

"I said no, Violet. Now I need to work."

I picked up the files and headed out of his office. I turned as I opened the door. "Think about it." He had to see how this made sense.

He rolled his eyes. "Get out!"

TWENTY-FOUR

Alexander

I clicked on my inbox, and I could feel my pulse rate rise at the number of emails from instructing solicitors that I hadn't even opened, let alone dealt with. I was too busy for house hunting this afternoon. If I had been going on my own to see the agent and hadn't said that Violet could come, I would have canceled. Which was how I'd ended up living in a hotel for three years. There was never enough time to find a place to move into. But I wanted to spend the time with her. I was looking forward to her bright smile and warm body.

I was behind, even more so than usual, and Lance had spoken to me—again—to tell me I needed to work with a junior. In the last four nights, I'd had fifteen hours sleep and I was exhausted. I'd been thinking more and more that maybe Lance was right. And if I moved someone into my office temporarily then I could track what they were doing more easily. I was weakening against the arguments put forward by Lance and Violet.

Despite my workload, I'd seen Violet most evenings,

although less than I would have liked. She was unsurprisingly undemanding of my time, but it only made me want to see her, touch her, hold her, breathe in that calming scent of India, get the easy perspective she had on the world.

It was the first time a woman had competed against work and stood a chance at winning. I looked at my watch. Even if I left now, I would be late, but Violet hadn't called to tell me where to meet. Had she forgotten?

Fuck it. I'd just work twice as hard tomorrow. I threw on my coat and bolted out the door. As I sat down in the back of the cab, I called Violet.

"Hey, sexy," she said.

"Look who's talking. I'm on my way to the agent's office, shall I pick you up?"

"No, that's fine. I can walk. I'll keep her talking if you're late."

"And you're still on for dinner?" I asked.

"Why? Do you have to work? Because if you do, I'm going to sulk."

Her words tugged at my chest. Sometimes I wondered if the reason she was so cool about everything was because she was indifferent. I was a selfish bastard who needed a woman who wanted me but didn't make demands of my time. Just like how I needed a junior barrister to take some of the burden of this case, but I didn't want to give up control. I wanted everything my own way. All the time.

I just didn't know how to be any different.

"No, I'm still on for dinner. Where do you want to go?"

"I don't care, nowhere fancy."

I always wondered if her lack of funds was the reason she never wanted to go anywhere expensive. Was she worried I'd let her pick up the bill? It would never happen, but maybe it was a concern. "What about Chinese? We could go to Hakkasan?"

"I've been in London a while now. You can't pull that shit on me. I know that's a super-fancy Chinese place."

I chuckled. "Okay. You name the place."

"I could cook. I make a mean mac and cheese."

"I know that about you. Sounds good." It felt good too—to have a woman want to cook for me, someone who wasn't interested in going to the latest restaurants but just wanted to spend time with me. I peered out of the window and saw Violet huddled under an umbrella outside the real estate agent's office. "I see you," I said.

The cab pulled up next to her just as she snapped her head around; her eyes lit up when she saw me. God, it felt good to provoke that kind of reaction in a woman that clever, funny, and beautiful. I jumped out of the cab and cupped her face in my palm, pressing my lips to hers, breathing her in.

The cab honked and she jumped. I grinned against her mouth, then released her. I paid the impatient cabbie, grabbed Violet's hand, and we made our way inside.

A smart woman, dressed in flat shoes and a navy-blue suit, introduced herself to us as Martha and we took our seats opposite her at a table by the window.

"So, Mr. Knightley, what exactly are you looking for?"

I really should have given this more thought than I had. It felt like such a big deal just to be contemplating moving from the hotel—I'd let myself off the hook from considering the details. "A place to live," I responded, unhelpfully. It was about as far as my attention had reached in relation to house hunting.

"Good. And what sort of place are you looking for?"

"A place around here." I liked the area, that much I knew.

"I see. And your budget?"

"It will depend on the place."

Violet squeezed my hand. "How many bedrooms?" she asked.

"Two plus a study."

The agent nodded. "At the top end of the specification for a three bedroom, we're talking around the ten to twelve million mark."

I'd looked at a couple of places when I'd left Gabby, but prices had gone up in the time since. I should have bought three years ago, but I hadn't been ready to commit to anything more than my work.

"A similar size and specification in Fitzrovia would be more like three to four," Martha said. "And Bloomsbury is even more affordable. Or we can look at something that might need a little more work, which would bring it down significantly. Shall we extend our search area? Many people are starting to move out of Mayfair."

People might be moving out of Mayfair but that didn't mean I would. I liked being so central. Convenience was key. "I don't want to do work or spend more than ten. I'd prefer freehold or a long lease. That's something I won't compromise on."

Martha didn't flinch. "I'm sure I can find something for you that will work. In fact, I have a couple of things in mind. Give me a few minutes while I arrange a couple of viewings."

As Martha walked away, Violet took in a deep breath.

"You okay?" I asked.

"It's stupid expensive around here." She glanced out of the window.

"New York's no better—it's the cost of living in the city."

"Well, I live in New York and I'm not paying ten million cents for the places I rent."

"Have you kept your place on while you're over here?" Was she desperate to get back home? I didn't think about her stay in London as temporary—was I taking too much for granted?

"No way."

"So what will you do when you go back?" I wanted to ask her how long she planned to stay. Her extended contract in chambers lasted until the end of January, but what would happen after that? I didn't want to push her, though. I wanted her to open up to me. Share things.

She began to pick at her thumbnail. "Not sure. Stay with Scarlett and Ryder for a while."

She wouldn't meet my gaze, and I wanted to ask her what was wrong but before I got a chance, Martha was back.

"I've just confirmed a few places are still available— they're in easy walking distance. Are you ready to go?"

The rain had stopped, and as we got out onto the pavement I slipped my hand into Violet's and we walked behind Martha silently—both with too much on our minds. Was she homesick or just horrified by real estate prices in Mayfair? I could understand both, but do nothing about either. Was she thinking about what she'd do when she got back to New York or whether she could extend her stay in London past six months? If Martha hadn't been with us perhaps I'd ask her, but for now, I'd settle for her being with me.

"I want your honest opinion, okay?" I told Violet as we approached the first place.

She glanced up at me and grinned.

As we walked in, Violet dropped my hand.

"It's newly renovated. Solid-oak, herringbone floors, three bedrooms, three bathrooms. Italian marble in the kitchen, integrated sound system. Twenty-four-hour porter." Martha's voice faded into the background as I watched Violet look over the flat. She inspected every corner in great detail from the floor to the ceiling and from the kitchen to the broom cupboard. Her face didn't give anything away, which was unusual. Normally I could immediately tell if she approved or disapproved of something I'd said or something someone else had done. I followed her around, failing to take in my surroundings, just more and more interested in what Violet thought.

"The third bedroom is the perfect size for a nursery," Martha said, opening the door to a small bedroom that overlooked the square. "And of course, the park is wonderful for children."

Did I look as if I was verging on procreating? Perhaps she thought it was the reason for the move. Martha couldn't know I was a selfish workaholic who had left his wife when she'd started talking about kids. Martha didn't understand that I didn't stay most nights with Violet because I had a habit of getting up in the early hours and clearing down my emails.

Like Gabby had said, nothing had changed—single or married, married or divorced. And that was how I wanted it, wasn't it? I was flat hunting for a place that would be empty eighteen hours a day, every day. Where there'd be nothing in the fridge and only *my* clothes in the wardrobe.

"So, what are your first impressions?" Martha asked, looking at me.

I glanced at Violet. "What do you think?"

"I think the third bedroom is too small. You spend a lot of time working. There isn't enough space for you in there, and if you took the second bedroom as a study then the third isn't big enough for a guest bed. The master en suite doesn't have dual sinks or a separate shower, and I think that could impact resale." Violet sighed. "It's also overpriced by about two hundred and fifty pounds a square foot for the area." She put her hand on her hip and glanced around again. "But I like the ceiling height and the views. I just don't think this is it. Maybe we should look at a mews house to compare. Plus I want to see inside one. We Americans don't have many houses left that were built three hundred years ago and shared with horses. I can't decide whether the horses were super lucky or the humans were just slumming it and I want to see for myself."

My God she was cute, sexy, and smart. And so caring.

I didn't have to think about what I needed from a house because Violet had done it for me.

"I have a mews house lined up," Martha said. "And a duplex. Shall we move on?" She turned and headed toward the exit.

Violet grinned as if to say *You thought I wouldn't do my homework?*

I had no reply but the beginning of a raging hard-on for this girl who was clever and prepared and considered everything I needed before I even knew what that was myself. She was always like that—the picnic in Lincoln's Inn Fields, the junior sharing my office. She cared about me and my needs and I wanted to do the same for her. I wanted her to feel as special as she made me feel.

TWENTY-FIVE

Violet

"This isn't shopping, it's hell!" I yelled at Darcy, who was plowing ahead in front of me while people coming from the opposite direction were banging into me on either side.

She dipped down a side street and I followed, but not before getting cursed at by a man wearing a t-shirt that didn't quite cover his belly. Given it was mid-November and freezing, I couldn't be mad because he was sure to be dead from hyperthermia by the end of the day.

"Christmas shopping season has started in earnest—I didn't think it would be this bad," Darcy said.

"But it's not even Thanksgiving until next week."

Darcy pushed my shoulder "But you're not in America. You get that we don't celebrate Thanksgiving, don't you?"

"I'm in denial about it, and anyway, *you'll* be celebrating because we're all going to be in Woolton."

She beckoned me into a shop. "I can't wait, actually. I found a place that sells yams."

"We just use sweet potatoes," I replied, stepping up through the door.

Darcy rolled her eyes. "Now you tell me. I've spent hours trying to track them down. And you really eat them with marshmallows?"

"Sure. Candied yams."

She shook her head. "If you say so."

"I'm sorry but no one in Britain can complain about candied yams when you people eat Marmite. I mean that stuff is heinous. It smells like fermented rat poop. Looks like it too."

"It's really good for you," she replied, acting as if it were totally no big deal to be spreading poop over toast in the morning.

"I don't care if it makes me look like Charlize Theron. It's disgusting." I glanced around at the sparse rails and gleaming white floors and ceilings. The place looked expensive, but then most places Darcy shopped in were out of my price range. "You promised me Forever 21," I said.

"It's further up. This place has great stuff."

Surreptitiously, I picked up one of the labels hanging off the sleeve of an ordinary-looking t-shirt. A hundred bucks? In another life, maybe.

"You've told me nothing about all the boys you're shagging," Darcy said as she trailed her fingers over the rack.

"Shagging?" I laughed. "Yeah, not many boys. But lots of kissing."

Darcy looked at me from over her shoulder. "What do you mean?"

"I'm kinda dating someone. Like, I have a boyfriend."

She put back the trousers she'd just reached for and turned to me, a huge grin on her face. "You have a boyfriend

—I thought you didn't believe in those? When did this happen?"

"I'm not quite sure how it happened."

"How did you meet? What does he do? You have to tell me everything."

"He's a barrister in chambers. It started off as a lust thing." I shrugged. "And I don't know, it morphed into something more. He's not like other guys. He feels more like a man. A grown-up—you know."

"I've never heard you talk about any man without a hint of contempt in your voice, not even your brother." She turned back to the rail, moving each hanger with a swipe. "It sounds like you really like this guy."

"Well Max deserves all the contempt I dish up, but Alexander's just a bit misunderstood. He's spiky on the outside, but he's kinda great when you get to know him— full of integrity and honor and super smart. I enjoy spending time with him. He makes me laugh, even if he doesn't mean to."

"It sounds serious," she said. "We get to meet him at the weekend, right? He's coming up to Woolton?"

I frowned. There was no way I'd invite Alexander. "God, no. He'd never take the time off work."

Darcy pulled out a blouse, inspected it on both sides, then shoved it back on the rail. "You've not asked him?"

"There's no point. I know he'd say no."

"But you'd like him to come?" she asked.

"I haven't thought about it," I lied. "You know me. I don't make plans with men." I didn't want to put Alexander in a position where he felt he was letting me down or not giving me enough time. And anyway, why would he want to meet my family? It was too much. Too serious. I'd be back in the US by the end of January and he'd still be here, working himself into oblivion. Our expiration date was looming. Even my extended contract had only bought us a few months and I didn't want to integrate our lives any more than they already were. I'd leave London in a few weeks, and Alexander with it.

"I'd love to meet him. He sounds perfect for you if he's 'spiky' on the outside but misunderstood. You pretend you don't care, but I'm not buying what you're selling anymore."

I laughed. "I never said I didn't care. Anyway, we're not talking about me. Alexander's far from perfect. He has a short temper and never says anything nice just to keep the peace." But he had a kind and generous heart and a wicked smile.

She paused at the rack and turned to me. "It sounds like you might have met your match. I've never known you to dial down an argument—you and Scarlett bicker constantly."

I rolled my eyes. "That's because Scarlett's always wrong."

She smiled. "I rest my case."

I looked through the rack in front of me. Hopefully Darcy would do the same and get distracted. I didn't want to talk about it anymore because it reminded me that we didn't have long left—that even if I wanted to, I couldn't make plans for a future with this man.

"You could just invite him. Tell him that you don't expect him to say yes. You never know, he might be offended if you *don't* ask him."

"I doubt it. He's happy when he's working. He's not the type to enjoy making polite conversation with a bunch of strangers." There was no way that Alexander would come to a Thanksgiving dinner in the country out of choice, and I didn't want him to do anything just to make me happy. I'd start to rely on him, expect things from him, and that could only lead to trouble.

"Hey," Darcy objected, focusing all her attention on me.

"Well, you are a bunch of strangers to him. Just because you're all my favorite people doesn't change that."

"I don't see what you've got to lose by extending the invitation to him."

"You're pushy for someone so little," I said, narrowing my eyes.

She grinned proudly. "I know. I really want to meet this guy. If you can find love, it gives me hope."

"It's not love," I scoffed. "It's *so* not love, you lunatic."

"What is it then?" she asked, holding an electric blue shift dress up to my body and shaking her head.

"It's good sex." But even I knew it was more than that. It felt like the real thing. Like something that wasn't all about the moment, but something I could imagine in the future. "And I told you, he makes me laugh." There were so many things I liked about Alexander. His integrity and the way he'd never said anything bad about his ex-wife. The way he'd said yes to my picnic even though I was sure it was his idea of hell. The way that if he was in the office he'd always call me just before I went to bed to wish me sweet dreams. The thoughtfulness of the gifts he had delivered to me at work. The way his grumpy, concentrating face turned into a smile when he saw me. He made me feel good. He made me feel smart. And he was loyal and decent. He'd never, ever do what David did to me.

It so wasn't just good sex.

Fuck.

"So, invite him. He can make us all laugh."

"He's not a circus monkey." I rolled my eyes. "I'll think about it. But only if we can go to Forever 21."

I wanted to stop contemplating all the things I liked about Knightley. I hadn't been looking for anything other than a kiss and a cocktail when I'd come to London. I certainly hadn't been looking for a boyfriend or a career. I wasn't here to find someone to introduce to my family. I didn't want to get attached to someone I would pine for when I went home. But at the same time I was going to be out of London for four days and already I'd miss him. We didn't have long left, and I wanted to make the most of the time I had with him.

I'd ask him to Thanksgiving. He'd say no because he knew the score. He knew everything we weren't. Then it would be over with, and I'd stop thinking about him in terms of the future and keep him in the present.

TWENTY-SIX

Alexander

I'd finally agreed to have a junior barrister in my office. As usual, it had been a selfish decision—ultimately it would assist me in progressing the cases I took on if I learned to work with juniors.

I smiled at the knock on the door. Not only was she persuasive, Violet King seemed to know everyone's movements at all times. She never came into my office when my roommate, Sebastian, was there. He'd left about ten minutes ago.

"Come in," I replied.

She slipped in quickly. "You have to bark more when you say it. Otherwise people will suspect something. Anyway, how did you know it was me?"

I chuckled. "You're ridiculous. What do you want?"

"I see Mr. Charm has returned. I'm going out for my lunch and just wondered if I could get you anything?"

I leaned back in my chair. "Actually, I'll come with you. I need to stretch my legs."

"I'm not going straight to get food," she said, a slightly panicked look on her face. "I'm going to a museum first. But I'll be back in an hour if you want me to get you something."

It struck me that Violet had a secret life that went on without me while I was working. She'd mentioned that she'd gone to the Museum of London a couple of weeks ago, but this was clearly a regular thing. I found myself a little envious, both that she had the time to take herself off and spend her time as she wished *and* that her time wasn't spent with me. "Why don't I come with you?" I asked.

"To the museum?" She frowned as if she'd misheard me.

"Yeah. Where are you going?"

"Some dude's house just over there." She pointed her thumb over her shoulder. "Sir John something."

"Soane."

"So, you've been. You don't want to go again, do you?"

Sir John Soane's museum had been one of my favorite places to go when I was junior, concerned that I'd never have enough work or have the career my father did. It had been a welcome distraction, something that reminded me that building a career, a legacy, was a life's work and not something that happened overnight. "I've not been for ages. I'd love to go."

"You have time?"

"In case you hadn't noticed, I have a junior now."

She grinned. "Is he helping?"

I winced. "Jury's out. I think we both need time to adjust. But I'm in the mood to carpe some of this diem with you."

She grinned and blew me a kiss. "I'll see you in ten minutes."

It felt good to see her happy, even better that I'd been

the cause. I couldn't remember ever having this warm feeling in my stomach because I'd made Gabby happy. Perhaps because I never did.

I pulled on my coat, scarf, and gloves and headed out of chambers toward the Fields. A prolific architect, Sir John Soane designed and built his house as part home, part school, part showcase for his clients. It was stuffed full of interesting art and architecture.

I grinned despite the biting chill of the wind. Six months ago, the idea of going to a museum at lunchtime would have been ludicrous. The notion of having a girl-friend laughable. But here I was, heading toward Sir John Soane's museum to meet Violet.

She came into view, leaning against the cast-iron rail-ings, her nose buried in something she was reading. Her hair fanned out over the shoulders of her coat that was the same glossy black as the railings and contrasted with her pale skin, pinked by the cold. She had that timeless beauty that would have been just as revered in the eighteenth century when the house was newly built as it was now.

"I like your hat," I said as I approached her, tugging at the pale pink beret she had on, which picked up the rosiness in her cheeks.

"Hi," she replied, beaming at me. My breath caught. I was so lucky I got to spend my lunchtime with this woman.

"What have you got there?" I asked as she stuffed what-ever she was reading into her bag.

I dipped to peek at what she was looking at. "Columbia University?" I asked, reading the title of the booklet just before she put it away.

"Oh, nothing, just some research. Ready?" She linked her arm through mine and we ascended the pale stone steps to the entrance.

Violet picked up an information leaflet from the dresser in the hallway. "Where should we start?"

I nodded, indicating that we turn right into the library-dining room. As she stepped into the room, Violet tipped her head back and turned three hundred and sixty degrees, taking in the blood-red walls stuffed with paintings and sculptures and the glass bookcases on either side of the room. "It's wonderful. Like he could still be living here."

"They have dinners in here sometimes. It's all served by candlelight just like it would have been when he was alive."

"Sounds romantic. You've been?" she asked.

"Yes, although it was a thing chambers did, so it wasn't romantic." Having dinner here with Violet would be romantic, though. Eating dinner by candlelight would be nice—perhaps I should suggest it sometime. I continued to watch Violet's reactions as she took in the room. I couldn't keep my eyes off her. It was like being with her energized me, filled me up, and I didn't want to spill a drop.

"What are your plans for this weekend?" I asked as we made our way out and into a cramped study that was nothing more than a through room. Perhaps I could take her to dinner somewhere nice, somewhere she'd think was romantic.

"I told you, my brother and sister are coming over from the States with all their kids."

"Oh that's right. For Thanksgiving." I wouldn't see her for the whole weekend. "You're not in London, right?"

"I have four days of vacation," she said, squeezing my arm, then releasing it and walking ahead of me as the corridor got narrower.

"Four days?" I asked.

"This place is crazy," Violet said, ignoring my question.

We were surrounded by exits to different routes, doorways, corridors, steps into smaller rooms.

"It's like Alice in Wonderland or something," she continued. "Yes, I'm going up to Woolton on Wednesday night." She grinned. "Darcy's cute; she's doing candied yams, cornbread—the whole nine yards."

"Sounds good. You looking forward to seeing everyone?"

Her eyes widened and she patted me on the lapel. "Of course. I never thought I'd say it, but I miss my sister."

My gut tugged at the thought of her having fun without me. At the idea of not seeing her for four days. "You'll come back humming the *Star-Spangled Banner*."

"If you're lucky, I'll come back wrapped in one." She winked.

I pulled her toward me. "You could dress up tonight." I dropped a kiss on her lips. My nights were increasingly spent with Violet. More and more often, I ended up at her place when I left work and I was staying over more frequently. It was where I wanted to be.

When I pulled back, she looked at me as if she wanted to say something but was stopping herself. "What?" I asked.

She shrugged and turned away, heading deeper into the house. "You could come if you want. I mean, I know you're too busy, but if you wanted to, just for an evening, you'd be welcome."

I swallowed. She was inviting me? Away for the weekend, to meet her family?

"I don't expect you to say yes. I just thought . . ." She gazed up at the wall covered in trinkets that Sir John had collected on his extensive travels. She was trying to avoid my eyes.

I had a lot of work to do. A huge amount. But the idea of

being with Violet and away from London had me mentally planning how I could rearrange things. "Maybe I could," I replied.

"It will be crazy. I don't expect you to say yes. I just—"

"I want to come, Violet."

She turned to look at me, finally. "You do?"

I hated that she was so surprised—that she assumed she wasn't important enough that I'd make the time. But she had no reason to react in any other way. Work always came first. "Yes. I probably can't come for the whole weekend, but maybe for Thanksgiving itself."

She stopped and looked at me as if she hadn't heard me right. "But that's on a Thursday."

"You sound surprised," I said as if she had no reason to be. She wasn't the only one who could tease.

She burst into laughter. "I have no idea why. I mean, you're forever slacking off work."

"I'm seizing the day, Violet."

She slipped her hands around my waist, and I pulled her toward me. "I'd like that," she said quietly, almost as if it were a confession. And my chest expanded, as if I'd scored a victory. Surprising Violet, making her happy, felt like the biggest achievement in my week. I'd never experienced anything like it outside of the law.

TWENTY-SEVEN

Violet

The dining room at Woolton had been set up buffet style so we could eat dinner when we liked, but we were all too busy talking and catching up and we had to save ourselves for a Thanksgiving feast tomorrow anyway. Even though there were only six of us and the kids, it seemed as though the entire house was full. As much as I complained and bitched about my brother and sister, I couldn't ever remember being so happy to see them.

I stood with my arm around Scarlett's waist. "You look fantastic, Duchess," I said.

She giggled. "Don't call me that. It sounds like you're trying to be down with the kids."

"I've called you worse."

"True. So how's England? I haven't heard from you this week."

"I'm enjoying it."

"Well you look fantastic. I love this dress." She glanced

down at my bottle-green, silk dress. "It's a bit of a departure from your normal boho thing."

The dress had been a gift from Alexander. I'd told him to stop buying me stuff, but he'd said that since he'd bought me the skirt, the retailer was following him around the internet with ads of things he thought I'd like, so he kept clicking. And I enjoyed how he always noticed when I wore them.

"That's what love will do," Darcy said.

"Stop it, Darcy. You know I don't believe in that shit." David had taught me that love really was blind and I'd taken my blinders off.

"I'm really hoping to catch a glimpse of this guy while I'm here. Any guy who's managed to hold your attention for longer than a week intrigues me. I'm going to come to London for the day and rock up to your work when you least expect it."

Darcy frowned and my stomach churned. I hadn't told Scarlett Alexander was coming tomorrow. Darcy knew, obviously, as she'd suggested it and had to know numbers for lunch tomorrow. I'd fully expected Alexander to drop out because of a last-minute work emergency, but so far nothing had come up, which was making me a little nervous —this wasn't like him. I didn't know what was scarier— Alexander showing up, or Alexander blowing me off.

"You won't have to wait until next week," Darcy said, interrupting my thoughts. "We all get to meet him tomorrow."

Open mouthed, Scarlet turned to me.

"I'm not sure if he'll make it," I said. "I did say it wasn't definite, didn't I?" I asked Darcy. It would be humiliating if he didn't come now people knew. "He's working on a huge case. He said he'll try, but I'd be surprised if he can spare the time." I released Scarlett and picked up my wine glass.

"Don't have so little faith," Darcy said. "You originally thought he'd never even consider it. He'll be here."

"You've never met him," I replied. "How would you know?"

"Just a feeling." She took a sip of her wine, grinning around the glass.

"This is big news, Violet," my sister said.

"It's really not." The last thing I wanted was for everyone to make a big deal out of this. We might have been dating a few months, but because Alexander was so busy and we both knew it was a temporary thing, it wasn't that serious. It couldn't be.

"Have you said 'I love you'?" Darcy asked, stirring up trouble.

"No! It's not like that." I doubted Alexander had even told his *wife* he loved her. He wasn't that guy, and I wasn't that girl. We were just hanging out. Enjoying the moment.

"You've been together months though, haven't you? I've never known you to be with a guy this long. You must like him."

"Of course I like him. I mean, he's a moody, brooding asshole at times but—"

"Who's an asshole?" Max came over, with a plate over-flowing with food. He must have heard the word asshole and assumed we were talking about him.

"Her boyfriend," Scarlett said.

"You're dating, Darcy?" Max grinned.

"No." Scarlett nudged him with her elbow. "Violet."

"What? You have a boyfriend?" he asked, looking at me as if I'd just told him I'd decided to donate a kidney. "A

British guy? I can't handle any more British blood in this family."

Oh my God, Max was fast-forwarding to the birth of my children. "Will you guys stop making a big deal about this? He's going to think you're all crazy when he arrives."

"What, he's coming to Woolton?" Max asked.

"Tomorrow," Darcy said.

The girl was dead to me after this weekend. She was spilling all my secrets.

"Are you pregnant?" Max asked.

I rolled my eyes and turned to leave this group to top up my wine.

"She's not pregnant; she's in love." Scarlett grabbed my arm. "You're not pregnant, are you?"

"No, I'm not pregnant, and I am definitely *not* in love. How many times do I have to say it?" I wished I'd never invited him. The whole thing was going to be a horror show. Except that I didn't really wish I hadn't invited him. I was excited that he might be coming, that he was giving up work for a few hours to spend time with me. I wanted to show him around the house and take a walk with him around the lake, wrapped up in our coats and scarves. Kiss him looking over the croquet lawn.

"You guys have to promise that you're not going to act like freaks."

"We'll be fine. We won't tell him he's your first boyfriend since college and the only guy who's *ever* made your eyes light up when he's mentioned."

"Scarlett, please. And anyway, he knows all about David."

"You told him what happened?" she asked.

"Well, yeah." It wasn't a big deal that I'd told him, was

it? I didn't want to keep things from him and after the Gabby debacle I didn't want him keeping things from me.

"About the business?" Scarlett asked.

I nodded. "Yes, I said. He knows."

"Wow." She took a sip of her wine, trying to disguise her smile.

"There's nothing 'wow' about it."

"Well, I hope he's not an asshole," Max said.

"Then I'm afraid you're going to be disappointed," I replied.

"Well, if he puts a foot wrong—" Max's chest expanded and I rolled my eyes.

"He can't be an arsehole," Darcy said. "Not if you like him as much as you do."

"Who said I liked him that much?"

"Has he signed his divorce papers yet?" Scarlett asked.

"The asshole is married?" Max asked, his mouth full of food. He swallowed. "Jesus, Violet. You're involved with a married man?"

"Thanks, Scarlett," I said, shaking my head. "Yes, he's signed his divorce papers, and he's been separated from his wife for over three years."

"I don't like the sound of this guy," Max mumbled.

"Well, you two have a lot in common. You're both workaholic assholes, so you should get along just fine."

I wasn't really sure Max and Alexander would get along at all. I'd never really seen Alexander interact with anyone other than me in a non-work public setting. But he was a good man. He might be brooding and moody, but that was just a cloak. When you got to know the real Alexander, he was decent and kind. I hoped my family could see that. I wanted them to like him because he was the first person in a long time that I'd cared about. And I wanted to be right about him. I wanted them to see what I saw in him. It was as if Alexander represented a new Violet—a woman who'd moved on from the scars of her early twenties. And if it turned out I was wrong about him, then what else was I wrong about?

I just hope he didn't cancel. Not now.

TWENTY-EIGHT

Alexander

For the second time in three months I was driving into the country for Violet King. When she'd left chambers on Wednesday, she hadn't complained that I wasn't leaving with her. And she hadn't asked me how long I'd stay, or even if I was sure I'd definitely make it. She just took each day as it came.

I'd found that the lunches we spent together didn't impact my workload as much as I might have expected. In fact, our stolen moments invigorated me, leaving me more efficient after time away from my desk. It made me yearn for more time with her.

I turned up the gravel driveway the map indicated. The Duke of Westbury's estate was beautiful. Violet King was full of surprises.

As I pulled up in front of the house, the door opened and Violet came tripping down the steps. I was only just out of the car when she threw her arms around my neck.

"You made it," she said, more delighted than I could have hoped for.

"I said I would, didn't I?"

"And you never say anything you don't mean." She pressed her lips against mine and I pulled her in tighter.

"This is a beautiful place," I said, scanning the gardens. "Capability Brown by the looks of it."

"Yes, we should take a walk down to the lake, but after lunch, which will last the whole day. So tomorrow. If you're going to stay?"

"I'll stay if you'll have me."

She tilted her head. "I really like you," she said.

I chuckled. "I really like you, too. Now come and help me with this," I said, opening the back door. I handed her two paper bags.

"What's in here?" she asked.

"I didn't know what to bring, so some booze for the adults and toys for the children." I closed the door and went 'round to the boot and pulled out my weekend bag. "What?" I asked as she stood there, her brow furrowed.

"You brought the kids gifts?" she asked.

"Don't get too excited. It's just a few things I ordered online. I have no idea if they're age appropriate." I nodded toward the door. "Let's get in; it's freezing."

"That's sweet of you."

I chuckled. No one had ever called me sweet before.

"Everyone's getting ready for lunch, so I'll show you up to our room." Violet set the gifts on a side table. As we climbed the stairs, a shriek echoed through the walls and a door slammed.

A petite girl with long brown hair bounded down the stairs to meet us in her stockinged feet. "You must be

Violet's boyfriend," she said, sticking out her hand. "I'm so happy you're here. I'm Darcy."

"How do you do?" I asked, taking her hand. "Thank you for inviting me to your beautiful home."

She lifted herself up on her tiptoes and then set herself down again. "It's a total pleasure. I think giving thanks is such a wonderful idea, and I'm so pleased we have another person from this side of the pond around the table. We're usually overrun!"

"Yes, these Americans are taking over," I replied.

"I'm just popping down to see that everything's running smoothly and that Mrs. MacBee hasn't had a stroke. Make yourself at home, and let me know if I can get you anything."

She bounded down the stairs and we continued to make our way up.

"You're so charming," Violet said, kissing my cheek.

"You have no idea what I'm capable of when I try," I replied, swatting her bum.

She laughed. "I'm enjoying finding out."

Violet was at her most beautiful when she was laughing.

"This house is so creaky. The floors, the walls, the doors. And the beds."

"Sounds like we'll have to get creative," I replied. "What time's lunch?" I'd missed sleeping next to her last night. Even though we'd not been staying over at each other's place until recently, I'd gotten in the habit of creeping around in the dark when I got up in the mornings, so it had felt odd to be able to have the light on and the news in the background as I padded around my hotel room.

"We don't have time," she replied, slapping my hand from her backside. "You're not a fast fuck."

"Good to know where I am on your scale, but we had to be pretty quick that first time, in the office."

"Sorry, I didn't mean—it was a compliment."

"Hey, lighten up. Live in the moment," I teased.

"God, you're annoying."

I bent and kissed her head as we arrived at a large oak door.

"This is us," she said.

I tried not to smile at the label. I hadn't been an *us* in a long time. I wasn't sure I'd really ever been an *us* before. With Violet, *us* was new. But it was the right description.

When we got in, I dumped my bag and took my jacket off. "Come here," I said, holding my arms out. I needed to feel her warmth, to enjoy the way her body fit so perfectly against mine.

"How was your conference call?" she asked, sliding her hands around my waist and putting her head on my chest.

I exhaled and tightened my grip. "Good. I've left Sebastian a list of stuff to get on with. I'm delegating. Are you proud?"

"Very," she said. "And pretty blown away that you're here."

A loud knock at the bedroom door interrupted us.

Violet groaned. "That will be my sister."

I released my arms and Violet went to answer the door while I slipped my jacket back on.

"Is he here?" someone whispered.

"Alexander, this is my annoying sister, Scarlett." Violet held the door open and Scarlett walked through.

Scarlett was slightly taller than Violet but they both had similar long, dark hair.

"I'm so happy to meet you," she said and we shook hands.

"How do you do? I'm Alex."

"Want to go downstairs? It's almost one," Violet said, hurrying us out. "Apparently we have drinks in the library before lunch."

I nodded and followed the girls out.

Violet glanced over her shoulder at me as I walked behind them down the stairs. She smiled, but it wasn't the same unforced grin I'd seen from her earlier.

"This must be Alexander," a British man said as we entered the library. "I'm Ryder. How do you do?"

I took his hand. "Please call me Alex."

"Gosh, all these introductions. I hope it isn't too over-whelming," Darcy said, handing me a glass of champagne. "Ryder is my brother and Scarlett's husband. That," she said, pointing at a man crouching to negotiate with a toddler, "is Max, Violet and Scarlett's brother—"

"And I'm Harper," a woman with brown hair inter-rupted. "I'm Violet's sister-in-law and the chief interrogator for the day."

"Don't mind my wife," Max said, joining the group. "I'm the protective older brother. I hear you're a barrister."

I glanced over at Violet, who was glaring at her brother.

"That's right. And you're on Wall Street?" I asked. I much preferred to learn about others than answer ques-tions. Most of the time, people were happy to oblige me.

"And you work in the same office as Violet?" he asked.

"Indeed."

"I'm a big fan of office romances," Harper said, patting her husband's chest. "It's how Max and I met. And here we are—married with three kids."

"And you're married?" Max asked me, his eyes narrowing.

I couldn't blame him questioning me about my

marriage. I was dating his sister, but it felt a little misplaced —Violet and I weren't about to have three kids. Our relationship was different. It was constrained by my job and my capacity to make time for a woman. "Gabby and I split up three years ago."

"Don't start, Max," Violet urged. "Can't we just have a nice time rather than reenact the Spanish Inquisition?"

Luckily, we were interrupted by someone coming in to announce lunch and we all wandered into the dining room. Violet and I trailed behind, and I picked up her hand and pressed my lips to her fingers. "I can handle anything they dish out. Don't worry."

She sighed. "But they're making such a big deal out of it." She shook her head.

"You're the little sister, but it doesn't matter. You and I know who we are together and that's all that matters."

Violet stopped and turned to me, her free hand on her chest. She searched my face with her gaze. "You're right. We do. We're living in the moment, just enjoying each other's company."

"Exactly. Stop worrying." I kissed her forehead and we headed into lunch, taking our seats as indicated by the name cards. It was just adults around the table, and I'd been placed between Violet and Scarlett. Food was passed around and the chatter and laughter seemed to relax Violet.

"Thanks for coming," Scarlett said as she handed me a plate of broccoli.

"It was very nice to be invited. I've never had a Thanksgiving before."

"I don't suppose you have. Something else that you and Violet don't have in common," Scarlett said.

"Sorry?" Was there subtext behind her statement?

"You and Violet seem to be quite different."

"You know what they say about opposites," I replied. "And we have plenty in common—neither of us suffer fools gladly, and she's not afraid of speaking her mind. We complement each other in lots of ways," I said, passing the plate to Violet, who was busy talking to Darcy.

"Complement each other?" Scarlett asked, handing me another bowl of something. "Candied yams," she explained as I spooned out a small amount onto my plate.

I nodded. "Yes. Violet doesn't like to plan and I'm so busy—it works quite well for us. And . . ." Our picnic lunch replayed in my mind. She knew I was busy. But she also knew I could extricate myself from my work for an hour. "You know, she challenges me—shows me how life can be different."

My world had been broadened with Violet in it—not least because I spent time with her but also because she had me trying new restaurants, taking picnics in November, and going to museums in my lunchtimes.

"She's helped me to seize the day a little more." Unexpectedly, Violet had made small changes in my life, cracked open my narrow view on the world, which meant I was enjoying each day more and more.

Scarlett smiled. "Spontaneity really is Violet's best quality."

"One of many," I replied.

My responses seemed to placate Scarlett, and we fell into casual conversation about her business and her life spent between Connecticut and England.

"I hear you've given up waitressing," Ryder said to Violet. "How's office life?"

"Different," Violet replied. "I like it though. I enjoy solving problems and sorting out issues."

"She's very good at it," I interjected. "Too good really. Way overqualified."

"What do you think you'll end up doing when you come back to New York?" Ryder asked.

Violet laughed. "You know me, Ryder, I don't think past the end of the week. I have no idea."

"You still thinking about Columbia?" Scarlett asked Violet, while spooning potatoes onto her plate.

I turned my head to see Violet's reaction. Columbia University?

She shrugged. "I have no idea. Maybe. I've filled out the application. They might not take me."

"I think going back to school would be an amazing thing for you," Scarlett said. "You have this big brain that you haven't used in so long."

Back to school?

I racked my mind, trying to think back about whether Violet had ever mentioned anything about getting another qualification. That was a huge piece of news. Why hadn't Violet said anything? Clearly, she was thinking about her future more than she'd ever disclosed to me. And she saw her future in New York at Columbia University. That was a positive step. I would hate to see her talent wasted doing any more waitressing or frankly any more administration. She should be doing something else with her ability. I was happy for her.

But hearing it stung slightly. More than it should have. More than I would have ever thought it would. Because Columbia University was three thousand miles away and her applying there was evidence that none of her plans for the future involved me.

I thought about my future all the time, but only ever in terms of my career. I carefully considered the work I aspired to do and how it would impact my desire to take silk early. I spoke to Craig and Lance about my career path and what I could do to step things up. I was constantly looking toward the horizon.

But when I saw myself in the future—the man with a career to rival my father's—the best at the bar, was all I saw. I didn't see a home or a wife or children. I never thought about the places I'd visited or the experiences I had—it was all about work. If I looked even two months ahead, Violet's contract would be up, and then what? Would my expanded world suddenly shrink? Would it become smaller in her absence? Less interesting. Almost certainly. But of course Violet had to consider her future, and I should be happy about that. But would I be sad if she disappeared from my life? If she wasn't in my future?

I realized I would, but there was nothing I could do.

Violet

"Who'd have thought you could be so charming?" I asked Alexander as I lay sprawled across the bed as he undid his tie.

"Who'd have thought you could be so sexy?" he replied as he came toward me. "This dress should be illegal." He smoothed his fingers over my cleavage and starting on my buttons.

"You bought it for me."

"Because I knew you'd look incredible."

My dress open, he abandoned me and began to undo his own shirt.

"Why do you have everyone call you Alex?" I'd never noticed it before, but whenever people called him Alexander, he asked them to call him Alex.

He smirked as he discarded his shirt and began to take off his pants. "That's my name."

"Very funny. I call you Alexander and you've never asked me to call you Alex."

"I know. I've never liked it. It was always the name I associated with my father."

"But you don't mind me calling you it?"

He shook his head as he stood completely naked in front of me. I squeezed my thighs together at the sight of him—his strong thighs and perfect cock. I knew what happened next, knew how he'd feel inside me. I shivered as an ache for him grew in my stomach.

"I like it when it comes from your mouth." He crawled over me and began to peel off my dress. "What I don't like is you keeping things from me." He lay beside me.

I frowned, unsure of what he meant. Before I had a chance to ask him, he'd moved my underwear to one side and shoved two fingers inside me.

I gasped at the unexpected action.

"I don't like being caught off guard like that." His thumb slid over my clit and he began to pump his fingers in and out of me. "So you don't get my cock. Not for this first orgasm."

He was denying me his dick because I hadn't told him about . . . what, exactly?

I grabbed at his wrist, trying to stop his relentless, driving rhythm. "What did I keep from you?" I asked, trying to beat back the waves of pleasure that were travelling up my body.

"Columbia, going back to university."

I let out a groan as my orgasm began to build.

"You see how easily I turn you on?"

I closed my eyes, unable to speak, reveling in his hard,

rough fingers between my legs as pulses of pleasure scattered under my skin.

"You want to come so quickly."

My whole body was throbbing within seconds of him touching me.

Without warning he removed his hand and moved away from me. My eyes flew open.

I'd been a second away from my climax. What was he doing? "Alexander. What . . ."

"You don't keep things from me." His face was dark and serious.

I'd had no idea he'd want to know. Why did he care what I did when I left London?

"I'm sorry," I said, smoothing my palm down his cheek.

He skirted his hand down my belly and across my pussy, pressing his fingers inside me more gently this time.

"That was the brochure you were reading when I met you at the museum," he said. "I asked you what it was."

I arched my back as his fingers resumed their pumping and circling. "You have so much to think about. It wasn't important." My voice was breathless as my body inched toward climax.

He read my body as though he'd been studying me for years. I didn't know how, but he understood exactly the rhythm I needed, the perfect amount of pressure, when to hold back and when to let go.

His fingers changed direction at exactly the right time, and I was lost as pleasure burst out of my every cell.

Before I'd caught my breath, Alexander crawled on top of me and his condom-covered dick nudged at my entrance.

"You tell me this stuff, you hear me?" he whispered in my ear, his hair brushing against my cheek, setting me on fire as he pushed inside. "I want to know."

Right then I would have told him everything. I wanted to say how thankful I was to have met him. How I'd never had sex that had me sated and yet craving for more at the same time as I did with him. How no man before him had ever made me feel as sexy and wanton, yet so respected at the same time. How his passion to succeed and build a legacy seemed to have burrowed into my DNA. Alexander had changed me, altered my view of the world.

The drag of his dick inside me brought me back to physical need. I watched as his forehead became sheened in sweat born of the effort to make me feel good, to make him feel good, to make *us* feel good.

I opened my legs wider, wanting him deeper and more connected to me.

He groaned and thrust harder, pressing his smooth fingers into mine, covering my hands and keeping us joined, as if our hands clasped together meant we'd share everything from now on—our hopes and fears, our feelings and emotions. I shouldn't, but I enjoyed him wanting to know about Columbia, about my plans—that he seemed to feel like he had some kind of stake in my future. I felt the same. I wanted him to do well, be happy, laugh more.

I'd never felt so close to anyone.

These feelings weren't meant to develop. I wasn't supposed to care for someone. What was happening to me? I'd promised myself I'd never open up to a man again. But I couldn't help it. I wanted Alexander, liked him, trusted him. I'd not just opened up a little. He owned me.

Before I could figure out what to do with all these overwhelming realizations, Alexander shifted back onto his knees with me on his lap, my legs either side him.

His fingers dug into my ass as he pulled me toward him, driving his hips at the same time, my breasts thrust up with the movement. Alexander's eyes dropped, taking in my chest. He groaned, pushing deeper and harder.

I gripped his shoulders as our hips pushed against each other, our bodies desperate and wanting, scrambling toward climax.

I glanced down and saw him gazing up at me, his perfectly blue eyes taking me in as if to memorize me.

The fucking felt different this time, as if we needed something more from each other, needed to prove something, break down some kind of barrier. As though we'd moved to a different level of our relationship.

"Alexander," I moaned.

"No hiding," he grunted, his movements becoming sharper and less controlled.

I wasn't sure if it was his demanding tone or his need for more of me that triggered my orgasm, but my entire body began to shudder at his stipulation.

He thrust into me three more times, his face contorted by his orgasm.

I wanted to give him everything he demanded of me.

What was happening to me? I'd promised myself that I'd never care about a man again, and yet here I was, wrapped in a man's arms, hoping that he'd never let me go.

TWENTY-NINE

Alexander

When I reached Violet's place, I lifted the brass knocker with my elbow, then released it, almost dropping the armfuls of black boxes I was carrying.

Violet swung the door open. The box at the top of the pile tumbled off, and she caught it.

"Alexander. What are you doing?"

"I'm taking you to dinner," I said.

Her eyes lit up. "You are?" She glanced at the clock on the mantel as I followed her into the sitting room. "You've finished work? It's barely seven."

Since we'd spent Thanksgiving together, I'd stayed at her place every night. Although I was normally back a lot later than this. Something had passed between us that weekend, and we were more connected than ever. I found myself aiming to leave chambers as soon as I could, which had never happened to me before. I never clock watched—I just worked my way through whatever it was I had to do and I stopped when I knew I needed to sleep. Spending time with Violet had become a reason to finish early.

"Yes, and it's a Saturday. I'm giving myself the evening off while I can." I put the three remaining boxes on the console table.

"I'm excited. Want me to find us a table somewhere?"

"I've booked the *fancy* Chinese," I said as I slumped onto the sofa.

Her smile faltered, but she nodded. "Okay."

"You'd prefer not to go there?"

She shrugged and put the package she was holding on top of the others. "It's just fancy doesn't really suit me. I always think fancy is Scarlett and Max's thing."

"This place has good food and we should be celebrating. I don't often take evenings off." It was Saturday night. No normal person would work on Saturday night as a matter of course. I really needed to look at my life.

She slipped onto my lap and slid her hand around my neck. "Okay. I'll be the girl that goes to a fancy restaurant tonight."

"And I thought you might want to wear something in that lot." I lifted my chin at the packages. At Woolton I only saw her in clothes I'd gifted to her. And it gave me an unfamiliar sense of satisfaction. I liked buying her gifts, and I liked that she dressed in what I'd bought her, as though we were interconnected in the smallest of ways.

"Alexander, you have to stop buying me things."

I circled my arms around her waist. "I like it, don't you?"

"I didn't say I didn't like it, but you don't need to spend your money on me." She pressed her lips to my jaw, and my muscles began to unlock from a stressful day.

"But I want to." Whenever I'd bought gifts for Gabby, it

had been out of guilt. I'd have missed dinner or worked all weekend. It had proved effective for a while—she was satisfied and I worked harder. But buying her nice things quickly became a sort of fine or penalty, and I began to resent it. The gifts I gave Violet were never given with an apology. She would simply admonish me for my extravagance and then look stunning in whatever it was I'd bought. "Scarlett told me your size, so there are shoes in that box," I said, pointing at the second box down.

Violet rolled her eyes. "She needs a time-out from her interfering." She loosened my tie. "You sure you want to go to dinner? We could stay in?" She smoothed her hand down my chest.

"We can *stay in* later. But I want to take you out. Talk. Table's booked for half past seven." We had things to discuss. Even though I knew she was thinking about pursuing her masters at Columbia, we still hadn't discussed it in any detail. I wanted to understand what she was planning to do next year. Would she start at Columbia straight away or stay in England a bit longer? I was sure Craig would extend her contract again or she could get a similar job at another chambers. For the first time in a long time I was thinking about something other than work in my future.

"Seven thirty?" She scooted off my knee.

I glanced at my watch. "We should leave in ten minutes, so get those boxes open."

She pulled out the cocktail dress first. It was cherry red and she'd look phenomenal in it. "Alexander, this is beautiful." She held it up against her. "It's short."

"It's a good job you have incredible legs."

I wanted her to open the shoes next. I really hoped they fit, because if it were up to me, she'd be wearing them a lot.

"Holy crap," she said, pulling out the shiny, black shoe with crisscrossed straps and higher-than-high heel.

"You like them?"

She gazed at them. "They're the sexiest thing that ever existed."

"Wrong. *You* are the sexiest thing that ever existed. I want to see them on."

"But you want me to be naked, right? Hell, *I* want to be naked wearing these things."

I chuckled, my cock twitching at the thought. "Later. I think the restaurant prefers its diners fully dressed."

"We could skip the restaurant," she said, stripping off her top and stepping in between my legs. She leaned over, pressed her hand against my hardening dick, and kissed me.

I grabbed her wrists. "Violet. Behave. I know you're using me for my body, but I want your mind for a couple of hours." She was hard to resist, but I was a master of self-control. I wondered if her deflection was deliberate. Was she avoiding a conversation about what happened next year? I knew she didn't like to plan, but if she was thinking about Columbia that meant she was considering her future, and I wanted to know where that left us.

I stood, held her hands behind her back, and crushed my lips to hers, taking the kiss from her as if it were my last one. "That will have to satiate you until we get back," I said, releasing her. "Now change and let's go."

She huffed and unzipped her skirt, letting it pool to the floor and reveal her legs and ass that I enjoyed so much. She knew what her body did to me. She was such a minx and never gave in so easily without a fight—she'd try to tempt me again, so I decided to wait in the hall.

She must have accepted defeat, because she was ready and by my side within just a few moments.

"You look fantastic," I said, my gaze skimming over the red fabric and her bronzed thighs down to the heels I'd fuck her in when we got back.

"Thank you. I'm styled by Alexander Knightley."

We put on our coats and I clasped her hand in mine and we began our short walk across Berkley Square to the restaurant.

"So I've been thinking," I said, glancing at Violet, trying to gauge her reaction. She kept her eyes firmly ahead. "I'm going to take every Saturday night off, at least when I'm not in the middle of a trial."

She nodded, but didn't say anything as we reached the entrance to the square. The trees had lost most of their leaves weeks ago, but a few clung on futilely. It was still one of the most beautiful squares in London.

"And I'm going to try to take at least half a day off at the weekend. Perhaps even a whole day."

"A whole day off work, Knightley?" She turned to me as we walked and clutched at her chest. "Won't the sky turn black and all the babies start crying?"

She was the only person I'd ever encountered who brought me back down to earth with such a tremendous thump. "I think it's good for my long-term health—mental and physical—and it will force me to work with juniors more often, so I can take on bigger cases."

She smiled and turned back to the path. "Good for you," she said.

"And it will mean I have more time for you."

She nodded. "You're not changing your working pattern for me, right?"

I'd expected her to be thrilled, but she seemed a little defensive. "Well, I want to spend more time with you," I said. Was that not what she wanted?

"I would really like that."

I relaxed my shoulders a little.

"I just don't want you to feel as if you're having to give anything up for me. If you have it to give, then that's great, but I don't want you to feel you *have* to do that. I don't want you to resent me."

I stopped and circled my arms around her waist. She was describing exactly what had happened between Gabby and me. In the end, I'd resented every moment my wife had taken me away from my work, every moment I spent with her. "I couldn't. You've never asked me for anything."

She tilted her head. "Not technically true. I beg for your cock a lot."

I chuckled. "Yeah, you'll never find me complaining about that."

"As long as you're doing what you think is best for you, then I'll very happily spend more time with you."

It wasn't the reaction I'd been hoping for. I'd been wanting to show her that I would have more time for her if she wanted to further extend her stay in the UK, even study here, but perhaps she'd not even considered it. "I don't understand. You're encouraging me to be selfish?"

"I don't want to expect anything and then be disappointed. Let down. You know? And I don't want to be a burden. I just want to enjoy things between us."

I dipped and dropped a kiss on her lips. I'd bring it up again at dinner. I wanted to really understand the reasons she thought I might disappoint her. "How could we not enjoy this? We're in Berkley Square." I glanced up at the almost-leafless trees. "Can you hear any nightingales?"

"Nightingales?"

"Yes. Singing in Berkley Square. You've not heard that song? Frank Sinatra sang it best."

"Anything he sings is always fantastic."

"Exactly." I grabbed her hand and slid my cheek to hers and began to move gently from side to side, humming the familiar tune.

"We're dancing?" she asked, grinning up at me.

"It's being here in Berkeley Square, with you. We have to dance cheek to cheek and listen for nightingales."

"Is that the law?" she asked as I twirled us around.

"Yes." I dipped her backward and she giggled, a sound more beautiful than any nightingale.

I cupped her face and placed another kiss on her lips before taking her hand and heading to the restaurant. I couldn't remember ever feeling like this before. I'd felt satisfied, proud. Content even. But I'd never felt this *happy*.

She shook her head. "How the hell did you get so romantic?"

A romantic was the last thing I'd ever describe myself as being, but that's what Violet King was doing to me. She was changing me into a man who took Saturday nights off and danced in a park.

"Holy crap. Bentley and Bugatti have stores on this street?" Violet asked as we walked by the glass fronts of the showrooms on Bruton Street. "How fancy is this place we're going?"

"Not very. But the food's good and you love Chinese."

"I do," she said as we grinned at each other.

"Alex," a man called from up ahead.

I looked up to find Lance and his wife coming toward us. Violet followed my gaze and tugged on my hand when she saw who was coming. I didn't release her. There was no point—they'd seen us.

"Flavia, this is Violet King," Lance said, introducing his wife. "And you know Alex."

After introductions and the obligatory cheek kisses, Lance said, "I'm so very delighted to run into you two like this. You've been very discreet. I had no idea about the two of you, although I might have wished it to be true." He turned to his wife. "Violet is the first person I've ever seen who was able to sort out Alex's billing. And now she's apparently persuaded him to take a Saturday night off. I'm surrounded by miracles every day."

"It was my idea. Violet doesn't need to persuade me to take her to dinner." From our earlier conversation, I suspected Violet wouldn't like the idea that I was spending the evening with her because she'd persuaded me to.

"Even better," he said. "I'm delighted for you both." He gripped my shoulder. "Look after her."

"Yes, sir."

"We'll let you get on with your evening. We're just off to the fish place around the corner," Lance said.

We said our goodbyes and headed into the restaurant. "You okay?" I asked.

"I guess. I'm glad he was cool about it, but I wish we hadn't run into them. I hope he doesn't tell Craig."

"He won't, but I can ask him not to if it will ease your concerns. But Craig wouldn't object."

"I just don't want the dynamic to alter."

I squeezed her hand. "No problem. I'll ensure Lance doesn't mention it."

I gave my name to the hostess and we were shown to our table.

"Let's just forget about it and enjoy our evening," she said. "Will you order for me? I have no idea what I want."

I chuckled. "Of course." I scanned down the menu. "Then you can tell me all about Columbia. Have you thought any more about it?"

"Nothing to talk about, really. I have to take the GMAT first, then see if I get in." I glanced up and she looked away, as if she hoped the conversation would change course before she looked back.

The waiter came over and I ordered for us as Violet scanned the dim restaurant. "This is fancy, Alexander."

"You're far fancier than this place. Your sister's a duchess."

She rolled her eyes. "Hardly. And anyway, I'm not my sister. I'm a waitress from Connecticut no matter what my brother and sister do. No matter my degree."

"And you're a very clever woman who's wearing that dress like a catwalk model." I reached for her hand across the table. "I don't see much waitressing in your future; especially if you're at Columbia."

"I have no idea what's going to happen. You know me, I don't like to plan."

I was going to have to press her on the subject of Columbia. She clearly wasn't going to volunteer information. I wasn't sure if she was really worried that she wouldn't get in or whether she just didn't want to talk to me about it.

I turned her hand over and swept my thumb across her palm. "Yes, I do know you, and I believe you're thinking about what's next, however much you want to deny it." I wanted to talk about this with her, discuss what she wanted to do, where she wanted to live. I needed to know if she saw me in her future. The more time I spent with Violet, the more I craved. My relationship with Gabby had felt as if it were stuck onto the side of my life like a cheap fridge magnet bought on holiday. Violet was fast becoming an integral part of my life in a way I never imagined a woman could be. I found myself asking her opinion of the morning's breaking news or wanting to hear more about her growing up in Connecticut. She never asked me to, but I checked in with her during the day when I hadn't seen her. I missed her scent and her smile when she wasn't around. She grounded me the way work usually did, but fulfilled me in a way it never had. I wasn't ready for her to go back to New York, and I wasn't sure I ever would be.

She bit the inside of her cheek. "I just thought I'd take the entrance exam and go from there. If I don't score high enough, that will make the decision for me."

"Violet, you're going to ace it. You're one of the cleverest people I know."

She glanced down at our joined hands. "Maybe. But you're right. I have been thinking about my future and what I want to do. This job, being in London, away from my old life—it's all given me room to breathe and consider things." She shook her head. "I can't go back to waiting tables. I was a shitty waitress at the best of times, and I don't want to live my life in reaction to some douchebag I dated in college, however much I thought I loved him at the time. Our business was my idea. I put together the majority of the business plan."

"It doesn't surprise me. You're very talented."

"And I've enjoyed working in chambers, but I think I could do more."

"I completely agree with you." She was far too clever for the clerical work she was doing in chambers.

"You do?" She looked confused.

"Of course I do."

"You don't think I'm too old to go back to school?"

I frowned. "If we're not learning every day, then we're doing something wrong. It's part of the reason I love my job so much. I'm constantly learning."

The waiter arrived with our food, and we held each other's gaze as he set down our plates.

"I think I'd like to set up my own business." She exhaled as if she'd just rid herself of the most tremendous burden. "At the moment, I'm thinking consulting. But maybe it's something else. I don't know, but I can't waitress again. If I can get my MBA then maybe I can figure out more what I want to do. I have my whole life to seize. Not just the day."

As I listened to her, I realized I wanted to support her however I could. She deserved a bright future, and however much I would miss her, if she wanted to go to Columbia and discover what her future was, then I'd whistle and cheer loudly from the sidelines. But was there a way she could chase after her future and be with me? Would she even want to?

"I think you'll be brilliant at whatever you decide to do."

"Just not waitressing." She grinned.

"Maybe not."

"You think Craig will write me a reference?"

"Absolutely." I nodded. "So you're thinking of applying for a general MBA at Columbia."

"Yeah, I figure I haven't decided exactly what I want to do, and I can test out some ideas while I'm there, do some internships and see where it leads me."

I nodded, my throat suddenly dry. I was dancing around the point, which really wasn't my style. I just didn't know what I'd do if she shut me down completely. "So it's not Columbia in particular you want to attend?"

"It's a good school, and I'm pretty sure I can live in Scarlett or Max's place while I'm there."

"I hear some of the British universities have excellent MBA programs," I blurted.

The corners of her mouth twitched, and she reached

out for her glass of wine. "Is that right?" she asked before taking a sip.

"Did you consider staying in the UK? Would you?"

She set her glass back down. "Would I consider staying?"

"We have some excellent universities. And I like you. I'll miss you if you go."

She laughed. "You won't notice I'm gone."

A sharp pain sliced through my gut. She couldn't really believe that. "That's not true. I would miss you tremendously. I was sort of hoping you might extend your time here in London."

"What are you suggesting? Give up on Columbia?"

I had no right to ask her to give up anything. I had a terrible track record with women and had never done anything successfully other than my job. "No. Not if you're wedded to going to Columbia. But if what you want is an MBA, then as I said, the UK and London have some excellent universities."

She didn't respond but she put down her knife and fork and leaned back in her chair, looking at me. Did she want me to say something?

"I like you, Violet. And I think you like me. I know I am a selfish workaholic, but I'd like to see more of you. I know you don't want me rearranging my schedule for you, but what if I chose to?" I looked into her eyes, trying to find some encouragement. "I want to work less so I can spend more time with you. Your contract is up just after Christmas and I'm not ready to say goodbye."

She sighed, which hadn't been the reaction I'd been hoping for. "Alexander, isn't the whole reason we work because I don't ask anything of you and you don't disappoint me because I'm not expecting anything?"

"But maybe I want you to ask things of me."

"But the whole reason that your marriage didn't work is that you always put work first and because your wife wanted too much."

"Agreed. But Gabby and I aren't you and me. And I said I can commit to spending more time with you."

"The problem isn't just that though. What happened with David hurt me. And for me this works because you are who you say you are. You never say things you don't mean."

"That sounds like a good thing."

"It is. It's one of my favorite things about you. But if this thing between us changes—you give more, I expect more—it will be so much easier for those lines to get crossed. For me to wind up disappointed, hurt."

I nodded. She was right as she usually was. "It's a risk."

She nodded and went back to eating as if it was settled, the discussion over. I was far from done.

"But it's a risk worth taking as far as I'm concerned," I said and she glanced up. "I want to eat out with you on Saturday nights and dance in the park. And the last thing I want to do is be on the phone with clients when I can be talking to you."

"But if it didn't work with Gabby, who you were married to, why would it work with me?"

"I feel more for you that I ever did for Gabby. You've changed the way I look at the world. You think six months ago I was dancing cheek to cheek in Berkley Square? Or spending lunchtimes in museums? I did neither with Gabby or any other woman."

She laughed. "Oh, that's my bad influence, is it?"

"It's your very good influence." I paused. If I'd thought for one moment that I'd be sitting here asking a woman to cross a continent for me just a few months ago, I would have assumed I'd lost my mind, but far from it. Violet had helped me find it. "You could always apply to some London schools and see what happens between us over the next few weeks. They all require the same entrance exam anyway."

She grinned at me. "They do, do they? Have you been doing some research?"

"Maybe a little," I admitted.

She twisted the stem of her wine glass. "I could fill out the application forms. See who, if anyone, accepts me."

"And we can spend some more time together, and I can show you I am the man I say I am. You don't have to decide right away."

"I'm nervous," she said, looking out from under her lashes at me. "This feels serious."

I nodded. "It does. But doesn't it feel right too?"

"Being with you right here and now feels right, and I don't want it to stop." She shook her head. "But looking into the future is never easy. It scares me. I don't want to get hurt again."

"It scares me too, but I'm really good at working really hard to be the person I want to be. I've just always wanted to be the best barrister. Now I want to be a man you deserve."

"And the best barrister?" she teased.

"Well, yes, of course I want both."

"And if anyone is capable of having everything they want, it's you."

"That's good to know. Because I want you." I reached out for her hand across the table.

A pink blush bloomed in her cheeks. Violet rarely got embarrassed, and there was something rather adorable about a woman so beautiful, charming, and clever being embarrassed by a man like me wanting her so openly.

"Let's take this slowly, okay?" she said.

"I'll follow your lead." It was the first time we'd talked about our relationship. The first time that we'd discussed more than what we were doing tomorrow. Adrenaline spread through my body. I was excited. Not about a new case I'd been assigned. Not about a courtroom win, but about my future with a woman. For the first time in my life I wanted more than to be the best at the bar. I wanted Violet King.

THIRTY

Violet

"I think I'm in love with Alexander Knightley," I blurted out as soon as Scarlett answered the phone.

"Of course you are. I think *I'm* in love with Alexander Knightley," she replied. "He's so charming, Violet."

I sighed and collapsed back on my bed. "I'm being serious. This is a *disaster*. You need to talk me out of it or recommend something I can get from the pharmacy to cure me." I'd been floating on cloud nine since Saturday, and I couldn't stop smiling. It seemed, without realizing it, I'd been waiting for Knightley to say he wanted more, that he didn't want me to leave. Dancing with him in the park, him talking about how he wanted me, it had allowed this rush of feelings to burst out of me. As though I'd been waiting to admit to myself that I was in love with Alexander.

Scarlett laughed. "I think it's wonderful."

"He danced with me in Berkley Square, the asshole. He said we had to listen for nightingales."

"Oh my, you mean like the song?"

I sighed. It had been the most romantic night of my life, and one I'd never forget. "He told me I was smart and beautiful and that I'd ace the entrance exam for Columbia."

"Which is true."

"He's really in my corner, Scarlett. He really wants me to do well."

"That's the kind of man you need in your life. So why is it a disaster?"

"Because of a thousand reasons." I'd been counting them since Sunday morning, as I tried hopelessly to climb down from my cotton-candy cloud.

"Okay. Give me your top three."

I held out my clenched fist and pushed out my thumb. "Well he lives in London and I live in the US."

"Easy. One of you can move."

I dropped my hand to my side. "If you're just going to say it's all easy, then I'm hanging up. This is not easy. There is no way he could come to New York—his whole career is here. He's not even qualified to practice law in the US. And all his clients and his reputation, it's all here in London."

"So? Move to London," she said.

"He wants me to think about doing my MBA in London."

"That's a great idea."

"But then what? What if I still love him at the end of two years? Then what happens?" I was falling deeper and deeper already.

"What do you mean what happens?"

"Well by then it's going to be difficult to leave."

"So you don't. Stay in London." She made it sound so easy.

"Just like that? Don't be crazy. Mom and Dad—"

"Mom and Dad want you to be happy, and anyway,

they're not in Connecticut half the time, and I'm in England a lot, too. The world isn't such a big place. We can video call. I might even persuade Ryder to get a plane."

I rolled my eyes. She said it like she was going to ask him to pick up some chicken from the market on the way home. "So I just move. Just like that."

"Yes, just like that. I've seen the way that man looks at you. He's going to go out and buy a flock of nightingales."

"It's a watch," I said as I tried to imagine him looking at me as Scarlett described.

"What's a watch?"

"The collective noun for nightingales is a watch. Not a flock."

"Jesus, Violet. Stop being a geek and focus."

"I am focused. On the thousand other reasons why being with him is a bad idea. He's impatient, short-tempered, and a complete workaholic."

"And you love him."

I did. There was no denying it.

"He's divorced," I said. "Because he didn't have time for a relationship." He'd said that he was going to try to achieve a better balance, take more time off, but he was hardwired to work. "Why would it work between us if he can't make it work with his wife?"

"You can't compare one relationship with another. Things change when you're in love. Look at Ryder and me."

I sighed. "Unlike yours, my life isn't a fucking fairytale."

"Dancing in the park with a man as charming as Alex sounds like the fairytale is yours if you want it to be."

If I allowed myself to hope for something for the future, even just for a second, it was Alexander I saw. I didn't plan. I didn't invest ahead of time. I hadn't been that girl for a long time. But Alexander had me applying for courses, thinking about the future, and needing him to be part of it.

"You never think two years in advance about anything. I know I bust your balls about it, but this is the one time you should just see what happens after the end of two years. *This* is the time where you need to be living in the moment. And it's not like you'll be putting your future on hold or anything. If at the end of two years things don't work out then you'll still have an MBA."

That was true. Studying abroad was a thing a lot of people did. Not just the people with boyfriends in a different country. Like Scarlett said, I wouldn't have lost anything by doing my MBA in the UK.

It would just be easier if I wasn't in love with him. My feelings left me exposed. I didn't want to be taken advantage of again, made a fool of. Knightley would never do that on purpose—he had more honor and integrity than David ever did—but that didn't mean it couldn't happen. Alexander was so focused on work. I didn't want to become an appendage to his life. So far things had worked for us, but changing things up left me vulnerable. But maybe the next two years could be a trial period. I knew I had a natural out when I finished if things weren't working.

"I could just apply for some programs in London. And then if I don't get in my decision is made." I'd already made the applications in London. I'd done it on the Sunday morning after the dancing in Berkley Square.

"Yes. And when you *do* get in, you can stay together for two years and worry about what happens after that then."

My sister was relentless but part of me hoped she was right. As much as it felt like a disaster to love him, I hated the thought of walking away from Knightley in just a few weeks.

THIRTY-ONE

Violet

I came out of the bathroom to find Alexander standing opposite me. It was a Saturday, but he still wore his suit to go into chambers.

"You're up early," he said.

I grinned, stood on my tiptoes, and kissed him. "You are *very* perceptive. Probably why you're such a great barrister." Alexander normally left me in bed on a Saturday morning, but today I had things to do. I had a day of grocery shopping and cooking planned.

"Have we decided what we're doing tonight?" he asked. "Do you want me to book somewhere?"

"We've had three Saturday nights of fancy, if you include Hakkasan," I said. I couldn't believe it had been three weeks since our discussion about me doing my MBA in London. Since then I'd applied to Columbia and two places in London. All three had responded this week. I'd been squirreling away the envelopes, ready for when I got my Saturday night with Knightley to open them. "I'd like to stay home tonight."

"We should be out celebrating." He circled his hands around my waist and pulled me closer to him.

I'd told Knightley that we'd open the letters together tonight. "We don't know if we'll be celebrating. I might not get accepted anywhere." If I got into Columbia but neither of the London universities, where did that leave us? Either way I wanted it to be just the two of us tonight.

"You are ridiculous at times. Of course they will all want you. You should have more faith in yourself."

However it went, my whole life was about to change, and I knew that I wanted Knightley there holding my hand as it did.

"I'd still like to stay home."

He kissed me on the forehead. "Only if you make your mac and cheese."

I laughed. "I'd been planning to go fancier than mac and cheese. We won't have another Saturday night before I fly back to Connecticut for the holidays. I fly on Tuesday." I wanted to make tonight special. I'd planned crystal and fine china. Flowers and a crisp white tablecloth. I might even try to cook venison.

"Are you sure you have to leave me for a whole week?"

I laughed. "You'll survive. I need to go back and see my family. I was only supposed to be here for three months and now it's going to be six."

"And maybe even more," he growled.

The last month together had been wonderful. We'd spent every Saturday night and Sunday afternoon together since. We talked about everything. His work, his ambitions and his time at boarding school. Even his regrets about his marriage—he said he should have never agreed to it. And I shared with him my crazy exploits from New York, and how I felt like a different person to the waitress I'd been there. Things had grown between us. And thinking about staying in London to be with him seemed less and less scary and more and more how things should be.

"Shall I get some wine?" he asked.

I laughed. "If you want it to cost more than about five bucks then I would say yes."

He shuddered. "Can you even buy wine for five pounds a bottle?"

I patted him on the chest. "You see what the rest of the world has to deal with while you're in your ivory tower."

"I'll get champagne. To celebrate."

I groaned. "Don't jinx anything."

"There's nothing to jinx. If you'd just open the bloody envelopes now, you'd see."

"I told you, I want to save them until we both have time."

He grinned. "We're going to celebrate all night." He glanced at his watch. "But now I have to head to chambers. Sebastian will be there already."

"You should go."

He released his arms from around my waist.

"I'll see you in just a few hours."

"Yes, I'll be back by seven. Half past at the latest," he said as he opened the bedroom door.

I blew him a kiss. "I can't wait." I'd thought he'd forget after our night out at Hakkasan. I'd suspected that work would engulf him, and I'd get pushed to the sidelines and his promise to take Saturday nights off would be broken. But just like Alexander Knightley promised, he did what he said and he didn't say things he didn't mean. It was why I liked him so much.

The front door clicked closed and I grabbed my cell phone. I wanted to get to the grocery store early. I had no idea how easy it would be to buy venison.

I'd been making mental adjustments in the last month. I'd been picturing myself studying in the UK. Darcy had said I could stay on in her townhouse for the entire time. Although Alexander had hinted that he was going to buy a place and wanted me to stay with him. I had images of us spending our free time together, even me managing to persuade him to have a vacation. Or holiday as he would say. I imagined us happy together. Because that's what we were now. But I hadn't allowed myself to actually plan anything. I'd not accepted Darcy's offer and I'd not looked into whether or not I could take part-time work on a student visa. I didn't want to let myself get too invested in case I didn't get accepted. When we opened the envelopes together tonight, then I could start planning.

Tonight was the start of something. It was the beginning of our future together.

Alexander

Violet was going to kill me.

There was almost as much paper piled up in this office as there had been when she'd first started.

"I just don't understand why the trial hasn't been pushed back until the New Year. It makes no sense to start it two days before Christmas and then have a break in the middle," Sebastian grumbled.

"They're trying to make the courts more efficient." There was no point in questioning the logic of the legal system. The trial was set for Monday and that was that.

"I'd be a lot more efficient if I wasn't here on a Saturday

night," Sebastian complained. He was going to have to adjust; this was how it worked.

"Wait, what's the time?" I asked, glancing out the window, trying to see how dark it was.

"Almost eleven."

How the hell had that happened? Shit, eleven? Last time I'd checked the clock it had been a quarter past four. Outside was dark, but it never got really light at this time of the year especially as it had been raining all day. It was difficult to tell what time it was. I stood up and started to pull on my jacket. "I need to go."

It was Saturday.

This was my evening with Violet.

She and I were supposed to have dinner.

We were meant to be opening her acceptance letters this evening.

Shit.

The enormity of what I'd done was suddenly revealed, as though a veil had been lifted on my memory. I grabbed my mobile and rushed out of chambers. Sebastian was muttering something, but I didn't have time to hear it.

I strode out toward the exit of Lincoln's Inn to get a cab and pulled out my phone as I went. I swiped the screen and saw the three missed calls. Fuck. I was an idiot.

The preparation for the Bar Humbug trial was almost complete, but we'd come across a number of issues today that had taken longer than expected to solve. Thank God Sebastian had been there, or I would have had to work through the night. I just hadn't expected them to have taken this long. I didn't know how I could have just let the time go like that. I'd been so immersed in my work I hadn't remembered Violet. I groaned and pressed dial.

It rang twice, and then I was abruptly cut off. Not like it

would have been if the phone had been turned to silent and my call had gone ignored. No, Violet had seen the call and cancelled it.

Christ.

I didn't know what to do. I needed her to understand that I'd just lost track of time and it wasn't a reflection on her. Except, what else could it be?

A dull ache in my stomach grew as I flagged the taxi down and began the short journey back to Mayfair.

I stared at the screen on my phone, willing Violet to call back. I had three unopened messages.

The first message, sent a little after five, asked what time I'd be back.

Damn. I should have picked up this message sooner and replied. I'd just been in the thick of it. But it was no excuse. I'd promised her and I'd broken that promise.

The second message—asking when I'd be back—had come in just after seven. And the final one was from twenty minutes ago. She said she was going to bed.

I grimaced. Ordinarily, Violet and I texted off and on during the day, more on a Saturday when she wasn't at work. But today had been overwhelming, and Sebastian and I were more than a little punch drunk from the hours we'd been working.

I typed out a message.

I'm so sorry. I didn't realize the time. I'm on my way home now. Work has been brutal.

She was probably asleep. But an uncomfortable feeling lodged in my gut.

The cab pulled up outside the Hill Street house. I paid and jumped out. The lights were off, so I fumbled in my pockets for the key she'd given me earlier in the week. She couldn't be asleep already, could she?

I entered the dark house and closed and locked the door behind me. Going into the living room, to check that Violet wasn't sleeping on the sofa, I glanced around the room, trying to find an explanation for my unsettled feeling. I set down my case and peeled off my coat and jacket, striding into the dining room to put them on the back of the chair.

My heart stopped.

The table was laid with a white tablecloth, crystal wine glasses, silver cutlery, candles, and white orchids. The whole thing looked beautiful. The table had been set for me, for us. In celebration of her future or our future together.

I hadn't turned up.

I hadn't called her.

I pressed my thumb and forefinger against my forehead. I had to make this better. I turned to find a speaker set up on the dresser with her iPad plugged in. I swiped it open.

A Nightingale Sang in Berkley Square.

Fuck. I was a selfish man who didn't deserve Violet King.

Violet

I opened my eyes as the faint click of the front door closing drifted upstairs.

Alexander had left.

I glanced at the clock. It was five after nine. He was late this morning. Maybe he'd lingered to see if I'd stir. Fact was, I hadn't slept much at all and had been awake for hours. I'd heard him come in, but had pretended to be asleep. I hadn't wanted to talk to him. Didn't want to have a conversation about where he'd been and why he hadn't called. I knew what he'd say. I knew he'd be sorry, but it wasn't enough.

I had a brother who was a complete workaholic, so it

wasn't as if I didn't understand what that meant. And in some ways, Alexander's devotion to his job had worked well for me. I hadn't felt suffocated and hemmed in, as I had when dating men who had more time on their hands. I'd been able to look forward to our time together while still having time to myself. Last night had brought things into focus for me. Our dinner together should have been symbolic, important—the start of our future together. I'd been accepted to all three programs that I'd applied to, and if Alexander had come back as planned, I would have been preparing for the next two years in London and a future with him.

At least this way I was able to walk away with my heart bruised but not broken.

This was why I didn't trust men. Why no man since David had lasted more than a few weeks before I walked away.

This was why I didn't fall in love. Until now, I got out before I could get hurt.

I should have trusted my instincts when they told me it could never work between us. I felt ridiculous for being so upset by being let down by him, because I knew who he was. I knew work always came first.

I didn't want to be the girl who sat around waiting for her man. That wasn't seizing the day, and it wasn't working toward my future either—it was just pathetic. I'd been clear with him that I needed him to be the man he said he was. By not turning up—not even calling me last night when he knew what a big deal it was, knew I was leaving for the US on Tuesday morning—he showed me he wasn't a man I could love. If Alexander didn't respect me enough to show up last night, or at least bother letting me know he couldn't, then I had to walk away. If my future, my heart, what was important to me, was so easily forgotten, then I *refused* to love him.

It would just take a little time for the feelings that had been creeping up on me for so long to wither and die. They would. I would make sure of it. But I couldn't stay in London while they did. I didn't want to hear Alexander's apology. Or even worse, hear an excuse. I didn't want to be the girl who was disappointed that a guy didn't show up for dinner on the night she was going to find out where her future lay. I'd rather be alone. I'd prefer to be with some nameless guy I *knew* didn't care about me than be with someone who pretended he did.

I wouldn't let it embitter me. Seeing Alexander's drive and purpose had inspired me in so many ways. London had opened my eyes to what my life could be like. I wasn't going to let this experience turn me into a gibbering wreck. And I wasn't going to let him affect my future.

I'd spent too long defining my life by the wrongs men had done to me. That time was over.

I sat up and grabbed my phone from my nightstand. I had a resignation letter to write and a suitcase to pack.

The phone buzzed in my hands.

I'm sorry about last night. I completely lost track of time. Did you get in? Call me when you're up.

I replied. *No apologies necessary. Maybe you should stay at the hotel tonight. I have a lot to work through.*

He responded right away.

You're awake. I missed you last night.

A dull ache spread through my body. I'd missed him too. I *would* miss him. But I'd get over him. Better now than two years down the line.

IT WAS ALWAYS the plan that today, Monday, would be my last day in chambers before I flew back to the US with Darcy. With just a few weeks to run on my employment with chambers after Christmas, Craig agreed to cut my contract short. I'd told him that I could start my course at Columbia in January if he let me go early. And being the man he was, he agreed. I didn't like to lie, but it was my plan to see if I could get my start day moved to January once I was back Stateside anyway, so I justified it by seeing it as rearranging the timetable of events.

I'd expected to miss Alexander while I was in Connecticut for the holidays, but I'd thought we'd only be separated for just over a week. I didn't expect to be walking away forever. He'd called me several times yesterday. Eventually I'd turned off my phone. I didn't want to have an argument. There was no point. My decision was made.

I was running away and although I knew it was cowardly I didn't know what else to do—I had to protect myself.

For a few blissful weeks I'd allowed myself to imagine being in London forever. With Alexander and an MBA from a London college—a glittering career and a handsome, charming man by my side. What had I been thinking? As I'd said to Scarlett—my life wasn't a fucking fairytale.

"Any questions, just email me," I said to Jimmy as I passed his desk for what would be the last time.

He bounced up from his seat and held out his arms. "I'm going to miss you." He pulled me into a hug. "Come and visit us next time you're in London."

I couldn't imagine there would be a next time. It would be too painful to come back and imagine what my life would have been like if things had gone differently, if Alexander had been a different man.

Jimmy released me and I said my goodbyes and headed into the corridor. There was just one final farewell to say. Court had finished for the day and Knightley would be back in his office. My pulse raced. I just had to hold it together for a few more moments. I wasn't such a coward that I was going to leave without saying goodbye, but I had timed it so I knew Sebastian would be in the office. This was the best time to let Alexander know I was leaving. He couldn't create a scene if there was an audience. Not that he ever would.

I fisted my hands, my fingernails digging into my palms, trying to distract myself from the emotions threatening to overwhelm me. I could do this. I was just saying goodbye to a man I *refused* to love.

I knocked on the door and couldn't help but smile forlornly at Alexander's familiar bark. "Come in."

He didn't look up. Both he and Sebastian had their heads bowed toward their laptops. It wasn't resentment I felt—it was pity. I was heading home to my beautiful family for the holidays and no doubt Knightley and Sebastian would spend most, if not all, of the festive season in this room surrounded by paper.

"I just wanted to call in and say goodbye before I left." I used my best singsong voice.

Alexander's head sprang up as I spoke, and when he saw me he stood.

"Bye, Violet," Sebastian said. "Have a good Christmas."

I forced an empty smile. "I see you're busy, so I won't keep you. Thanks for everything." I waved and turned to leave.

"Violet," Alexander snapped, and I froze.

"Sebastian, will you excuse us for a second?"

I hadn't expected Alexander to ask Sebastian to leave. The last thing I wanted was to be alone with him.

Sebastian didn't say a word. He just picked up his laptop, and I moved aside as he passed me.

I couldn't look at Knightley.

"Violet, please close the door."

I shook my head. "I don't think that's a good idea. You're very busy and I have—"

"Violet, what is the matter with you? Close the door."

I swallowed but did as he asked as he came around from behind his desk.

"I want to kiss my girlfriend before she leaves for a few days. I thought I might get to see you last night—"

I placed my finger over his lips to silence him. I didn't want to hear about how busy he was. I knew.

His hands slipped over my hips and I tensed. I didn't want to feel him again. I didn't want to be reminded of the good stuff.

"Good luck," I said, and my heart ached as if it were being ripped from my chest. "I hope you win."

He released me and ran his fingers through his hair. "We should, but I fear we won't."

He thought I meant the trial. I meant at life.

"I should have more time when you're back. What day are you home?"

I would be *home*, back with my family, tomorrow. I smiled and shrugged, cupping his jaw with my hand. He looked so tired and stressed. I should tell him I wasn't coming back to London, but I didn't want to add to his anxiety. Not today. He might not care about me the way I cared about him, but I knew that I had eased his burden a little, and he didn't have to find out today that I was leaving for good. The last thing I wanted to do was to leave on an argument. I didn't want him to convince me that what he'd done was okay when it just wasn't. I didn't want to weaken against his gravelly accent and strong hands. If he wasn't the man I needed him to be then I had to walk away now while I still had the strength.

"What did your letters say?" He ran his hand through his hair. "I'm so sorry about Saturday. I tried to call you yesterday but—shall I pop round tonight?"

I shook my head. "Darcy's here and we have to be up really early."

"Everything will calm down when this trial is over."

He was lying. There would be another trial after this one and another after that. I couldn't live my life wondering when he was next going to let me down.

One lie deserved another. "I haven't opened them yet."

He frowned but didn't question me further. "I'll call you later, okay?" he asked.

I nodded, but I wouldn't answer. Not until tomorrow, when he was out of court, and I was back where I belonged.

THIRTY-TWO

Alexander

London was emptying. Most people had left the city at the weekend, so the stragglers who remained were few and far between.

"Thank God that's over," Sebastian said, his barrister bag slung over his shoulder. Those things looked ridiculous. He should put his wig and robe in his case.

"Only until the third of January," I reminded him.

"In the meantime I'm going to remind my girlfriend and family what I look like. What are you doing for Christmas?" he asked.

I hadn't even thought about it. I usually drove up to see my mother, but she was visiting relatives in Switzerland. "Oh, you know, the usual family thing," I lied. Who didn't make plans for Christmas? Perhaps I could convince Violet to have me on speakerphone for the day?

I smiled as I imagined her face. I'd tried to call her a couple of times last night but she'd not picked up. She'd said she and Darcy were going to have an early night but I thought I'd have caught her.

"Right," I said as we entered chambers. "I'm just going to dump this"—I lifted my chin at my case—"and then head off. I suggest you do the same. I'll see you back here on the second to prepare."

Sebastian nodded.

I put down my case, took my laptop, and left. As I got back out into the cold December air, I realized that now I finally had some free time, I had nowhere to be. No one to see, no home to return to. My house hunting had been abandoned after I'd missed one too many calls from the real estate agent, so I was still in the hotel. Violet had gone back to America and my mother wasn't in town. I didn't speak to my brother from one year's end to the next.

Across the green lawn of New Square, I waved at Craig. "Finally leaving?" he asked, racing toward me.

I nodded. "Yes. I'll be back all too soon."

"You've had an excellent year. Not least because of all the billing Violet did for you."

"Yes, she's been great."

He nodded. "We'll miss her. Even a few more weeks and I'm sure she'd have worked miracles, but she's better off at Columbia. It's a great opportunity for her."

"It certainly is." She must have been accepted there. She can't have told him that she was also applying in London. "And you'll have a few more weeks of her when she comes back in January."

He frowned. "You haven't heard? She's not coming back —something to do with the date her course starts. Bloody shame for us, obviously."

His words began to merge together as if they were getting sucked into a bog and I couldn't hear what he was saying. Violet wasn't coming back? Surely he must have it wrong. I shoved my hands in my pockets, feeling the cold metal of my phone as I twisted it, desperate to pull it out and call her to ask her what Craig was talking about.

"You okay, Mr. Knightley?" Craig asked.

I nodded. "Yeah, I just remembered something about . . . something. Forgive me, I have to go." I sped off toward the exit of Lincoln's Inn to find a cab. When the taxi pulled up, I gave him the address of my hotel. Where else could I go?

After pulling my phone from my pocket, I sat down and dialed Violet's number. I'd thought she'd call before she took off or after she landed, but I hadn't heard anything. I'd assumed it was because she knew I was busy and probably wouldn't be able to talk for long. But maybe she'd never had any intention of calling.

The call went straight to voicemail. Where was she? She must have landed by now.

I'd never experienced loneliness before. It was almost the opposite to how I expected it to feel—time with nothing to do and no one to see had always been some holy grail, but now that I was here, it felt like a huge chasm that might swallow me up.

I stumbled out of the cab, my brain somehow disconnected from my limbs.

Had she not been accepted by the London universities where she'd applied? Or perhaps she had and was starting with one of those in January and Craig had just assumed it was Columbia. That must be it. There was no way Violet would just leave London without any intention of coming back and not tell me, even if I had missed our dinner on Saturday. Surely.

I'D BEEN CALLING Violet every fifteen minutes since I'd returned to the hotel three hours ago. I had nothing else to do. I just wanted to hear her voice. I couldn't remember the last time I'd held her. It must have been Saturday morning before we were meant to find out that she'd been accepted everywhere she applied for the MBA. Fuck, I should have set an alarm or something on my phone.

I went to the small bar in the corner of the room and poured myself a whisky. If I was going to be alone with no one to speak to and no work tomorrow, I could at least be drunk. Perhaps it would slow down my brain, fill up the emptiness that grew bigger inside me with every passing moment. Preparation for the trial had increasingly over-taken my life in the past few weeks. Apart from Saturday nights I'd been completely consumed, and this Saturday night the volume had spilled over.

As I drained my first glass of whiskey, my phone vibrated from where I'd left it on the bed. Violet's name flashed on the screen, and I was so desperate to answer, so eager that she not give up before I accepted the call that I almost dropped the phone twice before managing to swipe the screen.

"Violet, are you okay?" I asked. An entirely ridiculous question, but I was just so pleased she'd called. For a few hours, I'd been worried she'd disappeared forever.

"Yeah, just got back to Scarlett and Ryder's place. Darcy and I are staying here tonight before going up to Connecticut tomorrow."

I held my breath as she spoke, wanting to hear every word, every nuance. "I'm glad you're okay. I don't feel like I've seen you."

The sounds of movement and closing doors echoed down the line. "You've been busy," she replied. "And I need to tell you something. I'm not coming back to chambers in the New Year. There didn't seem to be any point."

Craig had been right. She'd left. Left *me* for good.

"Any point?" I asked. Why hadn't she said something before she left? "I thought you were doing your MBA in London. I thought . . ." I'd thought we were going to be together.

"I'm planning to move my start date on the MBA at Columbia to the beginning of the spring semester, so that means I'll start school in just a few weeks. There didn't seem to be any reason to delay things."

The pressure bearing down on my chest threatened to crack my ribs. "So you're not coming back to London at all?" Surely I was misunderstanding. She couldn't have just left.

"Like I said, I was able to move the start date."

"You didn't get into the London universities?" Was she upset at being rejected and had just fled?

"It doesn't matter. I picked Columbia."

I cleared my throat. I was finding it difficult to read her mood—her voice was light and carefree, but what she was saying seemed so catastrophic. If she were here in front of me, I'd be able to see what was going on beyond the words. "Okay."

"I knew you'd understand."

I wasn't sure that I did. "So you're ending things between us?"

"It's a relief, right?" Her voice was breezy and light, as if she were giving me good news rather than saying we'd never see each other again. "You don't have to worry about having to find time for me. Not that . . ."

Shit.

"Violet, I'm sorry about Saturday. I—"

"Don't apologize. I know how work is for you. I get it comes first."

I exhaled as she said it. It sounded so shallow and feeble, but it was true. It had always come first.

"Anyway, I didn't want to throw you off your game. I know how important this trial is for you—hence the phone call."

"Wait, what? That's it?" I sat down on the chair by the desk.

"What do you want me to say?"

I wasn't sure, but the situation we found ourselves in seemed so ludicrous. If she was angry with me then I wanted her to shout and scream. I wanted to work through this, past this. Hadn't we shared something? Hadn't we enjoyed the time we spent together? I *cared* about this woman and she was just calling to say goodbye as if we'd merely been coworkers? This couldn't be the way things ended between us.

"It all seems so sudden. You've caught me a little off guard. I was hoping I'd see you before you left. I wanted to tell you how sorry I am about Saturday. You can't just end things between us and run away." I hadn't told her that I'd never felt for any woman the way I felt about her. I'd thought we had time for all this.

She didn't respond.

"So, that's it?" I asked.

"I don't see how it can be any other way," she replied. "You have your work and—"

"I've said I'm sorry and you know I had the trial coming up—"

"It's not about Saturday," she said. "It's about every

Saturday. It's about not wanting to be the girl who waits around for scraps of time that you're prepared to toss me."

I winced. She made it sound terrible. "I am really sorry. I never pretended to be perfect, and I'm so used to only having to worry about myself that it's going to take me some time to adjust. That's all."

"I can't let myself care for you, Alexander. I'm just about to get my life on track. I don't want to be derailed again. I don't want to allow myself to believe in someone only to find they are another person entirely. I've done that before."

The bottom fell out from my stomach.

"At first we were just fucking and then we were dancing in Berkley Square and somewhere in the middle of that, my feelings changed and I started to want more. I changed. The more time I spent with you, the more you could hurt me, and I can't let that happen. I won't be let down again."

I'd let Gabby down. And although I regretted what I had done, it hadn't caused me actual pain. But now the agony coursed through my body. "I'm so sorry. You deserve better." It was true. She was precious.

"You are a very special man. Someone who's taught me what I want in my life. You've shown me what I deserve—a man who's capable of putting me first."

"It was a mistake, and I wish I could take it back. Can't we at least try?"

"I can't, Alexander. I'm in too deep; it hurts too much already."

I had no response. I didn't want to hurt her—it was the last thing I wanted.

"I'm sorry," I said.

"Don't be. This way, we can remember the last few months and look back fondly at our time together. I feel like you breathed new life into me, and I will always be so thankful to you."

Breathed new life into her? That's what she'd done to me.

"Can we stay in touch? Be friends?" I was grasping at straws, but I wanted her in my world in whatever way I could have her.

She sighed and the loneliness inside me grew. I knew her answer before she said it. "Maybe one day. Right now, I need a . . . clean—"

"I understand." I tried to keep my voice steady when what I wanted to do was break down and beg for another chance.

"Thank you. I mean it; I think you're a wonderful man."

I just hadn't been good enough for her. I'd been less than she deserved, and rightfully, she'd left me.

———

I'D SPENT Christmas day alone in a hotel room. I'd ordered a club sandwich and a bottle of whiskey and didn't speak to anyone who wasn't working at the hotel in some capacity. Some years that might have been the perfect way to spend the festive season, but this year it just seemed like the life of a lonely, washed-up bachelor with an empty life.

I'd never been much of a drinker. I didn't like the way it clouded my mind and dulled my senses. But in the last week, since Violet had left, a clear head was the last thing I wanted. I longed to be drunk. Each morning, I woke sober and watched the clock until it struck noon, and I got out of bed to fix a whisky.

The news rattled on in the background as I poured my second glass. A rap at the door caught my attention. For a split second I thought Violet had changed her mind and flown back to rescue me. I checked the peephole and found a member of the housekeeping team standing outside.

I pulled the door open and the girl began to talk to me in what sounded like Romanian although it could have been Polish. She pushed her way past me and began clearing up my room. I ripped the Do Not Disturb sign from the outside of the door where it had hung since before Christmas and held it up. "Excuse me." I waved the sign. She turned, saw the sign, shrugged, and pulled the sheets from the bed.

Fuck me. I didn't have the energy to argue. No doubt the hotel staff were wondering what the hell I was doing in here. I pulled on some clothes and grabbed my wallet. Perhaps I could go and buy a bottle of my favorite whisky instead of ordering the stuff from downstairs.

As I stepped out of the lift, I raised my arm to shade my eyes from the light. I'd spent the last week in darkness; I should have brought my sunglasses.

Without knowing where I was going, I stepped outside. I'd not brought my scarf or my gloves and it must have been close to freezing. The air stung my whiskey-bruised throat as I turned up the collar on my coat and stuffed my hands into my pockets. I figured the housekeeper would be done in thirty minutes. I just needed to kill some time before I could go back and take a nap.

The last few weeks preparing for the trial had been brutal and it was catching up with me. Work had been relentless and then there was Violet. If I could find a way of getting to sleep without passing out from alcohol, then perhaps I wouldn't wake with pain tearing through my stomach in the middle of the night. It was like an illness, except I had no temperature or any other symptoms except agony buried so deep it was impossible to describe where it was.

I groaned as I came to the end of the pavement and saw where I was. Berkley Square.

There were no nightingales singing. No beautiful Americans to dance with. Just me feeling sorry for myself with nowhere to go.

I wandered through the gates and took a seat on one of the benches near where I'd danced with Violet just a few short weeks ago. Slouching, I put my head in my hands. How had things been so good and become so awful so quickly? How had I fucked things up so fundamentally?

I cast my mind back to the weeks after my separation from Gabby. It had never felt like this. How long would it last? Would this crushing devastation ever leave me? When Gabby and I parted there was guilt and regret, but I didn't recall pain. Or loneliness.

Chatter caught my attention and I sat up and saw a couple, hand in hand, strolling through the park, laughing and sharing their day together.

I had to get out of there. I headed in the opposite direction and turned left out of the park. But I wasn't done torturing myself. Hill Street was within sight and I wanted to see it, remember Violet's beautiful face at the door when I went to her after work, savor the memories of the night we first slept together and all the times since.

I slowed as the house came into sight. How had I let her go?

"Alex?" a woman called from behind me.

I resisted the urge to run. I didn't want to see anyone other than Violet but when the woman called my name again, I turned to find Darcy, laden down with shopping, coming toward me.

Her brow was furrowed and her eyes narrowed. "What are you doing here?"

"Just passing. I live just . . ." What could I say? My hotel was in the other direction. No doubt I looked like a stalker.

"Can you help me with these?" she asked, indicating the bags she was carrying.

"Yes, of course." Our fingers fumbled as she transferred the weight to me. She got out her keys and unlocked the front door.

"You growing a beard?" she asked.

I rubbed my hand over my jaw. I guessed it was time to shave. "No, I just . . . I've not been in chambers, so . . ."

I set the bags down in the kitchen, and tried not to look at anything but my feet. Already, memories Violet had left in this house threatened to overwhelm me.

"I'll make us some coffee," Darcy said, turning to put the coffeemaker on.

I didn't want to stay but I didn't want to be rude. I glanced over at the dining room, the starched white table-cloth had been removed from the polished walnut table. The flowers and cutlery had been cleared. What would have happened if I'd come back when I'd said I would?

Perhaps Violet would still be here.

"I should go," I said. "You seem busy."

"And you're not?" she asked. "I thought you were always busy."

"Courts are closed, but I'm back in chambers on Monday." Christ, that was only a few days away. I wasn't sure the fog in my brain, or the pain in my heart, would have left me by then.

"Okay, but before you go I want to say something even though I'm pretty sure Violet would kill me before she let me utter a word, but maybe it will help—you don't look good, Alex."

I nodded, unable to disagree.

"The Saturday night that you didn't come home—"

I went to speak, to say how sorry I was, but Darcy raised her hand. "She got into the two London universities she applied for. She loved it here and I think meeting you really made her see the world differently."

My heart ached. Violet had been accepted. If I hadn't fucked up, she'd be coming back and we'd be together.

"She loved you."

I couldn't hold it in. I let out a deep, rumbling groan. I bent over, sharp stabbing pains shooting through my gut. She loved me? How was that possible? Violet was the most beautiful, charming, effervescent woman I'd ever met.

And for some inexplicable reason she'd loved me.

And I'd *lost* her.

"I'm sorry, but I thought you would want to know. Should I have kept quiet?" Darcy asked.

I straightened, grasping the work surface for support. I shook my head.

"She said she had to get out before she got hurt," Darcy continued.

I nodded, breathless from the pain.

Violet had said as much on the phone.

"She's heartbroken, Alex. And you look just . . . broken. Isn't there anything that can be done?"

I cleared my throat and released my hands. "I'm afraid not. She was right to leave." I needed to gather myself. I was hurting but it was bound to happen at some point. It was inevitable. "She knew I could never make her happy in the long run." I should never have thought it could be any different. I wasn't capable of making her happy. I was too selfish. "I'm just sorry that I hurt her."

"Alex." She grabbed my upper arm. "I wasn't blaming you. You're both hurting. All I'm saying is if you love her, don't just give up. I've told her the same thing. You can't just walk away from each other."

"She said she wanted a clean break. I have to respect that."

"No! No, you don't. She upped and left without a discussion and you just let her go." She blew out a puff of air. "Don't you love her?"

"Of course I love her." I'd not admitted it to myself, but it was obvious, wasn't it? I'd never experienced anything like it—neither the joy nor the pain.

"She's hurting and trying to protect herself." Darcy gripped my arms. "You need to prove to her that even though you missed something really important to her, it was a mistake that you regret and won't repeat. Show her it doesn't mean she doesn't matter."

"She matters *more* than anyone ever has. She means *more* than I ever thought anyone could. I love her *more* than any man ever loved a woman."

"Have you told *her* that?"

I hadn't had a chance, had I? She'd come across as so decided in our telephone call. So resolute.

"Well it's obvious . . ."

"I can tell you, Alex, it is *not* obvious. Certainly not to her. You gave her up without a fight—you, a man who fights for a living. A man who's made it his mission in life to win just let her walk away."

I ran through my rebuttal in my head: I couldn't make Violet listen to me. She was three thousand miles away. She'd abandoned me.

And I didn't know how to work less.

She'd done the right thing.

They sounded weak. They were arguments a loser would make.

Darcy was right. I hadn't fought for Violet. I'd accepted defeat before I'd finished making my opening statement.

But some fights couldn't be won. "I don't know if I could ever be the man she deserved."

"You love her and she loves you—it's worth trying, isn't it?"

"For me, maybe." I glanced down at my feet. "But it's too late. She's gone."

"She's a plane ride away and it's been a week. Don't be a fool."

It felt longer and further than that. Was I giving up too easily? If I thought there was a possibility that I could make her happy, that I could convince her to come back to me— that was all I wanted. I looked up. "You think I have a chance?"

"You won't know unless you try. If she's as important as you say she is, then fight for her like it's the case of your career."

Violet was more important than any legal case.

I knew the law but I didn't know women. I didn't understand relationships. I also had no clue how to prove I could change.

"I don't know how," I confessed. Words wouldn't be enough. I needed something more.

"You have a simple choice. Find a way, or lose her."

Losing her wasn't an option if I had a choice. I had to find a way to demonstrate my love and I had no idea where to begin but one thing was for sure: I loved Violet King and I wasn't giving up without a fight.

THIRTY-THREE

Violet

It was the most ridiculous thing in the world. I was sitting here, in my assigned seat, having completed my first week of my MBA, wishing I could tell Alexander all about it. I should be soaking it in, not thinking about a man. Even if I'd thought I was in love with him, which I wasn't. Because that would be ridiculous.

Coming back to New York had been the right thing to do. I felt safer here. In the weeks since I'd left London I'd been busy with the holidays and then changing my start date and preparing for classes. It had helped keep my mind from wandering to Knightley. Mostly.

There were just under two hundred of us in the lecture hall—each in preassigned seats so the teaching assistants could tell who was in attendance and the lecturers could pick unsuspecting names from the chart on the desk to answer their impossibly hard questions. Two hundred complete strangers. I would have thought it was impossible to feel this lonely among so many people.

"Did you think it would be this much work?" Douglas asked from next to me.

I smiled and began to gather up my things. We had hours of prep work to complete for next week and had already been issued three assignments. "It's good to be busy."

The holidays had been exhausting. I'd wanted to spend them in bed, in a dark room with a bottle of vodka, but there was no chance of even a moment's peace at my parents' place. Dad was always up by six, crashing about in the garage just below my bedroom, and there was always some place to be—either at Scarlett and Ryder's, Max and Harper's, Grace and Sam's. So I'd plastered on a smile and gone through the motions regardless of how empty I'd felt inside. Looking back, leaving in secret had been immature. I'd run away rather than having a discussion. At the time I'd not seen any other way. There was nothing he could have said that would have changed my mind, so I'd done what I'd thought had been the best for both of us. The fact that Alexander hadn't told me what I'd wanted to hear as I'd said goodbye—that he loved me and couldn't live without me, and that he promised to make more time for me—made the breakup easier. There were no false promises to be broken, just a clean break before things got too messy, before I fell too hard.

At least he hadn't loved me. If he had told me he had, I wasn't sure if I would have been strong enough to walk away. But he hadn't and here I was, facing my future.

Being in college, even if it was under a mountain of work, was better than being surrounded by happy couples. At least here I was doing what I wanted to. School forced me to think about the future and not the past. I *refused* to think about what might have been.

"A bunch of us are going for a drink. You wanna come?" Douglas asked.

Did I? I wasn't sure. Homework beckoned, but I didn't want it to own me. I wanted to enjoy myself, too. I realized what I needed was balance between the future and the present. "Maybe just for an hour."

He grinned. "Perfect. By then, you'll be a beer in and hopefully I'll be able to convince you to stay for the evening."

The smile, the eye contact, the way his eyebrows pulsed when he talked—I'd seen it all before. I smiled, wanting to like him more than I did.

A group of us, wrapped in padded coats and wool hats, gloves, and scarves headed toward a bar on Amsterdam. The last time I'd been out for drinks in Manhattan had been the night Darcy had invited me to London. So much had happened since. I could never have imagined that I'd be studying again, let alone have ambitions to set up a management consultancy business.

It might never happen, but I was willing to take a risk, make an investment in the future.

"What can I get you to drink?" Douglas asked as we got inside. Pre-London Violet would have ordered a cocktail. I'd drunk wine with Alexander. Things had changed. Now I was open to something different. "Just a beer. Whatever you're having," I replied. Douglas and a couple of others went to the bar, while the rest of us secured a table, pulling off our outdoor clothing, already hot from coming inside.

"Thank God that's over," said one of the girls I hadn't met. "Hopefully things will ease up a little next week."

"I heard it gets worse," the girl from California said.

Luckily, I didn't have a long commute to contend with. I'd borrowed the money from my brother for tuition, so I wasn't forced to take a part-time job. I would have more time than most, so the volume of work didn't bother me. I didn't want any spare time. Too much space meant thoughts of Alexander would filter in and that just wasn't acceptable. Also, the last few years had been wasted. I needed to make up for lost time. I didn't want an easy ride—I wanted to squeeze every last drop out of this experience, learn everything I could.

"Beer," Douglas said, thumping down a huge jug of foaming alcohol on the table. Another student set down a jug and Christine, who also sat next to me in lectures, put down a tray of glasses.

"Here's to getting drunk," a dark-haired girl—Erin or Erica, I thought—said from across the table.

Douglas turned to me and tapped his glass against mine. "Here's to getting drunk with you."

I smiled. I'd have to put some distance between us. Before London I would probably have been naked with him before the end of the day, but he held no appeal. Next to Knightley, Douglas seemed like a boy. His eagerness, the way he was unable to disguise what he was thinking, it all seemed so juvenile compared to Alexander's contained passion.

Such bright images flooded my brain whenever I thought of him. He would have finished his trial by now. He'd be on to the next thing. No doubt the files were already piling up in his office. He may even have expelled Sebastian. Life would have gone back to normal for Alexander, as if I'd never even existed.

But my life would never be the same.

Loving Knightley had enabled me to unbind myself from the shackles I'd worn since college. It had shown me that my feelings for my college boyfriend were nothing in comparison. If Alexander had betrayed me in the way David had, I would never have survived—my view of the world would have been so completely shattered. But he'd never treat me like that. Alexander was a lot of things, and he may have hurt me, but he wasn't capable of betrayal.

Alexander Knightley had taught me what I was capable of, what I wanted, and who I was.

THIRTY-FOUR

Alexander

I slumped into my chair. I was done.

Sebastian sat and put his head on his desk.

"Go home," I said.

"I don't think I'll make it." He sounded pathetic. The trial had been exhausting, but it was done. The leftover adrenaline would see him into a cab.

I picked up a note that had been left on my desk from Lance, asking me to pop into his office before I left for the night. I glanced at my watch. It was only three but it felt later. I'd go and see him and head back to the hotel and book a flight.

We wouldn't get a verdict for days. Maybe longer, and I wasn't going to hang around for it. I needed to go and find Violet. It had been nearly a week since I'd seen Darcy, and I'd been rehearsing all my arguments carefully, building my case. Now this trial was over, I just needed to find her and start fighting for her. I just didn't know if I could win her back in a weekend. Any good barrister knows the arguments of his opponents before he hears them. I knew Violet would challenge me. She'd want to know how I could prove to her that I'd be different. How I could *guarantee* that I wouldn't hurt her again. So far I had no evidence.

I stood up. "I don't want you here when I get back," I said and stalked out to find Lance.

His office was further along the corridor in a quiet spot with a view of the courtyard. He'd been in the same space for the last thirty years, and before that, in the room next door.

I knocked at the half-open door and stepped inside.

"Good to see you, Alex, come in," he said.

I couldn't remember the last time I'd been in this office, or any room in chambers other than my room or the clerks' office. And of course, the admin staff's room when I went in to drop off one of the gifts I used to buy Violet. I took a deep breath at the thought of her. I had no idea where she was or what she was doing. If she thought of me, she'd know exactly where I'd be and what I'd be working on. It seemed unfair and uneven. I couldn't even properly imagine her— I'd never seen her on her home territory.

"Take a seat," Lance said, lifting his chin in the direction of one of the chairs opposite his desk. "This has been a very complicated case—you must be exhausted."

I nodded and sat, resting my arms on the mahogany arms of the chair. I was also as confident as one could be about the verdict. The arguments had presented well and the judge had seemed sympathetic. But Lance was right—I was shattered. I couldn't remember ever feeling this tired.

"I hear from Craig that your performance has been outstanding. Lots of people have been talking about how you're just like your father."

It didn't surprise me that Craig had been in to watch

me. It was a crucial case in my career and one that could have broken me. It hadn't. A flash of Violet's smile appeared in my mind. Maybe it had.

"But I am a little worried about you," Lance said, his brow furrowed.

Lance had been a constant mentor to me throughout my career, but I couldn't remember him ever saying he was worried about me.

"Don't concern yourself. I just need a good night's rest and a decent bottle of red wine." I smiled but Lance remained stony faced.

"We were very sad to lose Violet. I'm sure you were too," he said. He scanned my face as if he were inspecting me, looking for my reaction. Was he trying to gauge how I felt about her leaving?

I drew in a deep breath. "Yes, well, Columbia's a good school. I'm sure she'll do well." I was planning to fly out this weekend to put my case to her—to start my fight for her.

Lance nodded slowly. "I realize I'm speaking out of turn . . ."

I tightened my grip on the arms of the chair. What was he going to say? Was he going to tell me I'd been a fool? I knew that already.

"But I think Violet was good for you. Now, I don't begin to presume what went on between the two of you, but I do think she was the only woman who ever matched you stroke for stroke. You two are quite different, but Violet is your equal."

I swallowed. Lance and I rarely discussed anything personal, and I didn't quite know how to react. "I've no doubt that Violet is at the very least my equal." She was more than I could ever possibly deserve. "But you know how bad I am with women. I put work first like I always have done. And now Violet's back in New York."

"I'm not so sure you're bad with women. More that you're on unfamiliar territory as far as a woman as special as Violet is concerned. This job is demanding. And it can be a very lonely life—married or single. I've been lucky with Flavia. And not because she's understanding about my hours but because I *want* to get home to her. She is a sufficient counterweight to the pull of our profession. You need a woman who you yearn to see at the end of the day. If you've found that in Violet, you mustn't let her go."

I sighed and my shoulders dropped. That's exactly who Violet was, the only woman who could inspire me to give up Saturday nights at work. Now that she was gone, I wanted more than Saturday nights together, but how would I prove that to her? "I'm planning to fly over this weekend. I need to apologize properly. I messed up."

"But you're worried it won't be enough."

"I feel like I'm missing the evidence—how do I prove to her that it will be different? I'm going to try."

He nodded, and his gaze wandered around the room as if he were trying to come up with a solution for me. "Well I might have just the thing for you. One of the reasons I asked you to pop in was because I just had a call from an old friend of mine. You know I have lectured in New York before now?"

I frowned. "I thought you did that at Harvard?" What had that got to do with anything?

"Yes, Harvard and also Columbia. My old chum is the president of Columbia law school, and he needs someone to help him out of a hole. I was hoping you might be the man for the job."

"What does he need?"

"Someone to take the international law module at Columbia this semester. The person they had lined up has been taken sick at the very last minute."

I'd expected him to say that his friend wanted some advice. Maybe wanted me to contribute a chapter to a text-book. A teaching post was the very last thing I was expecting Lance to suggest. "Lecture? But I've never considered teaching. Why—"

"Maybe not. But you admit you're tired. And Violet leaving is upsetting news for all of us, not least for you. This could be a chance to reassess what you want from your life, your career. You can think about your practice, decide whether you need a change in direction."

I frowned, wondering why he'd think my practice would need a change in direction. "My career? That's the only thing I am certain of. I've spent so long laying the foundation. I think I'm finally on the right track."

"You mean your father's track."

I wanted to be the best at the bar, so of course it made sense that I would follow the footsteps of the best who went before me. Those footsteps just happened to be my father's.

"The thing is, your father's legacy is just that—a career left behind, seen with the benefit of hindsight. We can discard the parts that don't fit into his legend because it's in the past. But this isn't his career we're talking about—it's yours. Your time. Your life. You need to create something you can be proud of and stop measuring yourself against a man who isn't here to tell you that there were downsides to leaving the legacy he did, sacrifices he wouldn't make again."

I only measured myself against him because he happened to be the best. Not because he was my father. And he'd only ever regaled me with stories of the good times. I'd never heard him say anything negative about the choices he'd made.

"There are sacrifices in whatever choices one makes," I replied. "I just want to be the best at what I do." I leaned forward in my chair.

"But what does being the best mean? It has many interpretations. Does it mean earning a lot of money, acquiring a myth to equal Alexander the Great, getting the best cases? Maybe it means having a career that allows you to give back to the generation behind you. Perhaps it means being a loving father, or being well-travelled and experiencing as much of the world as it has to offer? It could be enough to be a dedicated, devoted husband who knows the love of his equal." He paused, bringing his hands together. "Being successful can mean a lot of things. I know your father felt like he failed you and your brother, but by the time he understood that there was more to life than law, he was too old to know how to do anything else. Too old to tell the people who looked up to him and relied on him that he wanted a change. Don't let it be too late for you."

I cleared my throat, beating down the emotion rising in me. I could never imagine my father failing at anything. The man I knew was a conqueror, a winner. He wasn't regretful.

I wasn't sure which way was up at the moment. Could my father have wanted more, something different? Had he ever lost anything as precious to him as Violet was to me?

"You don't need to have the same career he did for you to honor him, for him to be proud of you. I think he'd want more for you."

I couldn't speak.

"Watching you over the years," Lance continued. "I've often wondered whether your drive was really a desire to get your father's attention—no doubt you were starved of it as a child. But actually I wonder if you're searching for him in these walls, among the paper. You know your father's office was a similar mess."

"I remember." I smiled.

"Maybe working is my way of keeping him close." My father was all around me while I was in chambers—it felt as if he were still here and I was still eight years old, sitting at his desk, surrounded by paper.

"I think so." Lance nodded. "Maybe it's time to let him go and look to your future, not your past."

We sat there for a few minutes in silence as I thought back to memories of my father in this very building. I wished I'd had more time with him, gotten a chance to share an office with him the way I'd thought I would as a child. But Lance was right, working myself into the ground wasn't going to bring him back.

If I let my father and his legacy fade from the finish line in front of me, what was I left with? What did I really want? I couldn't bear the thought of not having seen the world before it was too late, to not love and be loved. As much as my career was important to me, I knew that there were other things out there—Violet had showed me that. I just always saw any other desires or goals as something I'd pick up when my race to be the best was over.

One thing was for sure. Being without Violet felt wrong and I had to make it right. There was no way she was going to hang around and wait for me to finish anything, and that meant something had to change. I had to change. I had to *show* her that I'd learned from her leaving. Not just *tell* her.

"I think you're right, Lance." I was like a supertanker going in one direction, deciding I might want to change course, head for the Med and transform into a yacht. Wasn't it just impossible?

"Teaching would be an experiment. An opportunity to try something new and decide if you want to change track or just slow down."

Was it really as easy as Lance made it sound? "It's a risk," I said.

"But not going, the risk is you lose Violet. Three months isn't a great deal of time in the scheme of things. It may be long enough for you to get some perspective. I'm sure we can rearrange things so you don't have to worry about anything while you're gone."

Changing the course of my career would certainly surprise her. I'd expected her to move continents to study in order to stay with me. It had never been a consideration that I would be the one to cross the ocean. It hadn't even occurred to me. But was it really possible? For *three months*? "Wouldn't that devastate my practice? This case will create a real buzz and I—"

He silenced me with a look. "Nothing in relation to your career will be devastated in three months. Teaching is very likely to enhance it. And you might even enjoy it. Columbia is one of the best law schools in America, but they need someone to start immediately."

I swallowed. Could I just abandon everything I'd built here and go off and become a professor? "What do I know about teaching?"

"You'd have assistants to help you prepare. They like to have guest professors. When I retire, I'd like to do it a little longer. It allows me to remember what it was to be young. And I like to feel as if I'm sharing my knowledge."

"You think I can just walk away for three months?"

"You're not walking away from anything. You're moving

towards something. At the very least it would allow some room in your life for conscious thought, to uncouple your father's myth from your destiny."

I blew out a puff of air, leaned forward, and rested my head in my hands. Perhaps it would be what I needed. At the moment I was hurtling toward my target at a million miles an hour, but was using so much energy I wasn't sure I'd survive until the end. I'd already lost Violet along the way—what was next? My sanity?

"You wouldn't be sitting on a beach doing nothing. You'd make new contacts, and add an impressive post to your CV."

Whether or not I believed it, I could tell Lance thought this was a tremendous opportunity at the time I needed it most. And I trusted him. He'd been a guide throughout my career and never steered me wrong. Perhaps this was the day I needed to seize. Three months would go by in a blink of an eye and before I knew it, I'd return, reinvigorated and refreshed. I might have even won Violet back.

"Three months. Just seize the day," I said out loud but to myself. Saying the words was like tipping weight from a sinking raft. Instantly I felt lighter and more energized. It would be a new challenge, something completely different, and it might prove to Violet how much I loved her.

"I think I'm interested. You think the clerks can rearrange things here in chambers?"

He smiled. "The graves are full of indispensable men."

I nodded. It was arrogant to assume my caseload wouldn't be easily distributed between other members of chambers. "I could go this weekend even," I said. I'd planned to fly to New York this weekend anyway. I didn't want to wait a moment longer than I must to see Violet again, to apologize in person. "This president friend of yours. He just happened to call you? It seems like rather a coincidence."

"I spoke to him last night," he said and smiled. It was the perfect lawyer's response—a careful description of the truth.

"You never know, it might be the best thing to ever have happened to me."

"Or that might happen while you're there."

The longer I was without Violet, the more I realized how much she meant, how foolish I'd been to spend any time at work if I could have spent it with her instead. Lance was right—she was the only woman who could pull my attention away from work, show me there was more to life, and I needed to win her back and then hold on to her. I hoped going to New York and lecturing was the evidence I needed to show her how important she was.

THIRTY-FIVE

Alexander

Lance had been right about coming to New York. I'd known it the moment I'd agreed to come, but as I'd stepped off the plane yesterday a weight had lifted, not from my shoulders but from my very soul. Teaching was something my father had never done. There was nothing to live up to, and I had no caseload to manage, no concern that the work would dry up, no pleadings to draft, no strategy to create. For the first time in my life I was *excited* about my job—not pleased because something had gone well or relieved I'd got some work in, but genuinely *excited*.

Campus was quiet as I wandered across the South Lawn Saturday morning. I'd wanted to take a look at the place before I started on Monday.

The place reminded me a little of the Inns of Court. It was relatively peaceful among the bustle of Manhattan. But the buildings were larger—a pastiche of various eras rather than the organic mishmash of Lincoln's Inn. I enjoyed the difference and took comfort from the similarities.

The law school and the business school were quite separate, but it felt odd to be so close to Violet, yet for her to have no idea I was here. Perhaps my exploration today was really a desire to bump into her. I hadn't decided how to tell her I was here or even what to say.

The campus was big, but it wasn't beyond the realm of possibility that we'd run into each other, and I didn't want her to be caught off guard. I had to let her know as soon as possible.

And of course, I wanted to hear her voice.

I wanted things to be different between us.

Would she see that me being here was proof I was capable of creating a future with her? She was the only thing that had ever been important to me other than my work, and her leaving had wounded me deeply. It had changed me forever.

I pulled out my phone. I'd call her. Warn her I was here.

My heartbeat thrummed in my ears as I dialed.

"Alex?" She sounded confused, as though she couldn't begin to think why I'd be on the other end of the line. I clenched my teeth at the idea that I had no place in her life anymore.

"Yes. It's me. It's good to hear your voice."

I sighed at the sound of her breathing on the other end of the line.

"Are you okay?" she asked. Her voice was sad, as if I were torturing her, and I hated it.

"I just wanted to let you know that I've taken a teaching post at Columbia law school. It's only for a few months. And I was wondering while I was here whether you'd agree to meet with me. I would really like a chance to apologize face-to-face."

"You're teaching?" she asked.

I wanted to tell her all about it, but I didn't know if I should say any more. "Yes. Someone's taken sick."

"And so you've left your job? You're not a barrister anymore?"

I took a seat on the steps in front of Butler Library. "I've not abandoned the bar. I'm just taking a sabbatical. I need time to reassess my priorities. A chance to redeem myself. I miss you."

"I had to protect my heart, Alexander."

"I know, and you were right to do so. I'd never provided any indication that I could give you more than snatched moments here and there."

"But I shouldn't have run away and I'm sorry for that. I should have found the courage to tell you I wasn't coming back," she said and paused.

"I don't blame you for running. I understand."

"And now you're in New York," she said.

I sighed. "I am. I was burnt out. Exhausted. I'd lost something important to me and it affected me in a way . . ." She didn't need to hear about my pain. I'd caused her enough. "I spoke to Lance, and he suggested I take this teaching post to reassess things."

"It seems like a big coincidence that it's at Columbia."

"Lance is friends with the president of the university."

"I didn't know that," she said, her voice quietening as if she were thinking while speaking.

"A happy coincidence, I hope." I paused, hoping she would agree with me. At least she didn't hang up. "I was wondering if you'd meet me. I'd like us to talk and if possible work through what happened in London. I realize I was an idiot, and I want to make it up to you."

She sighed. "I don't have a lot of time. I'm just trying to focus on the program and get settled."

I closed my eyes, trying to block out the pain of her rejection. But I was here for three months, and I wasn't about to give up without a fight. "Maybe later in the semester then, when you have a little more time."

"Maybe," she replied.

I swallowed. "I miss you."

There was a pause before she spoke as if she were carefully considering her response. "I should go. I hope you enjoy the teaching thing."

It sounded so final, as though she had no intention of seeing me again while I was here.

"Okay, it's been good to hear your voice. And I'm free anytime when you feel ready to talk."

"Goodbye, Alexander."

I couldn't say goodbye. I wouldn't.

I waited for her to hang up and then put the phone back into my jacket pocket. Today was just opening arguments. My fight for Violet hadn't even begun.

THIRTY-SIX

Violet

The call from Alexander was the last thing I'd been expecting. Knightley wasn't a man to chase after a woman.

But here he was. In New York.

I couldn't help but be flattered as well as surprised.

The reason I'd left London, left him, was because I didn't think he was capable of being anything other than a man who thought only about his work. It never would have occurred to me that he might come to New York, albeit for three months. It seemed so out of character.

Because it didn't seem to make sense, I decided that I had to see it myself. After an annoying amount of time on the law school website, I'd managed to uncover Knightley's teaching schedule.

I was a little older than most of the students filing into the lecture hall, but no one said anything as I took a seat at the back of the class, tucked away in the shadows.

Knightley stepped to the front in his beautifully cut, handmade suit as if he might have been on his way into chambers. The titter of the female students echoed through the hall. I bet there had been few more handsome lecturers in Columbia's history.

He addressed the room in a loud, confident manner and seemed to know the material despite being only a couple of weeks into the job. He was just so hopelessly clever. So annoyingly charming.

I barely focused on what he was saying—seeing him brought everything whooshing back. I'd been testing myself, seeing if my feelings for him had passed. I'd hoped I'd be cured, but no. I loved this man. Still.

Since his call a little over two weeks ago, I'd done nothing but think about what him being in the US meant— could mean—for him, for me, for us.

He'd made no attempt to contact me in the days since his last call. I'd know because I hadn't been more than a foot away from my phone at any point. Just in case.

I couldn't get over how a man so devoted to his career had so easily put that on pause. Rightly or wrongly, it made me wonder if I'd done the right thing by leaving. Should I have told him what I needed? Should I have told him I loved him? Given us more time?

Clearly, there was so much more to the man at the front of the hall than I'd ever known. But I yearned to learn it all. Watching him, it felt as if he was not just my past but perhaps part of my future.

When the lecture was over, a host of students lined up to ask questions. There was no lack of admiration for this man even without me in the room.

My feelings hadn't changed, I was sure of that. And now I'd seen the evidence that he had changed his whole life, I was ready to talk. Ready to hear what he had to say.

Alexander

The teaching assistants were good at helping me fend off questions at the end of lectures, but that still left me with a string of students out the door, which after thirty minutes since the end of my lectures, I was only just finished with. I enjoyed their enthusiasm and clever questions. They had time to think, discuss, and debate—I'd forgotten how thrilling and stimulating being a student could be. I'd felt like them once, back when it hadn't become a job, when it hadn't taken over my life. Occasionally, the questions got a little personal. I was surprised at how confident some of the women were in asking me about my relationship status, but I managed to be suitably vague without encouraging them or lying.

When the final student had left, the teaching assistants and I picked up the leftover handouts and headed out. Ready to lock up my office, I was looking forward to my second full weekend in New York. For the first time in as long as I could remember, I had nothing specific to do.

"Is this your first time in New York City?" Gideon, one of the teaching assistants, asked.

"I came once as a student, but that was a long time ago. I've never worked anywhere but London."

"I would love to work in England. And France," he replied. "Perhaps in Asia. I see myself as some kind of nomadic law professor eventually."

I hoped he'd fulfill his dream. It seemed so much more sophisticated than mine had been at his age. I'd just wanted to get a tenancy and start earning some money. I never thought beyond that—I'd simply walked the path my father had walked. Looking back, it seemed so pedestrian.

"We're all going for a drink, if you'd like to join us," he

said as we came out of the double doors and into the main corridor.

"I—"

I stopped dead in my tracks. Violet stood directly opposite, leaning on the wall looking straight at me. My heart began to pound. Christ, she was beautiful. Had she been waiting for me? Was she here to talk?

Whatever she wanted, I didn't want to hear it in front of my TA. I turned to Gideon, and he held out his hand to take the papers I was carrying. "I'm sorry; I can't make this evening. Another time. Enjoy your weekend," I said.

He nodded and went on his way, the chatter of the TAs mellowing the further away they got.

I turned back to Violet. She smiled, but it wasn't her breezy office smile. This was intimate, knowing. "Hi, Professor Knightley."

"Violet King, fancy meeting you here." It was so good to see her, to reanimate the memories I constantly replayed in my mind. It comforted me to see she was still the same, to know her curves would still fit against my body in the perfect way they always had.

She tilted her head. "I had to come and see if it were true. Had *the* Alexander Knightley really decided to come Stateside to *teach*?"

God, I'd missed her teasing—she never let me take myself too seriously. "Well, here I am."

"You were very impressive in there." She lifted her chin in the direction of the lecture hall.

Had she been in my lecture? "I'm not sure what you expected." I wanted to reach out and touch her, to pull her close and never let her go.

"I suppose you were who I thought you'd be."

I smiled. "I'm very glad that your expectations weren't completely dashed."

"Not completely." She held my gaze as if she wanted to say more. "Anyway," she said, pushing off the wall and standing straight. "I heard you were new on campus. I thought you might need a tour, an orientation of sorts."

I narrowed my eyes. Was she trying to be my friend? Did she want to talk? I didn't care as long as she was here. "I was just thinking that an orientation was just what I needed."

Silently, we started toward the exit.

When we got to the doors, I held one open as she walked through and out into the frigid, fresh air and toward the quad. I followed, and as we started down the stone steps she began to speak. "Before I left London, on that Saturday night when you came back late—"

"You will never know how sorry I am. If I had just set an alarm—"

"I know. But I need to say I'm sorry to have left like I did. I was trying to act like it was no big deal."

I exhaled, conflicted because as much as I missed her, I knew that she'd been right to leave. I was desperately sorry I'd let her down, but her leaving me had been exactly what I needed. "You did the right thing," I said.

We stopped at the bottom of the steps, and I watched as she looked out over the quad, avoiding my stare.

"You didn't want me to stay?" she asked.

I took a deep breath, keeping my hands in my pockets to stop myself from reaching out. "I have learned a great deal since you came into my life. First and foremost that you deserve to have a wonderful life with someone who worships and adores you. I also learned that I didn't know how to do that, not properly at least." I sighed. "I don't think you made the wrong decision by leaving, Violet. I wouldn't have been the man you needed me to be. The man you deserved. Not then."

"And now?" She lowered her gaze to the floor and balled her hands into fists.

"I want things to be different. I'm trying. I want to prove that I'm more than a barrister."

She gazed up at me, a crease between her eyebrows as if she wasn't sure she'd heard me.

"I'm just trying to take each day at a time; to spend these weeks in New York proving to you that I can be a man who deserves a woman like you. I know I want to be that man. But I need practice. I just know that I'm not ready to let you go. I won't ever be ready."

"That's why you left London?" Her gaze dipped to where I had my hands pushed into my pockets.

"I didn't want to pursue a profession that required me to sacrifice everything else in my life. And . . ." I couldn't hold back any longer. I reached out and trailed the back of my finger down her cheek, then lifted her chin so she was looking at me. "I came for you. To show you how I feel. I've never wanted a woman like I want you—I didn't realize I was capable of these feelings."

The delicate blush that bloomed across her cheek was something I'd savor forever.

"You leaving was a huge wake-up call for me. It almost broke me. I'll never be the same again. But when you left, it forced me off the relentless road I'd been on. For the first time, I'm doing what I *want* to do rather than what I feel I *should* be doing."

"And now you're here."

"I am, for you and for me. I want to prove to you how serious I am about you."

She put her finger on my lips, silencing me.

"I left London because I knew that however much you wanted to do anything else, you were hardwired to put work first."

I nodded. She was completely right.

"But now you're here . . . I don't know what to think anymore. I never imagined you'd leave chambers for a weekend, let alone three months. It makes me think that you're right, that maybe something has shifted for you. Maybe there's a chance . . ."

My instinct was to push, to ask her to take me back, to try again to see if we worked. But I wanted her to want it as much as I did.

Her gaze fluttered around the campus behind me as if she were searching for answers. "You've switched on this part of me that lay dormant for a long time—the bit that wants to look forward to the future. But whenever I picture what lies in front of me, I'm always standing next to you."

I had to close my eyes for fear that I was dreaming. Did this beautiful, accomplished woman want to take a chance on me?

"I can't guarantee anything," I said. "Except that I will love you for the rest of my life."

I knew that if I focused on anything, I could make it work. If I made her the center of my world, everything else would fall into place.

Her eyes were glassy with tears. She reached up and smoothed her fingers across my cheekbone. "How about we seize each day together for the rest of our lives?"

DID I *expect* to be lying in bed in my New York hotel room, watching as the love of my life slept peacefully beside me?

Never.

Had I *hoped* it might happen?

Always.

"Hey," Violet said, her eyes closed and her voice croaky with too little sleep. She extended her arm, and I caught her hand and pressed a kiss to her palm.

She smiled and stroked my face. "I love that you're here with me."

"I love *you*, Violet King. You are the most important part of my life."

She pulled me over her, slipping her hands down my back, pressing her lips against mine.

I braced my arms on either side of her and pulled back to look at her. "I'm the luckiest man on Earth. I swear I'm going to do everything I can to make you happy."

She pushed my hair away from my face. "I believe you. I believe *in* you."

My heart skipped. Whatever happened, I would always try to put us and our relationship first. "I believe in us. And I love you." Now that the words were out, now that she knew, I couldn't stop telling her, over and over.

"I love you, too," she said.

"Still?"

"Always," she replied.

I smiled and dipped my head, licking across her collarbone.

"But only because of the things you can do to my body —you get that, don't you? I mean, if your dick was ever to fall off, that'd be it for me. I'd be outta here." She grinned as she opened her legs and I settled between her thighs, my hard cock teasing her wetness.

"I'm okay with being used," I replied. I wasn't sure if she was just teasing me or if she was trying to hold back a part of her heart that she wasn't yet willing to relinquish— maybe she wasn't ready to trust me entirely quite yet. But that was okay. I knew myself well enough to know I'd never give any reason for her to regret giving her delicate heart to me. I knew how to work hard to get where I wanted to be, and in Violet's arms, between her thighs, sharing her world was the only place for me.

I slid my lips against hers and braced myself for being inside her again without a condom. Last night we'd agreed nothing should be between us from now on. She was on the pill and the only woman I'd slept with since that first time in my office. She'd be the only woman I'd sleep with for the rest of my life.

She tipped her head back and dug her nails into my shoulders as I slid into her. Fuck she felt good. Tight. Wet. Perfect.

With Violet, I understood for the first time in my life how good sex could be. How it was so much better because of how I felt about her. A delicious gloss on a fundamental feeling, an intimacy I'd never shared with anyone before her.

As I moved above her, slowly at first, my skin sang as she traced her toes down the back of my thighs, fluttered her fingers down my spine, and arched her back.

Lazily, I rocked in and out of her, wanting to stay like this forever, in this blissful state of pre-orgasm fuzz—the place only Violet had ever brought me.

"Alexander," she half whispered, half groaned. "Alexander."

I savored every word, every moan, grunt, and gasp from her lips. I'd missed them all. I'd been without them too long.

She flung her arms over her head and tightened around me. She was always beautiful, but it felt as if I possessed her when she came. Violet's orgasms were mine.

Her sexy, sultry smile of post-climactic satisfaction gave me the signal that she was ready for a little bit more. Her first orgasm had been slow and lazy, a wake-up call.

She swept her fingers across the top of my brow, tracing the edges of effort that lay there. Her soft and subtle touch disguised how wicked I knew she could be. And then, as if to prove my point, she clenched my cock and grinned. "More," she whispered.

She'd once warned me not to be too gentle with her, and although she liked me to be tender at times, I knew she enjoyed hard and sharp—the rough with the smooth. I wanted to notch up the pleasure. I pivoted my hips and pushed in deeper. Her eyes widened and she bit her bottom lip. I slid my hand under her bottom, holding her, pressing my fingers into her perfectly soft flesh, pushing her against me as my body slammed into hers.

She gasped as I dipped my head and grazed my teeth across her neck, tasting her, drinking in that scent of Indian summer I'd thought I'd lost forever. I drove deeper, faster, harder, desperate to show how much I wanted her, how good I could make her feel. I wanted to prove to her she'd never need anything else but this.

Pleasure circled at the base of my spine and began to rise. I closed my eyes, trying to concentrate, dampening down this overwhelming need. Sensation ricocheted across my body, from her fingernails scraping against my jaw to the sound of her groan beneath me.

Fuck.

This woman.

I drove deeper, and each time she got a little tighter, a

little wetter, and my climax gathered pace. My jaw tightened. I didn't want to get there without her. Violet's eyes widened, as if she were shocked that anything could feel this good, this big, this all-consuming. She clawed at my chest, her body clenching, her movements beneath me becoming jagged and desperate—her eyes watered as she gazed at me. She came beneath me—she was fucking beautiful. Finally I gave in to my orgasm, calling out her name, desperate for her to know everything I did was for her.

I lifted myself up from where I'd collapsed on top of her, my heartbeat still clattering against my chest. I dropped a kiss on her lips.

"I love you," she said, her palms pressed against my chest. "The way I feel for you is . . ." She pulled her brows together. "Binary. Permanent. I'd never felt it before you. It's as if what I feel has been specifically invented. Just for you."

I groaned at her words, so earnest and open. I would spend my whole life protecting this woman's heart, doing everything I could to show her how much I loved her in everything I did. That was my job now—she was my priority, my future, my destiny. It was all her.

EPILOGUE

Violet

Six Months Later

"Bicontinental," I repeated, slower this time, making exaggerated shapes with my mouth so hopefully my brother would catch on.

"I don't even know what that means," Max replied, handing me the potato salad.

I took it and put a spoonful on my plate before passing it to Alexander. "I thought you were the smart one? The King of Wall Street or some other such bullshit." I rolled my eyes.

"She just means she and Alex are going to be living between New York and London," Scarlett added, putting down a huge bowl of mac and cheese in the center of the table before taking a seat. All of us were here tonight—one final dinner in Connecticut before Alexander and I headed back to London after nearly six months in New York. Alexander had extended his break from chambers until the end of the academic year. Then we'd planned to spend the summer and the next semester of my MBA degree at a university in London on an exchange program. Then I'd head back to New York with Alexander in January to finish school.

"You as well?" Max asked. "Can't any of the women in this family pick a side?"

"I think it works. You get to appreciate the best of both worlds," Ryder said.

"Exactly," Alexander said. "We squeeze more out of life this way."

I rested my hand on Knightley's knee, still shocked by the way he'd embraced his teaching and a whole new way of life. He insisted it was entirely selfish on his part, because it meant he spent more time with me. I wasn't going to argue —it worked for us.

"Columbia has agreed to let me teach from January to April each year, then I'll practice law from April for the rest of the year back in London. It forces a balance in my career," Alexander said.

"Where does that leave you, Violet?" Max asked.

"Happy," I replied. "After I graduate, I can take on assignments in London and New York and I'll make it work."

"I'm proud of you," my brother said. "And glad you went back to school."

"We need to write your brother a check." Alexander nudged me. "For your fees."

Alexander had suggested a couple of times that he repay my brother the money I borrowed for tuition, but I'd always been good at changing the subject. Still, I couldn't help but enjoy the way he said "we" and considered us a unit.

"I'll pay him back when I start earning," I muttered, taking a forkful of cucumber in my mouth.

"What's mine is yours, Violet. Even if you have refused to use the cards I've had put in your name. There is no yours and mine. Only ours." He twisted toward me and cupped my neck with his hand.

I sighed. His touch hypnotized me.

"It's not like we can have separate bank accounts when we're married," he added.

The noise and the chatter of the table stopped, and the whole room stared at us.

"Do you have something you want to tell us?" My dad asked from the top of the table.

"No, it's just—"

"Violet and I will be married," Alexander said. "When she finally agrees."

It wasn't that I'd *disagreed* exactly. I just hadn't said *yes* to Knightley's three hundred proposals.

My dad looked at me. "You don't want to marry him? You don't have to, you know."

I laughed. My father didn't give a crap that Alexander was sitting right beside me. "I do want to marry him, Dad. I just want to finish school first."

"Don't let him push you into anything," he warned.

Alexander went to speak, but I patted his thigh to stop him. "He's really not. I swear, Daddy, if I asked him, he'd fly up to the moon to straighten it out just to make me happy. I love him, and I really want to marry him. I just . . ."

Why was finishing school so important to me? Maybe I felt the need to prove to myself that I could do it on my own. Whether or not we were married wouldn't change anything between us. I was his forever, and I knew he felt the same way about me. I turned to Alexander. "I won't be Mrs. Knightley, you know. I'll still be Violet King."

He looked at me as if I'd gone bananas. "Of course

you'll still be Violet King. I wouldn't expect you to change your name. I'm happy enough to be Alexander King if that's what you want."

I snapped my head around at the choking sounds coming from my brother and father, and I began to giggle. "I don't think that's necessary. We have plenty of King men around here."

"I'm still Scarlett King," my sister said.

"And I'm still Harper Jayne."

"Is that what you were worried about?" he asked.

"No. I'm not worried. I mean, of course I'm going to marry you."

His eyebrows shot up and his smile began to threaten the corners of his mouth. "But what?"

"But nothing." I shrugged. "I'm just not sure it means anything. I know how I feel about you, how you feel about me. Isn't that all we need?"

"I guess so. Having children when we're not married won't bother you?"

"Kids?" Max barked. "Are you pregnant?"

"No, but yes, we want kids together," I snapped back at him. "We're sharing the rest of our lives together. Of course we've talked about this stuff."

"I love your sister, Max, and I'm going to spend the rest of my life trying to make her happy just as I see you do with Harper and the way Ryder does with Scarlett. I hope that's clear to everyone."

"Good man," my dad muttered.

Darcy sighed. "So romantic."

"You next," Scarlett said. "I know he's out there for you."

Darcy shrugged. "I've lost hope." She tipped back her drink.

If I could find love, it would happen for Darcy, no doubt in my mind.

"Everyone needs to understand, we're just figuring out the logistics," I said. "We're in love, and married or single, in New York or London, with or without kids, we'll be together forever."

"I'll drink to that," Darcy squealed.

"Welcome to the family," Max said, raising his glass.

I gazed up at Alexander, and he dropped a kiss on my lips.

He was my Knightley in shining armor and our fairytale was as real as it got.

Alexander

Six Months Later

I glanced up from where I was sitting, reading the paper. Violet came into the kitchen and looked around.

"She did a really good job, don't you think?"

I shrugged. "If you like it, I'm happy." We'd moved into our new townhouse on Chesterfield Hill in Mayfair and had it completely redecorated. Violet and I had both been too busy to be involved and had left the interior designer to make most of the decisions. The free time we had we liked to focus on each other and not wallpaper.

"Are you packed?" she asked.

I closed the paper and folded it, placing it on the work surface. "Packed and ready to go. The car should be here any moment."

"I'm so excited for Christmas in Connecticut. Everyone in my family goes all out with the decorations."

We were headed back to the US after spending the last six months in London. When I'd come back to chambers after Columbia, I'd found I was more able to walk away in the evenings and at the weekend. A connection had been snapped while I'd been in New York, and I was no longer pushing myself to do more and work harder. It was ironic that the quality of work I was getting now was far beyond what I could have expected before I'd adjusted my priorities. Lance had been right—introducing variety in my life had made me approach the law in a different way. I spotted issues earlier, worked more efficiently, was more creative in finding solutions. Even better than that, I was enjoying it more.

I spun on my stool to face her. "We're going to have to find a place in New York as well."

Violet slid her arm around my shoulders. "I know. But can we buy something new that doesn't need decorating? I don't want to live with the smell of paint any longer. And I want to travel. Get away."

"Where do you want to go?" I asked.

She shrugged. "Anywhere I'm with you. Maybe South Africa? Or Thailand. Is there any place you'd like to visit?"

"When I was younger I wanted to go to Sri Lanka." It was difficult to remember what came before the relentless decade I'd spent at the bar.

She froze, her eyes wide. "Are you kidding me? I really want to go there. Let's book it for the spring after Columbia?"

"Sounds good to me." Who would have thought that I'd be living and working on two continents, and travelling with the love of my life?

She turned in my arms, her back to my front. "And we'll have to think about a honeymoon at some point."

She held her hand out and glanced at the engagement ring we'd picked out last week.

"You're not having buyer's remorse, are you?" The ring was unusual—three thin bands, all different styles, with a central diamond that looked more like a flower than a stone. It suited her perfectly—it was delicate, beautiful and precious.

She laughed and I couldn't help but smile at such a beautiful sound. I'd take it over a nightingale any day of the week. "Not likely. You're worth marrying for a ring like this," she said, still admiring it.

I pulled her between my legs. "Good to know. Are you going to tell your family when we're over there?"

She grimaced. "Which bit?"

"Any of it."

She huffed out a breath. "Maybe just as we're leaving. I can say it really fast 'Mom, Dad, Scarlett, Max, Alexander and I are getting married but we're going to do it in London and there's going to be twenty people, max.'"

"I think they'll be fine about it." Violet's family adored her, and from what I knew of them would be happy so long as she was happy. "They're not going to force you to have a big wedding."

"And then I'll tell them I have no intention of getting pregnant any time soon." She shook her head. "It might just kill my mother."

"Your mother has plenty of grandchildren keeping her busy." I pressed a kiss to her forehead and she smoothed her hands over my shoulders.

"And you're sure you don't mind waiting for a few years?" she asked. "I just want to spend some time with you. I want to travel and start my business and then see where we are."

"I want to do all those things too. I'm not sure I'm ready to be responsible for a tiny human quite yet."

"I think you'd make an excellent father," she said, tracing my eyebrow with her fingertip.

I pulled her closer. "Let's just take each day as it comes."

"Excuse me?" She pulled back. "Who are you and what have you done with my fiancé?"

I chuckled. "I told you. You've changed me."

She tilted her head. "Maybe just brought you to the center a little more."

I nodded. "Yes, that's right. I'm still more of a planner than you."

"But I'm more of a planner than I was. You've changed me as well."

"We've met in the middle."

She bit back a smile. "Exactly. And I like where I'm standing."

"Me too." I'd gone from knowing exactly how my life would be until I retired to looking forward to change. It had taken adjustment, but I was getting there. Being with Violet made everything worth it. She was the very center of my world. "As long as we're side by side then everything else will fall into place."

Violet was the only woman in my life I'd ever fought for and I'd keep fighting, keep loving her, keep doing whatever it took to stay by her side for the rest of our lives.

ACKNOWLEDGMENTS

Dear readers, I do hope you enjoyed being back in London for this book as much as I did. I really enjoyed showing Violet around! This couple were fantastic to write and I enjoyed hanging out with them. I wish it had lasted for longer. I've just met many of you at FBBF 2017 and it was a complete thrill! Chatting to you about your favorite characters and hearing about your love of reading is always simply wonderful! I appreciate all the love and support from all of you, whether or not I've met you! I wish I could hug you all!

Thank you to my mini pupil-master, Lance Ashworth, who guided me through my first experience at the bar. It's been twenty years since we first met on that train, not knowing what each other looked like! Are we really that old? It's been so rewarding to watch your career flourish— all that hard work has paid off. Your namesake in this book is indeed a kindly mentor. It's what I know of the Lances I've met ... thank you for your kindness toward me.

A tip from the author, if you ever find yourself at one of the award ceremonies as described in the book—drink plenty of alcohol and find the clerks to hang out with. They are so much fun and I've found myself in plenty of trouble with that particular combination—the good kind of course.

Elizabeth—thank you is never enough. Your commitment to my writing is beyond what I could hope for and I will be forever grateful. Like Jessica said, meeting you was like winning the lottery. I feel the same, even when you're collecting my author tears for your collection. In just a few days *Defenseless* will be kicking ass and you'll have the success you deserve.

Nina—thank you for all your help and support. It's always appreciated.

Stevie—I've said it before and I will always say that you really are one of the best people I know. I'm so incredibly lucky to have you in my life again. While you were guarding the legal department stationery cabinet did you ever think you'd be heading up #TeamBay ? We need to get Neillette on board and the dream team would be back! Next year!

Najla—I say it every time but I think this cover is my favorite! Hehe. You're so talented and I love working with you!

To Charity, Davina and Ruth—thank you for your help at the last minute of course! And Jules—Love you babycakes!

To all the amazing bloggers and reviewers who connect me with readers. You are amazing! Thank you for all your help.

I am always overwhelmed at the generosity of the author community—I'm so proud to be a part of such a great community of women. Thank you.

I can't wait to start 2018!

OTHER BOOKS BY LOUISE BAY

Sign up to the Louise Bay mailing list to see more on all
my books.
www.louisebay.com/newsletter

Duke of Manhattan

I was born into British aristocracy, but I've made my fortune
in Manhattan. New York is now my kingdom.

Back in Britain my family are fighting over who's the
next Duke of Fairfax. The rules say it's me--if I'm married.
It's not a trade-off worth making. I could never limit myself
to just one woman.

Or so I thought until my world is turned upside down.
Now, the only way I can save the empire I built is to inherit
the title I've never wanted-- so I need a wife.

To take my mind off business I need a night that's all
pleasure. I need to bury myself in a stranger.

The skim of Scarlett King's hair over my body as she
bends over . . .

The scrape of her nails across my chest as she screams my name . . .

The bite of her teeth on my shoulder just as we both reach the edge . . .

It all helps me forget.

I just didn't bargain on finding my one night stand across the boardroom table the next day.

She might be my latest conquest but I have a feeling Scarlett King might just conquer me.

A stand-alone novel.

Park Avenue Prince

THE PRINCE OF PARK AVENUE FINALLY MEETS HIS MATCH IN A FEISTY MANHATTAN PRINCESS.

I've made every one of my billions of dollars myself— I'm calculating, astute and the best at what I do. It takes drive and dedication to build what I have. And it leaves no time for love or girlfriends or relationships.

But don't get me wrong, I'm not a monk.

I understand the attention and focus it takes to seduce a beautiful woman. They're the same skills I use to close business deals. But one night is where it begins and ends. I'm not the guy who sends flowers. I'm not the guy who calls the next day.

Or so I thought before an impatient, smart-talking, beyond beautiful heiress bursts into my world.

When Grace Astor rolls her eyes at me—I want to hold her against me and show her what she's been missing.

When she makes a joke at my expense—I want to silence her sassy mouth with my tongue.

And when she leaves straight after we f*ck with barely a

goodbye—it makes me want to pin her down and remind her of the three orgasms she just had.

She might be a princess but I'm going to show her who rules in this Park Avenue bedroom.

A stand-alone novel.

King of Wall Street

THE KING OF WALL STREET IS BROUGHT TO HIS KNEES BY AN AMBITIOUS BOMBSHELL.

I keep my two worlds separate.

At work, I'm King of Wall Street. The heaviest hitters in Manhattan come to me to make money. They do whatever I say because I'm always right. I'm shrewd. Exacting. Some say ruthless.

At home, I'm a single dad trying to keep his fourteen year old daughter a kid for as long as possible. If my daughter does what I say, somewhere there's a snowball surviving in hell. And nothing I say is ever right.

When Harper Jayne starts as a junior researcher at my firm, the barriers between my worlds begin to dissolve. She's the most infuriating woman I've ever worked with.

I don't like the way she bends over the photocopier—it makes my mouth water.

I hate the way she's so eager to do a good job—it makes my dick twitch.

And I can't stand the way she wears her hair up exposing her long neck. It makes me want to strip her naked, bend her over my desk and trail my tongue all over her body.

If my two worlds are going to collide, Harper Jayne will have to learn that I don't just rule the boardroom. I'm in charge of the bedroom, too.

A stand-alone novel.

Hollywood Scandal

HE'S A HOLLYWOOD SUPERSTAR. SHE'S LITERALLY THE GIRL NEXT DOOR.

One of Hollywood's A-listers, I have the movie industry in the palm of my hand. But if I'm going to stay at the top, my playboy image needs an overhaul. No more tabloid headlines. No more parties. And absolutely no more one night stands.

Filming for my latest blockbuster takes place on the coast of Maine and I'm determined to stay out of trouble. But trouble finds me when I run into Lana Kelly.

She doesn't recognize me, she's never heard of Matt Easton and my million dollar smile doesn't work on her.

Ego shredded, I know I should keep my distance, but when I realize she's my neighbor I know I'm toast. There's no way I can resist temptation when it's ten yards away.

She has a mouth designed for pleasure and legs that will wrap perfectly around my waist.

She's movie star beautiful and her body is made to be mine.

Getting Lana Kelly into my bed is harder than I'm used to. She's not interested in the glitz and glamour of Hollywood, but I'm determined to convince her the best place in the world is on the red carpet, holding my hand.

I could have any woman in the world, but all I want is the girl next door.

A standalone romance.

Parisian Nights

The moment I laid eyes on the new photographer at work, I had his number. Cocky, arrogant and super wealthy— women were eating out of his hand as soon as his tight ass crossed the threshold of our office.

When we were forced to go to Paris together for an assignment, I wasn't interested in his seductive smile, his sexy accent or his dirty laugh. I wasn't falling for his charms.

Until I did.

Until Paris.

Until he was kissing me and I was wondering how it happened. Until he was dragging his lips across my skin and I was hoping for more. Paris does funny things to a girl and he might have gotten me naked.

But Paris couldn't last forever.

Previously called What the Lightning Sees

A stand-alone novel.

Promised Nights

I've been in love with Luke Daniels since, well, forever. As his sister's best friend, I've spent over a decade living in the friend zone, watching from the sidelines hoping he would notice me, pick me, love me.

I want the fairy tale and Luke is my Prince Charming. He's tall, with shoulders so broad he blocks out the sun. He's kind with a smile so dazzling he makes me forget every-thing that's wrong in the world. And he's the only man that can make me laugh until my cheeks hurt and my stomach cramps.

But he'll never be mine.

So I've decided to get on with my life and find the next best thing.

Until a Wonder Woman costume, a bottle of tequila and a game of truth or dare happened.

Then Luke's licking salt from my wrist and telling me I'm beautiful.

Then he's peeling off my clothes and pressing his lips against mine.

Then what? Is this the start of my happily ever after or the beginning of a tragedy?

Previously called Calling Me

A stand-alone novel.

Indigo Nights

I don't do romance. I don't do love. I certainly don't do relationships. Women are attracted to my power and money and I like a nice ass and a pretty smile. It's a fair exchange—a business deal for pleasure.

Meeting Beth Harrison in the first class cabin of my flight from Chicago to London throws me for a loop and everything I know about myself and women goes out the window.

I'm usually good at reading people, situations, the markets. I know instantly if I can trust someone or if they're lying. But Beth is so contradictory and confounding I don't know which way is up.

She's sweet but so sexy she makes my knees weak and mouth dry.

She's confident but so vulnerable I want to wrap her up and protect her from the world.

And then she fucks me like a train and just disappears, leaving me with my pants around my ankles, wondering which day of the week it is.

If I ever see her again I don't know if I'll scream at her, strip her naked or fall in love. Thank goodness I live in Chicago and she lives in London and we'll never see each other again, right?A stand-alone novel.

The Empire State Series

Anna Kirby is sick of dating. She's tired of heartbreak. Despite being smart, sexy, and funny, she's a magnet for men who don't deserve her.

A week's vacation in New York is the ultimate distraction from her most recent break-up, as well as a great place to meet a stranger and have some summer fun. But to protect her still-bruised heart, fun comes with rules. There will be no sharing stories, no swapping numbers, and no real names. Just one night of uncomplicated fun.

Super-successful serial seducer Ethan Scott has some rules of his own. He doesn't date, he doesn't stay the night, and he doesn't make any promises.

It should be a match made in heaven. But rules are made to be broken.

The Empire State Series is a series of three novellas.

Love Unexpected

When the fierce redhead with the beautiful ass walks into the local bar, I can tell she's passing through. And I'm looking for distraction while I'm in town—a hot hook-up and nothing more before I head back to the city.

If she has secrets, I don't want to know them.

If she feels good underneath me, I don't want to think about it too hard.

If she's my future, I don't want to see it.

I'm Blake McKenna and I'm about to teach this Boston socialite how to forget every man who came before me.

When the future I had always imagined crumbles before my very eyes. I grab my two best friends and take a much needed vacation to the country.

My plan of swearing off men gets railroaded when on my first night of my vacation, I meet the hottest guy on the planet.

I'm not going to consider that he could be a gorgeous distraction.

I'm certainly not going to reveal my deepest secrets to him as we steal away each night hoping no one will notice.

And the last thing I'm going to do is fall in love for the first time in my life.

My name is Mackenzie Locke and I haven't got a handle on men. Not even a little bit.

Not until Blake.

A stand-alone novel.

Hopeful

How long does it take to get over your first love?

Eight years should be long enough. My mind knows that, but there's no convincing my heart.

Guys like Joel weren't supposed to fall for girls like me. He had his pick of women at University, but somehow the laws of nature were defied and we fell crazy in love.

After graduation, Joel left to pursue his career in New York. He wanted me to go with him but my life was in London.

We broke up and my heart split in two.

I haven't seen or spoken to him since he left.

If only I'd known that I'd love him this long, this painfully, this desperately. I might have said yes all those years ago. He might have been mine all this time in between.

Now, he's moving back to London and I need to get over him before he gets over here.

But how do I forget someone who gave me so much to remember?

A long time ago, Joel Wentworth told me he'd love me for infinity . . . and I can't give up hope that it might have been true.

A stand-alone novel.

Faithful

Leah Thompson's life in London is everything she's supposed to want: a successful career, the best girlfriends a bottle of sauvignon blanc can buy, and a wealthy boyfriend who has just proposed. But something doesn't feel right. Is it simply a case of 'be careful what you wish for'?

Uncertain about her future, Leah looks to her past, where she finds her high school crush, Daniel Armitage, online. Daniel is one of London's most eligible bachelors. He knows what and who he wants, and he wants Leah. Leah resists Daniel's advances as she concentrates on being the perfect fiancé.

She soon finds that she should have trusted her instincts when she realises she's been betrayed by the men and women in her life.

Leah's heart has been crushed. Will ever be able to trust again? And will Daniel be there when she is?

A stand-alone novel.

KEEP IN TOUCH!

Sign up for my mailing list to get the latest news and gossip
HERE

Website
Twitter
Facebook
Instagram
Pinterest
Goodreads
Google +

Made in the USA
Lexington, KY
17 February 2018